With a *thump!* she contacted the ground. When she could no longer keep the nose off the ground, she let it sink.

Suddenly Taylor heard a *crack!* and felt the airplane's nose dip. Completely out of control, the plane swerved to the side and began skidding through the dirt on its nose. Crackling and popping filled the air as rocks and loose gravel pelted the metal of the cowling.

"Daaaaamn!"

The last thing she felt was the forward inertia of a thousand pounds of cargo driving her forward, forcing her against the stranglehold of her shoulder harness.

RED LINE

And don't miss

DEAD STICK

The first mystery featuring Taylor Morgan

MORE MYSTERIES FROM THE
BERKLEY PUBLISHING GROUP . . .

CAT CALIBAN MYSTERIES: She was married for thirty-eight years. Raised three kids. Compared to that, tracking down killers is easy . . .

ELENA JARVIS MYSTERIES: There are some pretty bizarre crimes deep in the heart of Texas—and a pretty gutsy police detective who rounds up the unusual suspects . . .

FREDDIE O'NEAL, P.I., MYSTERIES: You can bet that this appealing Reno private investigator will get her man . . . "A winner."—Linda Grant

BENNI HARPER MYSTERIES: Meet Benni Harper—a quilter and folk-art expert with an eye for murderous designs . . .

HANNAH BARLOW MYSTERIES: For ex-cop and law student Hannah Barlow, justice isn't just a word in a textbook. Sometimes, it's a matter of life and death . . .

PEACHES DANN MYSTERIES: Peaches has never had a very good memory. But she's learned to cope with it over the years . . . Fortunately, though, when it comes to murder, this absentminded amateur sleuth doesn't forgive and forget!

RED LINE

To Charline—

Megan Mallory Rust

Allegan Rust

BERKLEY PRIME CRIME, NEW YORK

RED LINE

A Berkley Prime Crime Book / published by arrangement
with the author

PRINTING HISTORY
Berkley Prime Crime edition / May 1999

The Penguin Putnam Inc. World Wide Web site address is
http://www.penguinputnam.com

ISBN: 0-425-16897-2

PRINTED IN THE UNITED STATES OF AMERICA

10 9 8 7 6 5 4 3 2 1

DEDICATION

To Sue Henry, with thanks for the leg up.

ACKNOWLEDGMENTS

My thanks go out to: Bill Redmond, who took time out of his busy flying schedule to remind me of some of the nasty properties of Ni-Cad batteries; Chuck Jamieson and Bill Kunkler, pilots for Rust's Flying Service who prompted me when my memories of my own days as a pilot failed me; and the numerous nameless characters I met while flying in Bethel that served as fodder for my hungry writer's hand.

RED LINE

ONE

The somber skies threatened trouble.

The dense cloud layer covering the fifty-thousand-square-mile Yukon-Kuskokwim Delta blanketed the entire area in gray flannel. On the eastern border of the delta, the tallest spires of the Alaska Range jutted up through the cloud ceiling like stalagmites piercing the surface of a subterranean lake. To the west the flat tundra plain stretched for miles and miles of dismal monotony. Inside the clouds, moisture began to coalesce into minute spheres. Shortly, raindrops would fall.

Sitting in the pilot's seat of the single-engine Cessna 207 operated by Tundra Air Charter, Taylor Morgan skirted the low hem of clouds. She surveyed the dreary skies. "This weather hasn't changed," she muttered. "Why the hell did I agree to come back out here?"

When Tundra Air Charter, a former employer, called and asked her to resume her flying duties in Bethel, she had laughed. Why would she want to give up a job she loved performing medical evacuations with LifeLine Air Ambulance? After three years with them, she had earned some seniority and was captain of a sophisticated twin-engine Beechcraft King Air B200. Transporting sick and injured people from remote parts of Alaska to urban med-

ical centers made her feel wonderful. Her flying skills
meant something when they were used to save lives.

The idea of repeating her days as a bush pilot, guiding
a low-tech Cessna 207 from village to village on the treeless Yukon-Kuskokwim Delta (called the Y-K Delta for
short) did not appeal to her.

Eventually, though, she agreed to return to Bethel. Not
permanently—there was no way she'd quit her wonderful
job with LifeLine—but she'd use a few weeks of vacation
time helping Tundra Air Charter restart their air-taxi service.

She owed them, in a way. Not only did they take a
chance hiring her when she was a neophyte pilot, but their
eventual bankruptcy was the push she needed to find her
job with LifeLine. Now that they wanted to restart the air
taxi—and they needed her to substitute briefly for one of
the newly hired pilots—she couldn't begrudge them a few
weeks of her time. Tundra Air management assured her
that her stay would be short-lived.

Touching base with old friends might even be fun.
Looking back at the good old days would be nice, but
knowing that she had a better job waiting for her return
would be even better.

Turning back to business, she squinted at the deterio-
rating weather ahead of her. She didn't like the looks of
it. Staying below the cloud base was requiring a descent
to a lower altitude every five miles or so. That was not
particularly problematic out over the flat tundra plains, but
as she flew farther south to her destination, the small village of Goodnews Bay, more and more hills cropped up.
The combination of lower clouds and higher terrain was
not a good one.

As the settlement of Quinhagak disappeared behind the
Cessna's tail, Taylor got more bad news—the visibility
had dropped sharply, indicating the presence of rain or
snow showers. Certainly those showers held icing conditions, where super-cooled raindrops formed and froze on
the aircraft wings as soon as they hit the aluminum skin.

A tiny flutter of apprehension stirred in her. Her Cessna

had none of the equipment needed to handle icing conditions, and icing posed a severe and often fatal problem for aircraft.

Taylor made a snap decision. "Back to Bethel for me," she grunted, and began to execute a turn to the north. She didn't want to be dodging mixed rain-and-snow showers when navigating the hills near Goodnews Bay. "My life is worth more than those groceries I'm delivering down the coast. They can wait."

But when the Cessna completed its one-eighty, her mild trepidation blossomed into full-blown anxiety. The skies between her and her home base held the same rain-and-snow mixture she had just turned her back on. The weather had moved in behind her, effectively cutting off her escape route. Adrenaline shot through her system.

"Oh, shit," were the only words that could fit the situation. Snap decision time again. She could assume that the showers were scattered and head back to Bethel, steering clear of the icing danger. That'd be easy enough, she told herself. It was daytime and she could see where she was going. Most of the time.

But what if the showers formed a continuous line? As they appeared to be doing? She couldn't get through that. There was no way she'd fly through known icing conditions; she wouldn't even do that in the King Air she flew for LifeLine, and that aircraft was much better equipped than the Cessna cocooning her.

Nope, she decided. She had to land and wait out the showers. If they moved out as quickly as they'd moved in behind her they'd evaporate shortly and she could continue to Goodnews Bay with her cargo. She had just passed Quinhagak—she could cool her heels at the airstrip there. Discretion was the better part of valor.

Thumbing the push-to-talk button on her radio she spoke into the boom mike centered over her lips. "Quinhagak traffic, Cessna nine-six-uniform is nine southeast, landing to the north." She pushed an annoying strand of hair behind the left earphone of her radio headset and scanned the area.

No one around. Apparently everyone else had the sense to stay out of the inclement weather. When she left Bethel earlier, the Goodnews agent hadn't mentioned anything about the rain-and-snow showers, and that annoyed her. If he had told her about the trashy sky she wouldn't have come.

Maybe that's why he didn't say anything.

As she turned onto a straight-in approach to the northeast-southwest gravel runway, she saw a woman running down the trail from the village to the airstrip. Following her was a small band of people who appeared to be huddled around some larger object. Taylor stared out the window at her for a few seconds, then caught herself and turned back to address her cockpit duties.

After pushing the mixture control forward she throttled back. She moved the prop control forward next. When her airspeed dropped below one-forty she added ten degrees of flaps, and once her velocity slipped below one hundred she selected twenty degrees more.

Once she'd performed the mechanical parts of the landing procedure, the success of the touch-down was all the result of talent.

It was all up to her—did she still have it? It'd been a while since she flew a single-engine Cessna, and commanding an airplane wasn't like riding a bicycle. Feeling her way down to the strip's surface, Taylor flared the aircraft and eased it onto the gravel.

With the wheels planted firmly under the Cessna, it thumped down the pothole-pocked runway as pebbles pinged off its aluminum cowling. When she braked gently to slow its progress, she broke out in a smile.

She still had it.

She flew a much more technologically superior plane with LifeLine but she hadn't forgotten how to handle the small ones. Her moves were still there.

Taxiing into the unloading area, she braked to a stop and killed the engine. Seconds later, a pounding started on the pilot's-side window. It was the woman Taylor had seen running toward the airstrip as she set up for landing.

The woman, wearing a white lab coat and a panicked expression, was mouthing something inaudible.

Taylor jerked the pilot's door open.

"Are you the medevac?" the young woman stammered when her words spilled through the gap. The stethoscope dangling from her neck and the white lab coat indicated she was the village public health aide, and it looked like she had trouble. Spots of blood peppered the cloth of her coat as though they were a pattern stenciled on the cotton. A name tag pinned near the spray of crimson read "Cathy."

"We called for a medevac," Cathy shot out, her words set on rapid fire. "But you're here faster than we expected. We thought the weather might slow you down, but you made it okay. Good. The patient's just down the trail, the others are bringing him." She pointed at the small group Taylor had noticed during her landing. The object they protected from the wind and rain was a body supported by a stretcher.

Taylor gaped at the sight. "I'm not the medevac," she protested. "I just stopped to wait out the weather. I've got a cabin full of groceries for Goodnews."

Cathy stared at her, disbelieving. "But can't you unload them here?" she pleaded. "This guy is dying! He has to get to the hospital in Bethel, and if you're not the medevac I don't know when it'll get here. You're here already, you've got to help."

Taylor shook her head. "What makes you think I can make it in through the weather if they said they couldn't get out?" None of the aircraft flying out of Bethel, other than a few operated by a competitor of Tundra Air, had the capability to handle icing. But even if they had the necessary equipment they'd choose not to challenge that kind of weather. "Who'd you call, anyway?"

"I just contacted the hospital; they were the ones that called for a medevac. The nurse on duty called me back and said that the medevac would be delayed, but we can't wait. This guy's going to die if you don't fly him back to Bethel." The dark-haired Cathy looked like she just got out of high school, and her solicitous, feathery voice broke as she begged for Taylor's services.

Without realizing it, the health aide had just ensured Taylor's assistance with those words. Even when things looked grim for a flight, a pleading voice always launched the young pilot into action.

"Okay," Taylor offered. "I can try. Get some of those guys with the stretcher to help me off-load this cargo." Jumping out of the pilot's seat, she strode to the other flank of the Cessna, where she opened the two-sided cargo door and clambered inside. The entire cabin was full of boxes of food earmarked for delivery to the Goodnews Bay store, but she began to toss them on the ground.

As she flung cartons of evaporated milk and pilot bread out into the waiting arms of Yup'ik villagers she thought about what she'd just agreed to do. Was she suicidal? Who knew what kind of weather awaited her on her flight back to Bethel? She loved performing medevacs, being part of the team that saved lives, but she was used to doing that work in LifeLine's sophisticated aircraft with a copilot, nurses, and medical equipment on board.

However, no service like that existed on the Y-K Delta, and the residents there had to take whatever they got. And in this instance, it was her.

She bent to her work.

Within minutes the Cessna cabin was empty and piles of groceries sat on the gravel loading area. Sprinkles of rain bounced off their cardboard tops, and Taylor hoped that someone would have the sense to throw a tarp over them. No way of knowing when she could return to pick them up.

However, soggy supplies and stale crackers were the least of her worries. The weather continued to swirl around her, propelled by a gusty wind. She hadn't felt much turbulence when she'd landed—being distracted by the rain-and-snow showers and the peril they presented—but by now it was making itself too obvious to ignore. The wind told her that the clouds were part of an atmospheric system on the move—any idea of what it would do to her on the trip to Bethel was nothing better than a guess.

"Okay, guys," Taylor called out to her helpers as she straightened the seat belts on the floor, "we're ready to go. Bring the patient over and load him in." Jumping down from the Cessna's cabin, she whirled to face the onlookers and gasped.

The injured man due to be medevac'd back to the hospital lay on a stretcher in front of her, held by two village men. His face—badly beaten, bruised and cut—was barely recognizable as that of a Yup'ik. His normally dark beige coloring had turned black-and-blue with wounds starting to scab over. His black, coarse hair lay in a tangle over swollen eyes. A flannel shirt and jeans covered his short, stocky body, but many pieces of the cloth had been cut away to expose the deep slashes and punctures that had needed attention from the health aide.

"He's been unconscious since I found him," Cathy muttered as she felt for a pulse at his wrist. Looking up at Taylor, she pointed at the red-stained flannel shirt. "He's losing blood, too. But I'm most worried about his head. They beat him pretty bad."

"Who's *they*?" Taylor asked. "What happened?"

The young woman shook her head. "We don't have time to get into it. Let's get going and I'll let you know on the way." She gestured for the men supporting the stretcher to load it into the airplane. Only three seats remained in the Cessna's cabin: the pilot's, the front passenger's, and one behind the pilot's. The litter went into the open area to the right side of the cabin, and Taylor buckled seat belts over the injured man's chest and knees. A blanket she extracted from the rear cargo compartment went over him, replacing the one that had blown off as they'd raised the litter into the plane.

Stepping back, she closed the double doors. Leading Cathy to the other side of the Cessna, she opened the pilot's door and pointed. "Go ahead and climb into the seat behind mine. You'll be able to watch over your patient easier from there than the seat next to me." She helped the health aide into the passenger seat, then jumped into hers behind the control yoke and rudder pedals. Slamming the door, she opened the window and yelled at the onlookers. "Cover up those boxes as soon as I leave, but not until I'm gone. Stay away from the prop until then."

Closing the window, she scanned the area to be sure everybody had obeyed her orders to stand clear of the prop, then engaged the starter for the Continental IO-520.

As the engine started its throaty hum, she glanced at her hand on the throttle. What had she just gotten herself into?

TWO

With the Cessna's engine running and her feet on the brakes, Taylor sat quietly in the loading area of the Quinhagak airport without moving. This would be her last chance to back out of a potentially deadly flight. Yes, she had a man in the cabin behind her that would die if he didn't get to medical help quickly, but she also had two innocent bystanders—herself and Cathy—that would suffer the same fate if they crashed on the way to saving him. Was it worth it?

She narrowed her eyes and glanced out at the dark skies surrounding the Cessna. The trickle of rain had metamorphosed into a steady downpour—one of the storm cells had moved right on top of them. Not a good sign.

But even with the risk looming ever larger, she decided yes, taking the medevac was worth it. Flying medevacs was her job in Anchorage, and sometimes that involved taking risks. Of course she hadn't anticipated flying a medevac during her short stay in Bethel, but she couldn't say no just because it was unexpected. And as far as risks go, she was smart, she was a good pilot, and if anybody could shoot through the storm line, she could.

Hoping her ego wasn't setting her up for a monstrous fall, she released the brakes and added power to taxi toward the runway. The beacon on the plane's vertical tail intermittently tinted the puddles on the ground emergency-flasher-red as she maneuvered into position.

She hoped that didn't portend tragedy.

"You all buckled in?" she asked Cathy. "How's the patient doing?" She peered over her shoulder to check on the injured Yup'ik man and gagged at the sight of his black-and-blue face and bloodied lips. In the closeness of the cockpit she could smell the acrid odor of booze breath and she wrinkled her nose. She doubted it came from the health aide; it must be coming from her patient.

That bothered her. She thought Quinhagak was dry: no alcohol sold or imported into the village. But some had made it in. Was that how he'd gotten beaten within an inch of his life? Because he'd smuggled some liquor into Quinhagak and refused to share? He was lucky he hadn't been thrashed to a pulp before any help arrived—worse things had happened in the bootlegging business.

She'd ask about the origin of his injuries once they were on their way to Bethel, *if* she could tear herself away from her airplane long enough to talk to Cathy. She wasn't sure she'd be able to do that, if the weather continued to threaten.

Words from the seat behind her broke her out of her thoughts. "Come on, let's get going," pleaded Cathy as Taylor maintained her position on the end of the strip without initiating a take-off. "This guy isn't doing well. We have to get him out of here."

"Okay, Cathy." Taylor nodded and cinched down her seat belt before she spoke into the boom mike pressed against her lips. "Quinhagak traffic, Cessna nine-six-uniform is taking off to the north, straight-out departure." Once any aircraft in the vicinity knew of her intentions, she taxied onto the gravel runway, made a perfunctory check of her engine instruments and firewalled the throttle.

This is it, she thought. Do or die.

Die being the operative word.

The pistons of the Continental IO-520 thundered as the

Cessna sped down the runway and leaped from the gravel surface of the runway. With the engine snarling it clawed its way into the air, venturing closer and closer to the looming snow-and-rain showers.

By the time the Cessna had gained seven hundred feet of altitude after take-off, Taylor had swung it to the northwest toward Bethel. At that point she got her first glimpse of the anticipated trouble. The showers—intermittent farther to the south—had strung together across the horizon like a fortress. There'd be no going through the storm line without escaping the treacherous icing conditions, and the icing could reduce an airplane to an object with as much flying capacity as a rock.

It was time to try one of the tricks that had saved her butt on occasion when she started out as a bush pilot years ago. If the air was cool enough at altitude to support formation of ice, wisdom dictated going to where the air was warmer. And if the air was warmer closer to the ground, you went there.

Reducing power to the engine, she dove to a lower altitude. At four hundred feet the outside air temperature gauge read thirty-one degrees—still too cold—so she descended to one hundred feet.

There the OAT showed thirty-five degrees. That was above freezing, but just barely. Even so, no pilot with any brains in her head would go any lower, which meant she had to quit at one hundred feet. An altitude that low was a stupid place to be, and she knew it—one little burp from the engine could send the plane shoveling into the vegetation below—but the alternative was even less desirable. At least there was nothing to hit between her present position and Bethel, since the tundra plain was so flat. No trees grew on the west side of the Y-K Delta, and the closest hills sprouted from the ground more than one hundred and fifty miles to the north.

Glancing over her shoulder, Taylor saw Cathy staring at the ground shooting past below the Cessna with an obvious look of anxiety in her eyes. "Aren't we flying awful low, miss?" she asked.

"Call me Taylor," she replied, feeling as though she and Cathy should be on a first-name basis considering the circumstances. "And yes, we are flying pretty low, but we have to in order to stay out of the rain." That wasn't the real reason, but she didn't have time to give a meteorology lesson about icing at the moment. Navigating while flying only one hundred feet above the muskeg called for complete attention from a pilot.

The poor visibility existing in the midst of the showers also warranted mindfulness. When Taylor had taken off from Quinhagak she could see for about a mile or two, but once she'd flown into the downpour the visibility had dropped to less than a quarter-mile. She was well aware of the fact that she was breaking nearly every regulation in the FAA rule book by continuing her mission, but she couldn't see any way to toe the line and still get the dying man to the medical help he needed. She realized that performing a medevac gave her no special dispensation for flying illegally, but there was nobody out there to catch her anyway. She had to bend the rules to save a life.

The tundra-covered terrain flashed past the Cessna as Taylor guided it to Bethel. She hoped the showers would subside before she reached the airport; if the visibility and cloud ceiling had not improved dramatically she wouldn't be allowed into the airspace around it. There was no way she could fudge on the regulations once she approached Bethel without receiving a violation from the FAA. She'd probably lose her license for that.

Once the Cessna was nearly half-way to the town of Bethel, she began to slack off on her watchfulness. She knew there was nothing tall enough to hit out there, and she had assured herself that no one else would be so stupid as to be out in that weather. She swiveled in her seat and spoke to Cathy, leaving her post of attention.

"So, Cathy, tell me how your patient got so carved up. I smelled booze on his breath—did that have something to do with it?"

The health aide nodded as she monitored the Yup'ik man's pulse with fingers against his carotid artery. "Yup,

you got it. Jimmy here sold some of his stash to a couple
of the other villagers, and when they ran out of the stuff
and went back for more he refused to sell to them. I guess
he was a bit low himself.'' She reached down to mop his
brow with a handkerchief. ''Anyway, they were none too
pleased by that, and tried to beat him into telling them
where the rest of his liquor was. When they started on
him with a knife, his wife ran to a friend for help and the
men were gone when she and the friend returned. Jimmy
was lying on the floor of his cabin, bleeding from his
wounds and unconscious. He hasn't regained consciousness the whole time I've been with him, and I'm afraid
the blows to his head may have given him a concussion.
Or worse. I need to get him to the hospital, get his head
checked out. The trauma could be serious, even fatal if
his brain is hemorrhaging.''

''Well, don't worry. We're heading that way as fast as
we can. I nearly have it red-lined right now.'' Taylor
swung forward and checked the plane's airspeed indicator
for its reading. The white arrow showing nautical-miles-
per-hour—knots—sat slightly below the red line marking
the maximum.

Taylor squinted out the pilot's side window, then
brought her eyes up to peer forward through the windshield. The picture filling the Plexiglas nearly gave her a
seizure.

Bearing down on Taylor's Cessna at twelve o'clock
was another single-engine plane, the twin of nine-six-
uniform. The two aircraft were closing in on each other
at about three hundred knots; the white strobes on the
other plane's wingtips flashed rhythmically as a warning
for those that ventured too close.

''Holy shit!'' yowled Taylor as she jerked her Cessna
to the right of the oncoming plane's path. The panicked
heave on her control yoke sent her aircraft careening
down toward the tundra and at the last second she yanked
it back into the air before impacting the ground. A shriek
blasted out of Cathy's mouth and she grabbed onto the
back of the pilot's seat in terror.

"Jesus Christ!" screamed the health aide. "What was that?"

With her heart hammering in her chest, Taylor fought to regain control over herself and her plane. Adrenaline had her pulse pounding in her ear drums, and a sheen of sweat had erupted on her forehead. Her bowels felt like they had turned the consistency of pudding. Breathing deeply, she slowly steered the Cessna back onto its proper course to Bethel.

"That," she stammered as she righted her plane, "was somebody else doing the same thing we're doing. Flying low to stay out of the icing. He probably figured nobody else was out in the weather, just like I did." Not taking her eyes off the view through the windshield—nobody ever said Taylor Morgan was a slow learner—she asked about the welfare of the injured Yup'ik man. The spasmodic maneuver she'd just put the Cessna through had likely not done *him* any good.

"He's still unconscious," Cathy reported, "so he probably didn't feel anything, but I'm checking on the IV needle to see if it came loose." After some rustling of the blanket covering the patient's body, she grunted. "It's okay, Taylor. The IV bag was caught under his body so it didn't get flung across the cabin and rip the needle off. But having the stretcher slam up against the seat rails didn't help. Please don't do any more wild aerobatics if you can help it."

Since Taylor refused to look behind her, she didn't know if Cathy was smiling when she said that or not, but most likely she wasn't. That stood to reason. The instinctive wrench on the control yoke prompted by the sight of another aircraft in her face had rattled more than her nerves.

Her face burning as she digested what had just happened, Taylor tried to console herself. That other pilot shouldn't have been out in the dangerous weather—didn't he have any sense? Surely he'd know of the dangers of icing in showers of mixed rain and snow. Nobody should be out in this.

Then she shook her head. Of course the other pilot knew of the hazards related to icing. That's why he'd been wallowing around only one hundred feet in the air, trying to stay out of it.

And she was out in the same dangerous weather as he was. However, she reassured herself, she had a reason: the injured, maybe dying, man she flew to safety.

Wriggling in her seat—Taylor needed to pee badly, perhaps due to the scare she'd given herself—she checked her engine instruments again. The manifold pressure gauge—the one that showed the amount of power generated by the engine—was still hovering close to the maximum. The Cessna was flying nearly as fast as it could.

A stirring in the rear of the cabin alerted Taylor to Cathy's monitoring of the Quinhagak man's condition. She was probably reassuring herself that the wild turn-and-dive used to evade the other airplane hadn't done any harm to her patient. Suddenly a wail ricocheted across the still air in the cabin.

"Taylor!" cried the health aide. "Crank it up! Jimmy's heart just stopped! We've got to get to Bethel right away!"

Cathy's urgent call was matched by the sounds of her climbing out of her seat, and Taylor craned her head over her shoulder. She saw the younger woman straddle the injured man's torso and begin applying the rhythmic strokes of CPR to his chest. After ten compressions, the health aide tilted his head and with two short breaths forced air into his lungs. When she removed her own mouth from his, blood from the wounds on his face tattooed her cheeks. "Come on," she urged. "Can't we go any faster?"

Knowing she shouldn't look away from the windscreen, but unable to pry herself away from the life-or-death scene evolving just feet behind her, Taylor croaked, "We can't! I'm running almost at red line as it is!"

"How close . . . are we?" Cathy gasped as she pressed down on his sternum. "How much . . . time?"

Taylor glanced at her distance measuring equipment and relayed the DME reading to the other woman. "Twenty miles," she acknowledged matter-of-factly, trying to bring calm back to the atmosphere. "About eight minutes. Hang on." Reaching for the throttle, she inched the power up an iota, but was unable to increase it more without ruining the engine.

"God!" Cathy clamored as she leaned all of her weight onto her straightened arms to compress his chest. "I hope he makes it!"

Staring out the windshield into the gray, menacing skies, Taylor hoped so too.

THREE

The gray, flat light surrounding the storm line filtered into the windows of the Bethel airport terminal. One hundred miles to the southeast—near Quinhagak and Goodness Bay—the foothills of the Kilbuck Mountains were submerged below the clouds.

A mile away, an aircraft was heading in from the southeast. Its lights flicked on as it entered the airfield's landing pattern, the white beams framing the distinctive red-and-gold colors of the Tundra Air Cessna 207. Water sprayed from the wheels as it descended onto a runway wet and slick.

It decelerated and taxied hurriedly toward the terminal. An ambulance waited nearby, its beacons flashing. Two paramedics stepped out of it and stood at the ready, waiting for the plane's propeller to stop its rotation. Even before the spinning ceased, the Cessna's cargo door opened and Taylor Morgan poked her head out of the cabin and frantically beckoned to the men.

They rushed forward and reached through the door, pushing Taylor aside to get into the cabin. Seconds later they were easing a stretcher out of the plane. It held the Quinhagak medevac patient, with the village health aide still at his side giving him CPR. The IV bag holding

Ringer's lactate bounced on his stomach with every thrust to his torso. Tears streamed down the aide's cheeks as she worked, and she swiped at them repeatedly.

The paramedics strode determinedly to the ambulance, the stretcher balanced between them, the health aide continuing to work on the still form on it as they moved. With him and the woman secured inside the ambulance, the Emergency Medical Technicians jumped into its cab and the vehicle raced away.

Taylor was left staring at the departing ambulance with a grim and troubled expression on her face.

She was worried. It looked like the Yup'ik villager might not make it. The eight minutes it took to get to Bethel, with Cathy giving him CPR all the while, were the longest Taylor had experienced in a long time. In addition, eight minutes was a lot of time to supply a dying body with blood flow to a traumatized brain and air flow to still lungs. Chances were he'd die.

It seemed like such a waste to Taylor, losing a life due to the insidious nature of alcohol. Even though the Quinhagak man was not dying of an obvious result of liquor like cirrhosis of the liver, the attack on him prompted by the need for the stuff did virtually the same thing.

She shook her head. How had he acquired a stash of liquor in the first place? She still wondered about that. Cathy's explanation for the origin of his injuries made no mention of where the illegal stash came from.

Taylor continued to think about that, but finally, unable to come up with an answer to her questions, she shrugged it off. It wasn't her place to analyze the ways people wrecked their bodies and lives, anyway. Turning away from the sight of the disappearing ambulance, she sighed.

She tried to compose herself as she trudged to the terminal, but still found herself shoving its heavy glass door open more forcefully than necessary. After glancing around, she focused on the startled expression of Dan Mackenzie, the TAC dispatcher who stood behind the counter. A silent groan choked her when she thought of the interrogation she would get from him. That was the last thing she desired at the moment.

As he watched her approach he adjusted the patch over his left eye. The sculpted black oval hid a badly scarred eye and lid, injured in a freak accident that had quashed his dreams of becoming a pilot. Still frustrated by that turn of fate, he drowned his unhappiness in orgies of banana cream pie and toffee, and weighed in at nearly three hundred pounds.

On a five-foot-seven-inch frame.

"What the hell are you doing coming in with an airplane?" Dan asked, peering through the door at the Tundra Air Cessna 207 outside. "I thought you were stuck somewhere waiting the weather out. It's still pretty shitty to the south. How'd you get in?"

Taylor shrugged, then mumbled, "Trust me, you don't want to know about it. All you need to know is that I had a medevac from Quinhagak."

Dan squinted at her. "Huh? The hospital called earlier, while you were gone, wanting the twin for a Quinhagak medevac, but we said we couldn't go until the weather improved. That must've been the one *you* brought in. How'd you do it?"

A noncommittal sigh prefaced her reply, and she fixed her eyes on the floor. "Like I said, you don't want to know." As she stuffed her hands into her jeans' pockets, a vivid image of the scary mid-air near-miss flashed across her mind. However, as soon as the vision appeared she suppressed it. She didn't want to relive the experiences of the day.

"Okay, I won't ask," Dan reassured her. "I don't want to know which of the regs you blew to get home. The only thing that matters is that you got a medevac in. Good job." Noticing her glum look, he reached across the counter to pat her shoulder. His smile seemed geared to brighten her mood, though it didn't. "So, you just got back, huh? Did the guy die, or what?"

"Dan!" she exclaimed.

"Hey, I was just making a joke. You don't look too

upset, he must not have gotten hurt too bad. I can't ask any questions about the weather, so that's all that's left.''

Glowering at him, Taylor yanked her hands out of her pockets. He didn't have any business deciding on how she felt just by her superficial appearance. She could hide her feelings as well, or even better, than most. "He wasn't dead when we landed," she reported in a clipped voice, "but I'm not holding my breath for him. He was in pretty bad shape. On our way into Bethel his heart stopped—the health aide was doing CPR on him while I was landing—and his head looked like somebody went at it with a meat cleaver. Plus, he got stabbed in a fight.''

"Stabbed? Fight? What was going on?''

"The health aide said it was some drunken brawl. The injured guy was selling from his liquor stash and a few of the villagers got pretty tanked up. When they wanted more booze and he refused to sell it to them they beat the shit out of him—''

"He was selling? How'd he get booze? Quinhagak is dry.''

"Yeah, I know.'' Taylor stared out the window, surveying the nearly empty ramp, bewildered. All the settlements on the Delta prohibited liquor sales, and most forbid alcohol possession entirely. She realized that villagers could obtain booze, but that required conspiracy and money. Had that been involved in the Quinhagak event?

She swung her gaze to meet Dan's. "Anyway, what's up for me now? I know it's still raining, but that won't stop anything.'' She used her casual tone to mask her discomfort.

He shook his head. "It may not stop you, but it stops me. I'm not going to send you back out in that mess. You probably broke a year's worth of FARs getting home from Quinhagak, and I don't want to press our luck. Why don't you go get a cup of coffee or lunch? I'll get you if things start to break.''

Taylor snorted. She knew Dan was doing the right thing, but she wanted to get back in an airplane. Her outlook on life needed some repair—the earlier events of the day had done a real number on it—and climbing back in a plane always helped. "Okay," she acquiesced. "I'll be upstairs." She headed for the stairs that led to the small restaurant on the terminal's second floor.

When she entered the café she saw many of her coworkers and peers holding court at window tables. Everyone appeared to be eating and she waved at old friends Ed and Andy, pilots with Arctic Wings, then nodded at a Scandinavian-looking man who flew for Yup'ik Air. She couldn't remember his name—wasn't it something typically Swedish like Lars, or Sven?

After ordering and paying for a cup of Swiss Miss hot chocolate—she sure wasn't hungry after seeing the life of the Quinhagak man slipping away—Taylor carried the heavy ceramic mug to a table occupied by her Tundra Air coworkers. Hoisting the mug, she greeted the men. "Hi there, Carl, Stan. Scoot over, Bob, let me slide in there." She pulled a chair out and dropped down onto it.

Surveying the full tables near her, she said, "Looks like no one's getting out because of the weather today. Must be shitty everywhere."

Carl Roston frowned and pushed his baseball hat back over his dark brown hair. "Well, I hope today's no rerun of yesterday." His loud snort made his narrow mustache wriggle. "Dan better dispatch us, even if the weather's shit. I'm not making any money sitting up here, and I've got to put food on the table. I wouldn't have taken this job if I knew I'd be sitting on my butt when I could be flying."

Both Stan Searle and Bob Allum shook their heads at Carl's complaint. "Hey, I don't want to fly in this shit," Stan confessed. His sturdy, well-fed frame showed he hadn't had any trouble finding money for *his* groceries. "We're lucky Dan has some sense. He never pushes us to fly, he knows this country. It's not Snohomish Country, with nav-aids every few miles like you're used to." He

ran a hand through his shaggy, reddish mane and peered
out the window.

"Well, Dan's not a pilot," Carl grumbled. "He doesn't
know that we can handle this junk. He's just reading the
FAA regulation book like it's a Bible, but I know *I* can
cope with a lot of the stuff the FAA says I have to stay
out of." With an irritated expression, he shoved his chair
back and stood. "I'm going back downstairs. If Dan tells
me to cool my heels like he did yesterday, I'm going
home. I've had enough of this shit." His rubber-soled
boots squeaked wetly as he stomped off.

Stan and Bob looked at each other and shrugged si-
multaneously. "I think I'll go down and check the
weather too," Bob announced. "No sense in hanging
around the airport if it's not going to improve. I've got
things I can do at home. You coming, Stan?"

Stan nodded and grabbed his empty plate and coffee
mug. Taylor waved at the men as they departed.

A few minutes later, she tipped the mug up and drained
the last drops of chocolate. She wondered if she should
imitate her coworkers and take off. Apparently they didn't
anticipate a change in the weather before nightfall brought
an end to the flying day.

She glanced out the window at the dismal gray sky,
then decided she'd had enough of scud-running in the
clouds for one day. Time to split.

Grabbing her flight jacket off the chair back, she pushed
her arms into the soggy sleeves. Her expression contorted
when the clammy leather rubbed over her hands: Her
jacket felt like a cold, damp sponge.

Out of the corner of her eye she saw a group of men
queuing up in front of the café's grill. Some were ac-
quaintances she hadn't seen for years. She waved at them,
then dropped her hand when she saw the man at the front
of the line saunter toward her. The cheeseburger he carried was surrounded by a mountain of french fries. A fry
toppled off the plate with every step the man took.

Her head tilted slightly to the side in annoyance. The

man ignored her look and ambled toward her table in his
subtly macho strut.

A faint sneer of distaste distorted her lips when Jack
Shumock directed an insincere smile at her. Three years
had passed since she'd last seen him, three years free of
his torment. She hadn't missed him. Busying herself with
her jacket zipper, she quickly turned away from her view
of the Western Alaska Transport patch on his shirt and
the longish curls dangling over his jacket collar. Done
with the zipper, she glanced up at his six-foot-two-inch
frame, then stood and grabbed her mug.

"Look who's back," Jack taunted when he realized she
was ignoring him and leaving. "Couldn't make it in Anchorage, huh? Too much for you, all that heavy metal?
Figured you didn't have what it took."

She yearned to tell him that she *did* have what it took—
how the hell had she escaped the day's dangerous weather
and a near-miss if she didn't?—but she stifled her retort.
If he'd known what she'd attempted to fly in earlier, he'd
go directly to the Federal Aviation Administration and
accuse her of breaking the regulations. Which she had.
They'd pull her license in a heartbeat, even if she *had*
been on a medevac.

She pushed around him, glaring, and headed off to
dump her mug in the dirty dish tub. He gloated as she
stamped off, pleased with himself.

Fuming, she trotted down the stairs.

Marching up to the TAC counter, still furious with Jack
Shumock, she planted her hands on the faux-cedar Formica and glared at Dan Mackenzie.

He glanced up upon her approach. "What?" he stammered. "What did I do?" Surprise tinged his features.
"You look like you want to smack me. Real bad."

"Relax, Dan," she reassured him. "It's not you, it's
Jack Shumock up to his usual. He picked up right where
we left off three years ago." She narrowed her eyes and
looked back at the stairs to the café. "Anyway, I'm going
to bug out of here. It doesn't look like the weather's going
to break before we start losing daylight. I want to head

over to the hospital, check on that guy from Quinhagak.''

''Why? Do you think he made it?''

''Could have. We weren't too far out when the health aide started the CPR, and that might have been enough to keep him going until she got him to the hospital.'' She stuffed her hands into her jacket and turned away from the counter. ''I guess I'll see you later,'' she called over her shoulder.

Ten minutes later Taylor swung into the parking lot of the Bethel Public Health Hospital. The beater VW Rabbit she was riding in hiccuped and snorted, then died when she turned the ignition off. ''Piece of shit,'' she muttered as she exited the cab.

Walking up the boardwalk to the hospital, she remembered her earlier days in Bethel when she passed the two-story neon-yellow building every morning on her way to work. The overly dramatic appearance of the structure did add a dash of color to the gray-green tones of everything else around, but she still wondered what kind of drugs the architect was on when he designed it. Must have been something good.

She made her way into the building and stopped at the front desk to ask for directions to the emergency room. Most likely that's where the man would be—it hadn't been all that long since the ambulance whisked him away. The front desk directed her around the corner to another nurses' station in front of several rooms that served as the ER for the small rural hospital.

A black-haired Yup'ik receptionist who was typing on a word processor greeted her when she walked up. The lenses of the glasses that sat on her wide, flat nose glinted in the light. ''May I help you?'' the young woman asked with the slightly guttural accent found in the voices of many of the Yup'iks. English was not their native language.

''Yes. I'm Taylor Morgan, one of the Tundra Air Charter pilots and I just flew a medevac into town from Quinhagak. I want to check on the patient I had on board, see how he's doing.''

The receptionist picked up a clipboard and looked at it. "His name?" she asked as she ran her fingers down some kind of list.

Caught off guard, Taylor hesitated. "I don't know. I think the village health aide called him Jimmy, but I never got his last name.'' She leaned over to look at the clipboard the younger woman held. "But surely you can find him. How many emergencies do you have in a day? And how many just got flown in from Quinhagak?''

"Hmmm," the receptionist murmured. "I don't see anyone like that here. Let me get the duty nurse for you. She might know.'' She reached to dial a phone and punched in an extension. "Gloria? Do you have time to come out here to talk to somebody? She can't find a med-evac patient that just came in.'' After nodding at the answer to her question, she cradled the phone and turned back to Taylor. "Gloria'll be right out. You can wait over there.''

Plopping down in a chair as directed, Taylor jumped back up a few seconds later when a small forty-something woman pushed through one of the doors separating the ER from the waiting room. Green surgical scrubs dotted with blood stains identified her as an ER nurse.

"Can I help you?" Gloria asked when she reached the vinyl-upholstered waiting room chairs. "You missing somebody?''

Taylor repeated her story for the ER nurse, adding, "The patient's heart wasn't beating when he left the airport in the ambulance. He also had numerous stab wounds, and trauma to the head. I brought him in from Quinhagak.''

The blood drained from Gloria's face when she heard Taylor's words, and the young pilot's gut spasmed when she saw the look on the nurse's face. "Is he okay?" she quizzed in a panic. "Did he make it? I got him out of there as fast as I could—''

Gloria shook her head slowly and looked at her toes.

''The man you brought in was Jimmy, Jimmy Lincoln. He didn't make it, expired about ten minutes ago. We tried everything we could but he had massive head injuries. I'm sorry.''

Taylor sank back into the chair and waved the nurse off. She'd heard everything she needed to. Her fears had been realized—Jimmy had been on his last gasps of life when she'd loaded him into her Cessna in Quinhagak, though she didn't know that.

She bristled in anger. That hazardous flight to Bethel, fighting the weather and nearly dying in a mid-air, had been for nothing. Both she and Cathy almost paid the ultimate price for their willingness to aid another.

And the original trigger for all of the day's crises was alcohol. Where had Jimmy Lincoln gotten it, in a dry village? Had he obtained it himself, perhaps smuggling it in from Anchorage as so many did? Or did he get it from someone else?

Snorting, she rose to her feet. She had to determine where the booze was coming from, to head off more tragedies like the one to which she'd just been a witness. The loss of one life to alcohol was one too many, and she didn't want another pilot to risk his life in a medevac necessitated by alcohol-related trouble.

Then she hesitated. She was getting ahead of things again, charging into a situation without really thinking it through. How would she check into what had just occurred? That was a job for the troopers, not a charter pilot, and she doubted they'd appreciate some amateur like her poking her nose into their business. Maybe she should examine the problem further before she pulled on her investigator's hat. Even though the day's dramatic events had offended her sensibilities, she still needed to approach the issue more cautiously.

Slow down, woman.

Wrinkling her nose in distaste—she hated it when the logical part of her brain reined in her impetuous side—she zipped her jacket and left the ER. She'd had enough of tragedy for one day. With pursed lips, deep in thought, she headed for her vehicle.

FOUR

When she entered the terminal the next morning a familiar sight greeted her. She had seen the same thing day in and day out when she worked in Bethel three years earlier. People crowded the room waiting for the first flight of the day, probably one that would take them back to their own villages. Several of the passengers looked up when she clumped in, and appraised her appearance. The weather hadn't changed dramatically since the previous day, and it was still sprinkling outside even though the cloud cover had lifted somewhat. Her jog from apartment to car had left her hatless head wet. In addition, her flight jacket hadn't dried after yesterday's dousing. It still felt like a dead slug. She stared back at the people evaluating her, envying the warm, dry coats draped over their shoulders.

They hadn't been out in the nasty weather yesterday.

In one corner a white Husky snoozed on the floor next to several cases of pilot bread, the large saltine crackers used as a staple everywhere on the Delta. The dog guarded important goods.

Unzipping her jacket, Taylor maneuvered around a huge stack of canned food. An elderly Yup'ik man napped next to another large pile of groceries. She figured he'd gotten an early start that morning, and was taking a snooze to catch up as he awaited his flight's departure. She hoped he didn't oversleep; he'd be plenty pissed if his ride home left without him. His soft snoring amused her, and she chuckled affectionately.

The Yup'ik people amazed her, and had earned her respect from her first day with Tundra Air Charter years ago. They had been thrown into the unfamiliar and hostile world of the white man, but still maintained their serenity—the old man's contented look exemplified that fact. He looked like a baby resting in a hamper, oblivious to everything. He didn't worry about the theft of his belongings as he snoozed because that didn't happen in his world.

Part of her amazement stemmed from the Yup'ik's ability to eke out a life on the inhospitable terrain of Western Alaska. Her many flights over the Yukon-Kuskokwim Delta showed her how difficult living off *that* land had been.

Nothing but unmarked tundra covered the lake-dotted Delta. Most of it was virtually treeless, offering no protection from the howling winds. No large animals made the Delta their home, and the few small ones that did provided little in the way of a food source. The typical diet consisted of waterfowl and fish, supplemented by berries and edible vegetation.

Turning away from her view of the old man, Taylor stepped up to the Tundra Air ticket counter and greeted Dan Mackenzie. "Good morning, sir," she spoke in a formal, quasi-military manner. "Is the weather good enough today for you to dispatch some flights? Or have you forgotten how?"

He sniffed at her light teasing reproof. "Oh, get off my case, Taylor. If it weren't for me, you pilots would fly off in any kind of junk, and I'd be wiping your asses off the tundra when you ran into trouble and plowed in."

She nodded approvingly when he put her in her place. It was nice to think that she had enough sense to stay on the ground when the weather threatened, but look at what she'd done the previous day. That was sobering.

"Anyway, Dan, I'm ready to go. You got anything? Isn't Marshall and Russian first for this schedule? I like that run. You can send me there," she crooned, hopefully. Maybe if she batted her eyelashes . . .

He ignored her feminine wiles and grabbed up a clipboard. "Okay. You can do that one. You got a fairly good load waiting in the cargo hold, so go tell the guys to put it in nine-six-uniform."

"OK, I'll head out to the pen." A dead-pan look on her face, she glanced around the counter. "No passengers? I don't see anybody waiting."

Dan shook his head no. "No one out-bound, but one to pick up in Marshall." He handed Taylor her paperwork. She set off for the cargo area, tucking the paperwork into her clipboard. She was glad to be off on an ordinary flight, one she could do without scaring the hell out of herself.

Nine-six-uniform halted next to the numbers painted on the asphalt of Runway 18. "Bethel tower, four-six-nine-six-uniform is ready on one-eight, departing to the northeast." Taylor yanked on her seat belt to tighten it, and wriggled deeper into her seat.

"Niner-six-uniform, Bethel tower, wind is two-two-zero at six knots, cleared onto one-eight."

"Niner-six-uniform cleared onto the runway," Taylor confirmed, and pressed the throttle forward. The 207 moved onto the runway, as she looked down at her engine instruments and controls to check everything before takeoff. "Bethel, niner-six-uniform is ready to go."

"Niner-six-uniform is cleared for take-off, no traffic."

Once the tower authorized her departure, Taylor advanced the throttle to full forward. The pistons of the IO-520 engine growled as fuel flooded into their combustion chambers, and the airspeed indicator needle swept across the gauge to the upper reaches. The aircraft quickly accelerated down the tarmac.

"Niner-six-uniform rolling," she informed the tower.

Taylor relished the feeling of such a complex and powerful machine responding to her direction, her control. It helped to erase the distressing feelings left over from the disastrous day she'd gone through only twenty-four hours earlier. She also loved the flight she was taking that morning, it was such a treat. The vast disparity between the Marshall-Russian Mission area and the majority of the Delta was a pleasant diversion. Where flat tundra plains covered most of the Delta, the 2,500-foot high Kuskokwim Mountains cradled the two small settlements, and where no trees of any kind grew on the neighboring tundra bogs, evergreens peppered the hills.

Shifting her gaze from the terrain below, Taylor glanced over her shoulder at the cargo packed in the cabin. She sighed as she regarded the load. Disposable diapers and soda pop made up the majority of its contents, and every time she had to deal with bulky cargo like that she grumbled. Why had the Alaskan Natives discovered those particular urban conveniences? Why hadn't they become enamored by something light, like Kleenex?

Though the load wasn't particularly heavy, it overran the cabin of the 207. Cartons were even stuffed into the rear tail section. Her back muscles still ached from wedging the awkward boxes into the Cessna.

After spending the next half-hour grousing about her cargo, she could see the village of Marshall ahead, perched on the hills along the Yukon River. Its inclined runway sat in a small notch between the hills, spruce trees bordered its edges. She lined up for landing.

"Marshall traffic," she transmitted upon nearing the strip, "Cessna niner-six-uniform is four southwest, landing to the north." She scanned the skies around her to verify no one else was approaching the village at the same time, then busied herself preparing for touch-down.

Feeling her way down her final approach, she eased the Cessna onto the gravel, then added some power to climb to the loading area. Like at all of her stops, a TAC agent stood nearby, waiting with a wheelbarrow.

The middle-aged, portly Yup'ik man headed the wheelbarrow over to the plane when it had stopped. Taylor was already outside when he arrived, pulling the cargo out of the Cessna's cabin and throwing it into a growing pile. "Hi, John," she called out. "It's nice to see you again. I've got the usual big load for you, seems like things never change."

"I can see that, Taylor. Glad you're back, though, it's been a while." The thick lenses of John's glasses were so smudged that they nearly hid his dark brown eyes, and the scruffy material of his plaid shirt-jac showed the same lack of care. He slowly bent over to hoist the first carton of Pampers into his wheelbarrow.

Continuing to sling cargo out of the airplane, she talked to him over her shoulder as she worked. "You've got a passenger for me, don't you? That's what dispatch said before I left, but I didn't see anyone with you when I landed."

John pointed up the path from the village. "Here she comes now, she's a little late. Come on Kittie, hurry up!" he yelled. Taylor jerked her head up from the cargo to focus on a Yup'ik woman, about her age, jogging toward the plane. A large handled shopping bag bounced around her legs as she ran.

As the Alaskan Native woman came to a stop by the Cessna, Taylor broke into a grin. "Kittie? Kittie! What are you doing here?"

Kittie Avakana gaped for a moment before recognition broke into her expression. "Taylor! Taylor Morgan! I can't believe it's you, I haven't seen you for what, ten years?"

"Something like that," Taylor laughed. "Do you live here now? Last time we talked you were still with your aunt in Anchorage. What's happened since then?"

"All kinds of things. I'll tell you about it during the flight back to Bethel. I'm assuming you have a schedule to meet, I doubt we can stand here and gab for a half-hour."

"Oh, yeah." Taylor's gaze panned sheepishly over the boxes and cartons still remaining inside the Cessna.

"Thanks for reminding me. I better get busy, we can catch up once we're back in the air." She grabbed another box and lifted it out of the airplane's cabin.

"I'm going to take this first load to the village store," John said as he steered his full wheelbarrow away from the stack of goods. "Go ahead and take off once you're done unloading. I'll have to take several trips to get everything, so just leave the rest of the stuff in a pile, okay?"

"All right, will do." Taylor hefted a case of Shasta cola out of the plane, puffing as she dropped it next to the other cargo. "Go climb in the right front seat, Kittie, make sure you buckle up. I'll be ready to go in a few seconds." With a grunt she deposited another case of soda pop on the growing pile.

FIVE

As the Cessna lifted off the gravel runway at Marshall, Taylor turned to the east: her destination, the village of Russian Mission, rested between the knolls on the southern fork of the Kuskokwim Mountains. The route would take her through a notch in hills peppered by conifer forests, and she loved going that way—the trip to Marshall and Russian Mission was the only one she flew where she could see trees. She kind of missed them.

Leveling off at two thousand feet, she turned to her Yup'ik friend. She hadn't seen Kittie Avakana since their senior year of high school, and she needed to catch up with the woman's life. A *lot* had happened, at least for her.

"So, Kittie," she said, "do you still have the medal we won when we got the state basketball championship? I've got mine tucked away with my letter jacket, somewhere in the boxes I put in storage in Anchorage."

Kittie nodded, grinning. "Sure, I still have mine," she confirmed. "But I didn't leave anything in storage when I left Anchorage, I took everything with me to Marshall." She shifted her grip on her plastic shopping bag, rustling its contents. Staring pointedly at Taylor's hands grasping the Cessna's control yoke, she cracked, "How did you wind up out here with an airplane between your legs?''

Taylor laughed at Kittie's suggestive remark. ''Well, it's a long story. Suffice it to say this is my second tour-of-duty here on the Delta.'' She launched into an abbreviated version of her first stint in Bethel, then the tale of her short-term return to Tundra Air Charter from her job with Lifeline. ''Coming back here really makes me appreciate what I have waiting for me in Anchorage,'' she snorted. ''And *who* I have waiting for me in Anchorage.'' She thumped her chest to mimic a hammering heart, then gestured to prompt a reply from Kittie. ''But tell me what you're doing out here in the sticks. When we graduated from high school, I thought you said you wanted to be a nurse. What happened?''

Kittie cocked her head, a sly grin on her face. ''Well, I *am* a nurse, just not in Anchorage. I wanted to work someplace where you can't just drive downtown to find a doctor, a place where nurses are really needed. So I'm the health aide for Marshall.''

Impressed, Taylor stared at her friend. ''Wow! How do you handle that? I mean, that's a lot of responsibility, being the only trained medical person in the village. You have to be able to handle every kind of problem for what, a hundred and fifty people? I don't think I could do it.''

''Well, it's not too bad. Most of the stuff is minor, colds and the flu, fishhooks caught on someone's finger, things like that. If I have questions, I can call the hospital in Bethel, and with major trauma I call for a medevac.'' Kittie arched her eyebrows. ''Like the ones you do out of Anchorage.''

''Yeah, and the ones I have to do out here.'' Taylor frowned, the memory of the previous night's failed medevac hitting her like a sledgehammer. She thought she'd erased it from her consciousness, but apparently she hadn't. It was too fresh. ''I got called for a medevac just last night,'' she murmured.

''You did? I bet that was exciting! Where'd you go?'' As soon as Kittie had said that, she appeared to notice

Taylor's pained expression and she peered at her. "You look upset, did something go wrong?"

"Yeah." Taylor sighed heavily. She wasn't sure she wanted to go over it again, but Kittie was someone who'd understand. Surely the Yup'ik woman had lived on the Delta long enough to know how the weather could make a flight treacherous. She glanced at her friend and cleared her throat. "Was the weather pretty shitty in Marshall last night?"

Her eyes narrowing, Kittie shrugged. "No, not really, just kinda cloudy." Then she rubbed Taylor's shoulder soothingly. "But I'm not a pilot. What seems just kinda cloudy to me might mean something different if you had to fly in it."

"Yeah. Well, it was bad around Bethel and the south end of the Delta. So bad I couldn't make it to Goodnews Bay on a flight, so I stopped in Quinhagak to wait the weather out. When I taxied up, a bunch of villagers, including the health aide, ran up with a guy on a stretcher. They thought I was the medevac they'd called for, but I wasn't. The actual medevac was stuck in Bethel, waiting on the same weather I couldn't get through. Even though I knew better, I let them talk me into scud-running back to Bethel. On the way in, I nearly hit another plane doing the same thing going the opposite direction." The memory of the dangerous near-miss from which she'd barely escaped overpowered the current images around her. "I can't believe I did that. I was all caught up in saving that injured guy, and in the end he died anyway. I risked two innocent lives for no reason."

The other woman continued to rub Taylor's shoulder. "I'm sure you did everything you could, don't agonize over it." She withdrew her hand and dropped it in her lap. "What happened anyway? What kind of injury did he have?"

"He got beaten to a pulp. Head injuries, stab wounds, any kind of trauma you could think of. His heart stopped just out of Bethel. He was getting CPR to keep him going and I thought he'd make it, but he didn't. They lost him at the hospital.'' Taylor continued the story in a tentative voice, telling Kittie about the fight that caused the wounds, and what had prompted it.

"They got in a drunken brawl? Wanting more booze?'' Kittie's face twisted in horror. Undoubtedly she had heard similar tales. "Quinhagak is dry, how'd the dead guy get the booze?''

"I wondered about that, too.'' Taylor squinted out the window, then turned back to Kittie. "Somebody must've brought some back from a trip to Anchorage. For all I know, one of the passengers *I* flew to Quinhagak had it hidden in their baggage. There's no way to check for booze if they do that.''

"Yeah, I know. Once in a while someone brings it into Marshall, even though the village council tries to discourage that. I've seen the bad results of people getting drunk, but nobody has died. Yet.'' Kittie cocked her head and stared out the window, caught in private thoughts.

Taylor picked up on Kittie's somber mood, and tried to break the tension that was hanging in the air. "So, Kittie, what takes you to Bethel?''

Kittie continued to peer out the window, as though she hadn't heard Taylor, then abruptly swung around. "What? Oh, yeah, I'm delivering some baskets to the terminal gift shop, and I have to get some more supplies. Here, I'll show you what I've finished.'' She reached into the shopping bag and extracted a beautifully woven grass basket.

The basket stood six inches from its flat base to the tip of its handle. Stripes of red, orange, and olive were spliced into the tan grass plait of the cylindrical basket, and the same colors filled the geometrical patterns scattered at measured intervals along its side. A circular pad of leather was bound to the bottom of the basket to strengthen it.

Unconsciously releasing her hold on the aircraft controls, Taylor reached for the basket and cradled it in her hands. "This is gorgeous, Kittie! You made this yourself?'' She popped the lid off the top of the basket and looked inside, then snapped it back into its aperture. No fasteners connected the lid to the basket, nothing but the close tolerances between the two pieces held them together. "How can you weave this so tightly? The lid doesn't even fall off when you tip it over! God, is this intricate!"

Smiling shyly, Kittie shrugged. "I learned basket weaving from some of the older women when I arrived in the village. It took a lot of practice to get the weave that tight, but I had plenty of time to work on it during the winters. Not much goes on from November to March." She took the basket from Taylor's admiring fingers and eased it back into the bag. "I've got three more baskets in here. I'll sell them to the gift shop when we get to Bethel. The money will pay for some more supplies, and maybe some kind of a treat I can't get in Marshall." Then she laughed sarcastically. "I promised my nieces and nephews that I'd bring back some Eskimo Pies. They don't see the irony in that name; they just like the way the ice cream tastes."

Taylor joined Kittie in laughter, then patted her on the knee. She had forgotten how much fun Kittie could be, and how they'd really enjoyed their high school days together. It was surprising how easily they had slipped away from each other. Without going to basketball practices together, and sharing biology and math classes, they had just lost track of each other.

The two women spent some time reminiscing over their days together in high school—the afternoons of shooting hoops; the weekends of sprinting on the running track until their lungs burned; even the practical jokes they played in study hall.

The village of Russian Mission appeared ahead when Taylor guided the Cessna around the end of the Kuskokwim Mountains. With a short intake of breath, she looked out the windshield and cut her conversation short. Her gaze narrowed. With an index finger, she pointed at an odd sight: small, slate-colored plumes wafted up from the center of the settlement, the smoke rising in a nearly vertical line, unbroken by the calm air. "That's weird, Kittie," she said. "Why would the villagers light bonfires this time of the year? Or for that matter, this time of the day? They having some celebration?''

Kittie followed Taylor's gesture, confusion showing in her eyes. ''Not that I know of. There aren't any celebrations going on right now. Maybe that's the remains of a fire from a potlatch somebody had last night.''

Pressing the Cessna's control yoke forward, Taylor descended for a closer look. Most of the houses in Russian Mission crowded the lower reaches of the valley's mouth, and were hidden from view of Taylor's aircraft. But when the Cessna broke out of the hills, they came into focus.

Passing them on her way to the strip, Taylor peered down. Immediately she spotted the source of the smoke. ''It *was* a fire, Kittie, but more than for a potlatch.'' Her Yup'ik friend gawked over the back of the pilot's seat to catch a glimpse of it, and gasped.

At the edge of the village huddled the blackened remains of a dwelling, with small hot spots glowing here and there: the embers were the origin of the smoke.

The house had been gutted. Being familiar with the construction of the delta's cracker-box structures, Taylor guessed that its destruction had been nearly immediate. Fortunately for the town, the fire hadn't spread to any neighboring houses.

''What the hell . . .'' Taylor turned to look at Kittie and caught her strained expression.

SIX

After her startling discovery, Taylor made a quick approach and landing at Russian Mission. She needed some news from the TAC agent on the ground, who would know what had happened. She hoped the agent remembered her from before—some of the villagers were close-mouthed with strangers, and if the man didn't recognize her, he might not reveal any information.

The Cessna purred as she guided it to the small gravel unloading area, and she felt relief when she saw a familiar person perched on an all-terrain vehicle nearby. Silencing the engine, she unfastened her seat belt and hopped down from the plane. "I'll ask the agent about what happened," Taylor called back to Kittie. "You stay buckled up." The other woman just stared out the window, not acknowledging her—she had been strangely silent ever since they'd seen the smoking pile of rubble in the middle of the village.

Looking across the square, Taylor called to the TAC agent, a young Yup'ik man, perhaps twenty-five years old. "Bring your four-wheeler over, Max, I got plenty of stuff for you." She gestured at the aircraft's half-full cabin.

Tugging his knitted wool cap down over shaggy, dark hair, Max started the all-terrain vehicle and putted over.

"Hey, Taylor!" he called out as he approached and realized who stood in front of him. "Where you been? You
back for good?"

Taylor stood by the Cessna's cargo area, torn between
wanting to say hello to an old friend and needing to know
about the fire. Finally, she compromised, and did both.
"Max, good to see you. It's been a while, hasn't it?" she
said. "But don't get too used to seeing me, I won't be
here very long." She gave him a very brief version of
what had brought her back to the Y-K Delta, then prepared to ask about what she *really* wanted to talk about.

When he stepped off the ATV, she waved at the smoke
in the near distance. "Hey, I saw that burnt house on the
west side of the village when I came in. What happened
there?"

"Oh, damn. What a mess." Max snatched a case of
soda pop from the Cessna's open cabin, and with a disgusted expression he plopped it into a cart hitched to the
ATV. "A woman was smoking in bed and set her house
on fire. She got out in time, but she left her baby behind."

"Oh, God," Taylor muttered. "Is the baby okay, did
she go back for it?"

Snorting in distaste, Max shook his head. "No, she was
so drunk that she couldn't even do anything but stand
there and scream. When help came, they got the baby out,
but it had breathed so much smoke that it died in a few
minutes." His face crumpled. Obviously, the story was
getting to him. He roughly jerked another case out of the
airplane as though to distract himself from the memory.

Taylor reached into the Cessna's cabin to join him in
pulling the cargo out. She pursed her lips thoughtfully. "I
thought Russian was dry, Max. Did the town vote to go
damp? Did the lady bring the booze from Anchorage?"

The young Yup'ik's eyebrows fused together as he
scowled. "No, that wasn't it. Russian is still dry, and nobody's gone to Anchorage for a long time. It didn't come
from there." He angled his head, staring at the village.
"I think somebody flew it in, sold it to her."

"You think so, huh?" She chewed on her lower lip,

digesting the idea. "Whoever did that had to know that booze-running is illegal. None of the villages permit alcohol sales." Then she shrugged, realizing she couldn't do anything about it. "Anyway, if someone's bootlegging booze, the troopers will look into it."

Turning back to her work, she grabbed a box of Pampers. "Let's get the rest of this stuff unloaded. I gotta get back to town." She tossed the last box to Max, who loaded it in his ATV and motored off toward the village.

The Cessna's cabin empty, she jumped into the pilot's seat and stared at Kittie. Obviously, the young woman had heard snatches of the conversation between her and Max—her olive complexion was ashen.

Studying her friend, Taylor growled, "I can't believe that fire happened. That's two deaths back-to-back in dry villages—it has to be more than a coincidence."

Kittie gestured frantically at the runway as though to say, "Let's get out of here, right now." She was tight-lipped. Taylor realized the infant's death had really gotten to her, and for good reason. As a Yup'ik, and a health aide as well, she knew the insidious nature of alcohol and its effect on her people.

She said nothing for five minutes, did nothing but stare out the window while Taylor readied the Cessna for its takeoff. Not until the plane had climbed out and leveled off at a cruising altitude of three thousand feet did the upset woman utter a sound.

"You have to do something, Taylor," Kittie pleaded. She turned to her friend, her eyes bright with tears. "You heard what the agent said. He thinks somebody's smuggling booze into Russian Mission! In a plane! You're a pilot, you can figure out who's doing it. It may even be someone you know!"

Nodding, Taylor returned Kittie's look. "I was thinking the same thing. As soon as I learned about the fight in Quinhagak, I was wondering how the victim of the beating got the booze to sell to other villagers. Quinhagak is dry, too, they can't just go to the village store and buy a fifth of Wild Turkey." She reached down to adjust the plane's trim wheel, changing its cruising attitude. "These two so-called *accidents,* the one in Quinhagak *and* the one in Russian Mission, have to be connected. Somehow the booze is making its way to the villages, and it has to be done by airplanes. That's how everything travels. And once it gets into the villages it's leading to murder. Those guys from Quinhagak beat their supplier so bad he died. How many more times is that going to happen?"

Kittie's pretty face contorted into an angry mask. "Can't you discover who's bootlegging the booze, Taylor? You *know* the trouble alcohol causes. Ever since the fur trappers first brought it to Alaska, we've been fighting it. You've got access to information the troopers don't have, you can use that to help. I hate to see what's happenin—" Her wavering voice broke into sobs.

Taylor peered at her friend, unsure of what to say. She'd never seen the woman cry, not even when she'd broken her thumb in a hotly contested basketball game. "Kittie, what's wrong? That baby's death really got to you, didn't it?"

Shaking her head, Kittie protested, "No, it's not just that. I mean, a baby dying is bad, but . . ." She looked down at the bag in her lap, then back up to meet Taylor's puzzled frown. "I know a lot about how alcohol destroys families, firsthand. I guess I never told you why I was living with my aunt in Anchorage, did I?"

Shrugging, Taylor shook her head. "I just figured you wanted a better education to get ready for college. That made sense to me at the time." Her gaze narrowed as she searched her friend's eyes. "That wasn't it, though, was it?"

"No, it wasn't." A heavy sigh prefaced Kittie's next comment. "I was sent to stay with my aunt when my parents died. I was twelve at the time. They had taken our snowmachine to visit some friends downriver, and the machine broke through the ice. They couldn't get out. They drowned."

The skin on Taylor's cheekbones pulled back when she recognized what Kittie was implying. "They were drunk, weren't they? That's why they couldn't swim away from the snowmachine.'' She paused to search the other woman's face. ''And they got the booze from a bootlegger.''

Kittie nodded and swiped at a tear. ''Yeah. That's why I want you to find who's doing it this time.''

''But the troopers will do something about it. That's what they're for, to police the Delta.''

''Well, yeah, they probably will, but who knows when? You can start looking into things right away. Plus, you're one of the guys, Taylor. Nobody would suspect you. They might say something to you that they wouldn't say to a trooper.''

''Yeah . . .'' Taylor arched her eyebrows as she considered Kittie's words, then made another snap decision. ''Okay, I'm going to do it. I don't want to get in the way of the troopers, they probably wouldn't appreciate that. But maybe I can just do a little checking around.'' She nodded slowly, and looked out the window at the tundra flats disappearing behind her. ''Yeah, maybe I will.''

Daylight ebbed as the afternoon came to an end. As the color of the sky deepened to charcoal, the color of the runway lightened to dove gray as its surface dried.

At the end of her own day, Taylor secured her aircraft. Behind her, a blue-and-white DeHavilland Twin Otter approached the ramp area. The post light illuminating the airplane's tail shone down on the stenciled Western Alaska Transport logo. The Otter taxied onto the asphalt of the loading area and stopped. The engines' whine quieted as the propellers ceased their rotation, and the red and green nav lights on the wingtips flicked off.

Several handlers opened the Otter's cabin door, and began unloading baggage and escorting passengers inside. Taylor vaguely heard someone climb down from the cockpit, though she ignored the sounds and concentrated on her work.

A cry broke through the silence, grating on her ears. ''Hey, Taylor! Way to go! What the hell were you doing yesterday? Did you let that guy die on purpose, or was it just an accident?''

She spun around, feeling her features crumble. Then, upon realizing the words came from Jack Shumock, her expression changed into one of indignation.

''Oh, fuck off!'' she retorted, feeling the color rise on her cheeks. ''I did everything I could!''

''That's my point, you did everything *you* could!'' Jack grinned maliciously as she sucked in her breath and swung away, rummaging in the airplane for her flight paperwork.

Gripping the aluminum clipboard, she dashed from the ramp.

Once inside the terminal, she threw the clipboard on her company's counter and scowled. ''That asshole,'' she snarled. Her pulse hammered in her eardrum, and she felt like shaking something. She knew calling Shumock a vulgar name wouldn't do anything to shield her from his attacks, but it still felt good.

It took several seconds to compose herself. Once the pounding in her ears moderated, she snapped at the dispatcher. ''I guess I'm done, Dan.''

Dan's eyebrows flicked up, surprised by her tone of voice, and pulled her paperwork off the clipboard. ''Yeah, sounds like you *are* done, Taylor. Kinda frazzled, actually. Not a cool day, huh?''

''No, not a very cool *couple* of days.'' She scrunched her face into an ugly contortion, as she unzipped her jacket. ''First I get to spend yesterday fighting the weather and scaring the holy hell out of myself, then later I get a ration of shit from Shumock. Apparently, he does not approve of the way I handled that medevac from Quinhagak.'' She looked out toward the ramp, frowning. ''Oh, well, I have better things to worry about than his bullshit opinions. Forget it. I want to go home.'' Then a thought occurred to her. ''At least I have a home to go back to. Some woman from Russian isn't so lucky. Not only is her house gone, so is her baby.''

''What the hell happened there?''

"Same thing as at Quinhagak. Booze. The woman got drunk, started smoking in bed, and set the house on fire. The baby died from smoke inhalation." Her brow creased as the image of the smoke plumes came to her mind.

Dan looked puzzled. "But Russian's dry, just like Quinhagak. Where's the booze coming from?" He tapped his pencil eraser on the counter. "Sounds to me like somebody's bootlegging."

"Yeah, I agree with you." Taylor stared at the counter for a second, drumming her fingers on it, then looked up at Dan. She thought about telling him of her resolve to look into the booze-running, but decided to keep it to herself. He'd probably think it was stupid. "Anyway, that Kwethluk run was the last one, right? Can I go home?"

"Yeah, get outta here, go get some dinner. I know it hasn't been fun for you the past couple of days." Then he grinned. "Aren't you glad you agreed to come back out here for a while?" Getting nothing from her but a malevolent sneer, he shut up. "Never mind. See you in the morning, Taylor."

Taylor headed for the door to the parking lot, dragging her gloves out of her pocket. "Later!" she called over her shoulder. The day had been nothing like pleasant, and she longed to get home.

She walked to a dinged and dented Volkswagen Rabbit, the best vehicle Dan Mackenzie could find for her when he heard she'd be back in Bethel for a few weeks. He'd borrowed it from a friend who was out of state, since no rental cars were available in this town of five thousand residents.

Pulling out onto the single paved road in Bethel, she began the drive to her studio apartment. Her mind was far away as she distractedly steered the vehicle around the potholes and frost heaves.

After ten minutes of bouncing down the road, she swung into the small lot in front of the apartment building that contained the TAC crew quarters. Leaving her gloved hands in her jacket pocket, she shouldered her way into the building. The heavy door slammed in her wake and the inside air began to thaw her chilled features. She wriggled her lips to get them moving again.

Trudging down the hallway, she glanced at her surroundings. Sickly ochre walls bordered the hall, reminiscent of an abandoned army barracks mildewing at a faraway post. Just as it had years earlier, the obnoxious color on the hallway walls stupefied her—she was in no mood to appreciate the humor in it. Heavy-duty gray carpeting, stained by a winter's worth of dirty snow, covered the hallway she strode down.

The apartment she entered lived up to its name: an efficiency. The single room measured twelve feet by eighteen feet, with a tiny bathroom and shower near the hall entranceway. A narrow kitchen counter sat by a small refrigerator and sink, which separated the bathroom from something loosely called a living room.

Taylor tossed her jacket on a drooping beige sofa that looked like it came from Goodwill. Glancing around the room, her eyes fixed on the light-green tint of the walls. It looked, not surprisingly, like the place she had lived years earlier, three doors down the hall. "Don't they ever change decorators here?" she murmured, amazed by the tackiness of the place. She hadn't missed that part of living in Bethel, either.

A rumpled army blanket dangled off the edge of the double bed in the corner. Several magazines lay on a coffee table across from the bed, and a red, cubical clock radio displayed the time from a night table.

She sighed resignedly, then opened the tiny refrigerator to extract another frozen dinner. Time to eat, even though she still had no appetite. Staring at the frosty box with a glassy-eyed expression, she stood with her mind in neutral.

It'd been a long day.

A knock interrupted her trance. Pushing away from the door, Taylor reached down to turn its knob, a confused expression on her face. Who would be looking for her? None of her coworkers had shown any interest in getting to know a short-timer like her, and an urban occurrence like door-to-door solicitation didn't happen in Bethel.

As the door creaked open, it revealed a familiar form, and she gaped. Jeff Davidson's tall frame filled the opening, his large hands stuffed into his jacket pockets.

She hadn't seen her former lover for three years, and thought he'd moved to Washington State. But here he was, back in Bethel, looking for her. Their split hadn't been amicable. Why would he try to track her down? What did he want? Was he just looking to get laid, for old time's sake?

Think again, Jeff, she pouted.

"Hey, Taylor." His voice made her spine tingle. "Just got back from my week off, heard you were in town. Thought I'd go see if it was true. Looks like it is."

She set her lips into a straight, tight line. "Jeff," she acknowledged, attempting to wash any emotion from her words. "I thought you were in Seattle."

"I was," he laughed. "But I came back when Western offered me a better job. I'm an Otter captain now; couldn't very well turn that down."

"Ah, that's it." She tightened her grasp on the doorknob. "Well, I'm only here for a few weeks, and I'm not interested in picking up where we left off, if that's why you're here." She began to close the door, but he wedged a foot in front of it. She glared at it. That was one of the reasons she'd broken it off with him—he was a bit too aggressive.

"Hey, I'm not here to get you back. We've gone through that before. It wasn't any fun." He sidled inside the room and closed the door behind him. "If I recall correctly, we make better friends than lovers, so I thought I'd just stop by and say 'hi.' Nothing else."

Her eyebrows rose. "Well, that's nice, but I'm not in the mood for company. Had a hard day yesterday...."

"Yeah, I heard about it," he confirmed, his head canted. "You wanna talk about it?"

She scowled. News travels fast, especially when you want to forget it. But she wanted to clear her name, tell

Jeff what was behind the failed medevac. Even though their relationship had soured in a big way, she still felt compelled to paint herself as an attractive mate. If he thought her ability as a pilot had caused the patient from Quinhagak to die, he'd see her as his inferior.

She was *nobody's* inferior.

Studying his face, she sketched out the story of the previous day's disaster. He nodded as she spoke, seeming to understand her frustration. "I can see why you're pissed," he concurred, "busting your ass to save somebody, only to have them die once they get to the hospital. That sucks. Don't you wish you didn't have to go on medevacs because somebody got shit-faced and beat somebody up?"

She stared at him. Didn't he see the puzzle in what had happened? "Hey, Quinhagak is dry. Don't you wonder where the booze getting sold came from?"

He shrugged. "That's not my problem," he asserted. "If the villagers want the stuff bad enough, they'll find a way to get it."

Shaking her head, she snorted. "Hey, they got some help this time. Somebody's got a booze-running operation going. I saw other signs of it." She outlined what she'd seen in Russian Mission, and saw his expression change. Maybe he *did* see the mystery in it. "Anyway, I don't like it, and I want to do something about it."

Jeff's eyebrows rose. "Hey, what can you do? You have no authority, you're not a trooper. You're not even a VPSO. All you can do is get in the way if the troopers decide to start an investigation." He stepped closer and looked down at her. "Anyway, I don't want to see you get caught up in this. You'll be gone soon, and the smuggling will still be going on—that'll make you feel like shit 'cuz you hadn't stopped it. Don't set yourself up for that." He stroked her cheek lightly. "I remember how you used to feel when you didn't get something finished the way you wanted. You weren't much fun."

She glanced up at his solicitous expression. That hadn't been one of their problems, an inability on his part to understand how she reacted to different situations. Maybe he was right—she should leave it alone.

Then she shook her head. "No, I gotta try to figure this out. I'd feel even worse if I didn't."

SEVEN

The next morning the weather had changed noticeably, from three-thousand-foot cloud ceilings to a high overcast. Upon reaching the airport, Taylor glanced up at the sky and shrugged. The change didn't faze her a bit. As an Alaskan pilot, she found such a shift in the conditions typical, and she realized the only predictable thing about the weather was its unpredictability.

Thoughts of forecasting the weather flooded her mind as she pushed through the door into the warmth of the terminal. With the temperatures cooling, she looked back with regret on the warmer days of August, nothing but a memory now.

"Morning, Dan," she greeted the dispatcher when she reached the ticket counter. "Starting to get nippy out there. Good thing I put the engine and wing covers on my plane last night." She gestured outside with a thumb like she was hitchhiking. "Too bad there's no hangar to put the planes in, like I've got in Anchorage."

Dan glanced up from his paperwork, and smiled. "Well, you're not the only one that thinks that. The other guys are used to hangars, too, don't like this no-frills setup one bit."

"Oh, well. At least *I'll* be going back to Anchorage

soon. They'll still be stuck here.'' She zipped her flight jacket, and glanced out the terminal windows. ''Anyway, I better go unwrap my plane, Dan. I'll be back in a few minutes, check on today's schedule.'' She ambled off, humming tunelessly.

With the heavy glass door swooshing behind her, she tugged a knit hat out of her pocket and pulled it down over her hair. While attempting to blow mock smoke rings in the cool air with her breath, she headed toward the bevy of TAC aircraft parked near the terminal.

''Morning, Bob,'' she said to her coworker, who was pulling nylon wing covers off one of the Cessnas. ''You're here kinda early.''

Bob Allum looked over his shoulder, his chiseled cheeks tinged pink. Strands of blond hair poked out from beneath a blue baseball hat adorned with a TAC patch. ''Hi there, Taylor. I guess I am here early, but I figured I should be.'' He turned back to his work, raising his voice to carry over the swishing of fabric and the snap of elastic cords. ''I've never had to put wing and engine covers on before, and I didn't know how long it would take to get them off. I had to make sure I had enough time.''

''Well, you'll get used to it in a while. I went through the same thing when I started.'' Taylor smiled, remembering her first days as a commercial pilot years earlier, when she worried so much about doing everything correctly. Just like Bob, she had given herself extra time to become used to unfamiliar procedures.

The sounds of Bob stuffing the last wing cover into the Cessna's cabin jerked her out of her daydream. As he wriggled his gangly frame into the pilot's seat, he called out to her. ''Gonna go do my run-up, Taylor. I'll talk to you later!''

He started the engine and taxied from the tie-down area. The blast of air from the plane's propeller whirled over her and she grabbed her hat with gloved fingers. Turning toward her own plane, she prepared to begin her own tasks.

Ten minutes later, after stuffing her Cessna's covers into the rear cabin, she approached the terminal again. Blowing on her chilled fingers, she nudged the terminal door open with one hip. Cold air rushed past her as she pushed inside. Noises washed over the whisper of the closing door: the rustle of paperwork at the ticket counters, the thumps and thuds of baggage dropping down on a scale.

With a hand massaging her cold nose, she dodged around a passenger standing at Tundra Air Charter's desk. "Okay, I'm all ready to go, Dan, what's first?"

"Tooksook Bay," he said, glancing up from a ticket receipt. "You got some supplies for the village store to take out." Then he grinned mischievously. "Oh yeah, the agent also said that there was a youngster out there to bring back to Bethel. The kid's grandma took the agent aside and told him that she's pretty scared of airplanes. She figured her grandkid would die in a crash or something, and was worried enough to tell the agent to make sure the pilot that comes out is good. So, watch out for the kid and take good care of him. I'm sure Grandma let him know how frightened she was, and he may be scared shitless too. Give him a good ride. Maybe if he has fun, he'll take back a good word—a little PR can't hurt."

Gaping at him, she narrowed her eyes. "Oh, great," she complained. "How did I get stuck with that? I have zero experience with children, and I'm not really excited about playing nursemaid when I'm flying."

"Well, whatever. It's still on your schedule for the day," he chuckled. "Plus, he might be more comfortable with a woman."

A groan issued from her lips. She hated the assumption that every woman had an innate ability and desire to watch over children. She was a pilot, damn it, not a nanny.

"Well, I'll see what I can do, but no guarantees." She snatched the dispatch manifest from Dan, and snapped it onto her clipboard. Scowling, she stamped off.

"If he gets so scared that he tosses his cookies, I'm not

cleaning it up,'' she called over her shoulder. Dan laughed at her last remark, but she meant every word.

A John Cougar Mellencamp ballad warbled through the earpieces of Taylor's headset when she tuned the Automatic Direction Finder to the station KYUK, the ''voice of the Yukon.''

She tapped her fingertips on the control yoke, as she peered down at the gray-green plain below. Lakes dotted the tundra, a skim of ice bordering the edges of some of them. Not until she neared the village of Tooksook Bay, seventy-five miles west of Bethel, did the terrain differ. At that point, a line of thousand-foot-high hills sprouted from the muskeg. Just beyond them, the dull blue waters of the Bering Sea spread to the horizon.

She reached down and adjusted her trim wheel. Glancing over her shoulder, she looked over the boxes behind her, held firmly in place by a cargo net. After checking on her load, she gazed out her side window at the hills slipping past. No animals appeared on them: none of the Dall sheep found near Turnagain Arm, no moose, no bears. She pondered the lifelessness of the region as the plane droned on.

It amazed her that any animals lived on the inhospitable tundra plains, but she knew some did. Tiny marmots and pikas burrowed furiously under the ground as the 207 flew past, foxes trotted across the muskeg on their way to a den, and fur seals bobbed in the frigid water off the coast five miles away.

Taylor readied her 207 for a landing on the airstrip dug into the hills surrounding the village of Tooksook Bay, which clung to their eastern bank. Upon touch-down, she taxied into the small unloading square and jumped out of the cockpit. She smiled at the Yup'ik agent limping toward her, surprised to see someone else she knew from her previous days with TAC. Hadn't anyone moved in three years?

The old man didn't appear to be taken aback by seeing her for the first time in quite a while. It was as though

she hadn't ever left. Amused by his lack of excitement
for her return, she just pointed back at the fully packed
Cessna matter-of-factly—two could play that game—and
said, "I've got a bunch of stuff for the store, George. You
ready for it?"

George tugged the ear flaps of his beaver hat down over
his greasy, gray hair and trudged her way. His parka's fox
fur ruff framed an O-shaped face, and his rheumy eyes
spoke of a long, tough life. His squat body, typical of the
Yup'ik people, displayed nature's design for humans that
lived in cold climates.

After undoing the cargo net, Taylor climbed into the
cabin and began passing boxes out to George, one by one.
She dragged cartons of pilot bread crackers to the door,
following them with cases of soda pop and canned tuna
fish.

About five minutes later, the last case of Campbell's
chicken and rice soup got tossed into the large pile on the
ground. Stretching and twisting, she massaged her lower
torso. "Good thing I don't have a bad back," she muttered, eyeing the stack of groceries on the ground. Pointing at the pile, she asked, "You got somebody that can
help you with that stuff, George? It's a lot, and I don't
want you to hurt yourself."

Cracking a snaggle-toothed grin, the agent pointed at
an ATV moving toward them on the road from the village.

The sound of the approaching vehicle and the clatter of
its attached cart made her recall her previous day's trip to
Russian. She shuddered, then decided to ask the old
Yup'ik man some questions.

"Hey, George, have you had any problems with booze
getting into the village lately? You know, somebody
bringing it in by airplane?"

"No. . . ." The gray-haired elder frowned at her, looking like he didn't understand her question. "Nobody's
been bringing booze in, the village is dry. The council
voted on it, and nobody can bring it. Even when they
come back from Bethel."

Apparently, George didn't get it. She tried again.

"Well, that's not exactly what I meant. Has anybody flown in with a load of booze, and sold it? Maybe one of your friends bought some."

George continued to look perplexed. "But the village is dry. Why would anyone bring booze in?"

A tentative smile washed over her face. She found George's innocence disarming. He was so unfamiliar with criminal ways that it made no sense to him that someone would break rules. "Yeah, I guess you're right," she agreed. She must have gotten too disturbed by Kittie's unhappiness the previous day, and lost her objectivity.

Sticking her hands in her jeans pockets, she watched the ATV approach with a sturdy young Native man perched behind the handlebars. She pondered what George had said. Why *would* anyone smuggle alcohol into a dry village? Booze-running was a crime, and the Yup'ik people were not stupid. Eventually, they would discover what was going on and turn to the troopers.

Shrugging as she ended her conjecture, she glanced at a youngish Native boy lolling by the airstrip's edge. He appeared to be about ten or eleven years old. When he noticed she was gazing at him, he busied himself by tucking a Teenage Mutant Ninja Turtles T-shirt into his well-worn jeans.

"Is that my passenger?" she asked George, interrupting his work with the pile of groceries. When he nodded yes, she smiled in relief. The boy wasn't too young, so he wouldn't be much trouble to watch over. Nanny duty wasn't called for—it would be more like supervising.

"You ready to go?" Taylor called out to him, gesturing at the open passenger door.

A Seattle Seahawks cap appeared from the pocket of his torn acrylic parka, and he tugged it on as he trudged to the Cessna. He wavered as though something held him back.

She could tell that he was ready to pee his pants, he was so scared, so she stepped forward and led him to the door. "He'll be fine," she reassured the onlooking agent. "I can handle him, no problem."

"Hop up here," she said cheerfully, pointing next to the pilot's seat. "You can be my copilot, okay? What's your name, anyway?"

He stared at her like a zombie for a second, then muttered, "Nikolai," and climbed up into the cockpit. She joined him, clambering through the left side door.

"Nikolai, huh?" she replied. "Okay, Nikolai, here we go. Sit tight." The 207 taxied out of the loading area and she applied power to send it barreling down the rutted runway.

Forty-five minutes later, Taylor escorted an ecstatic Nikolai from the Cessna into the terminal, and approached the TAC counter. Carl Roston stood next to it, talking to Dan Mackenzie and pointing at the schedule board on the wall. The two men appeared to be arguing.

Carl had changed into a heavier down jacket and wore sturdy Sorel boots, appearing to be prepared for winter. Maybe the colder weather was making him cranky.

Sidling up to the counter, Taylor cocked her head and nodded at Nikolai, wanting to alert Dan to the boy's glee. The dispatcher smiled when he saw the beaming boy, but Carl just stared at him crossly.

"Did I do a good job with him, or what?" she whispered to Dan. "You trusted the right pilot with this job." She was pleased with herself. She realized handling children was not her forte, but she knew she could figure it out.

The parking lot door opened as they stood there watching Nikolai grin like an Indy 500 winner. A chubby Native woman dashed over when she glimpsed the boy, and wrapped her arms around him in a protective embrace.

"Mother, mother!" Nikolai squeaked, his cries muffled by her hug. "I flew the airplane! I flew the airplane! It was great!"

Nikolai's mother glared at Taylor, mistrust in her eyes. Taylor recognized the look, and realized the woman had the same unreasonable fear of planes as the Tooksook Bay grandmother.

"He was a bit nervous when we left Tooksook Bay," Taylor confessed, "so I let him do a little of the flying. He felt better then." She assumed that would reassure Mama Yup'ik, but the Native woman retained her unpleasant look.

The boy was still expounding on the flight as his tight-lipped mother paid for his fare. Even as she steered him toward the terminal exit, his excited stammering filled the air. Taylor watched them disappear through the door, and when she turned back to Dan she caught the expression on Carl's face. "What?" she snapped.

"You let that Native runt fly?" Carl sneered.

Taylor glared at him. "Yeah, I let him fly! He was frightened. I figured I'd let him rest his hand on the yoke for a few minutes, after it was all trimmed out. He was too busy with that to stay scared." Her eyes darted to the terminal door swinging shut, then back to Carl. "He couldn't have hurt anything, anyway, and you know that."

"Yeah, Carl, lay off Taylor." Dan squinted at the man, exasperated. He seemed to think Carl was being a snot. "I told her to give the kid a good ride, and everything worked out just fine."

"Yeah, I knew what I was doing," Taylor retaliated. "I wouldn't let anything happen to the plane."

Carl snorted. "Anything could've happened, though. Those Natives don't know shit about airplanes, especially the kids."

Taylor immediately realized his comment reflected a bigoted dislike of the Yup'ik people, and that surprised her. Not the prejudice—plenty of people were dumb enough to act that way—but she thought he'd come from Washington State recently. How'd he pick up that kind of attitude so fast? She scowled at the man. If it weren't for his Native passengers, he wouldn't even have a job.

"Oh, come on, Carl," she retorted. "I just let him put his hand on the yoke, it was no big deal." Her hackles rose, and she felt herself color. She had gotten pretty fed up with him, in just three days.

"You probably let him fly all the way back to Bethel," Carl sniveled.

"No, I didn't," she protested. "But both of us know that's nothing he couldn't have done. If you think this job is such a daredevil stunt, you better think it over again. It's no incredible feat; we're just glorified bus drivers." She knew that her job as a pilot made her different from other people, but did not make her better than anyone.

She added another comment to irk him, eager to poke at a sore spot. "Think about it, Carl, even a *woman* can do the same thing you do! That bothers the hell out of you, doesn't it? That means you're not the stud you thought you were!"

Carl scowled at Taylor, then stomped off across the terminal to the ramp exit.

"You know, Dan," she laughed as Carl disappeared, "he doesn't have much tolerance for jabs when they're aimed at him. He's pretty good at poking at me, but he can't handle equal treatment."

She arched her eyebrows as the ramp door swished closed. Turning back toward Dan, she asked, "So, what were you guys arguing about when I walked up?"

Dan coughed and waved a hand. "Oh, you know, Carl's always pissing and moaning about getting short flights on his schedule. I told him things'll change in a week or so—he's only been flying here for three days—but he says he can't make any money if all he gets is short runs. He seems to think he has a right to fly nothing but the long ones. I keep telling him that the short runs are divided between all the pilots, he's not singled out to do them, but he still squawks."

"Well, that's typical. He's been a pain in the ass ever since I met him when I got in." She peered at the schedule board on the wall. "Anyway, what's next for me?"

EIGHT

The next morning dawned clear, with a bite of cold in the air. Fall was packing its bag, ready to head to another clime in the southern hemisphere. Winter stood by the door, eager to accept an invitation to stay for a visit.

A red-and-mustard-gold aircraft appeared in the sky to the north of the village of Tuntutuliak, known locally as "Tunt." The village's twenty-five small wooden houses huddled together on the tundra plain near a small creek, with a short gravel airstrip running between the town and the water.

The whine of the airplane's engine eased as it began the descent toward the airstrip. A minute later, the Cessna touched down firmly, tiny fragments of gravel pinging off its belly as it decelerated. It rolled into a small, cleared square at the end of the strip, and a Tundra Air Charter agent pushed a wheelbarrow toward it to receive the incoming cargo.

As the agent stopped nearby, the propeller spun to a halt and the colored wingtip strobes flicked off. Taylor Morgan zipped her jacket and climbed out of the airplane, waving at the waiting man. "Hi there, Herman. What's up?"

The Yup'ik man pulled work gloves out of his parka as he ambled over. His tobacco-stained teeth glinted in the morning sun, and he grinned at her. "Hey, lady. Got some stuff for me?" he asked in his gutturally accented English. He spit a dark brown glop of chew out of his mouth.

She matched his wide smile. "Sure do, Herman, all kinds of stuff." She liked Herman, as she liked most of the agents, and they seemed to delight in seeing a woman jump down from the cockpit of an airplane. As she slammed the pilot's door shut, she glanced at a figure who paced the edge of the strip twenty feet away.

When the anxious man saw her, he approached the airplane. His cheeks were battered and bruised, and his whole face was puffy and swollen. Undoubtedly more black-and-blue marks hid under the beaver-pelt hat he wore.

"Good Lord!" Taylor gaped at him. "You look like something the cat dragged in," she joked.

The young man looked away, red-faced.

"James got into the bottle last night," Herman grumbled, "and got into a fight." The older Yup'ik's glare made the younger one cringe.

"Got into the bottle?" Taylor's gaze narrowed. "Tunt's dry. Where'd the booze come from?" She looked at James quizzically, but Herman chose to speak for him.

"James says somebody flew it in, sold it to his friends."

Startled, she turned to the young man. Somebody flew it in? Booze-running had happened in Tuntutuliak? In the past few days as she thought about it, she had come to the conclusion that the liquor-fueled trouble in Quinhagak and Russian Mission were unrelated incidents, not part of a pattern. But it had happened again here, in Tunt. Her first hunch, that someone was smuggling liquor into the villages, *was* true.

"Who was it that flew it in, James?" She raised her hand to quiet Herman, who was posed to answer again. She wanted to hear it from the person involved.

James squinted at her, then looked away. "I don't know. I just went to a party, it was there. I guess my friend bought it, I don't know who sold it."

Shaking her head, she was fairly sure James knew the answer to her question, but wouldn't divulge it. He was holding back. Even if he really didn't know where it had come from, he certainly could find out easily enough.

She tried again. "But didn't you see anybody, a stranger, maybe, bringing the booze in? Did you see *anything?*" The need to discover the origin of the contraband made her want to lean forward, pull the words out of his mouth. If her guess had been correct, she had to support it.

"No, I didn't see nothing." James stubbed his boot into the ground for a few seconds, then looked up. "Well, I did see some airplane taking off last night, right before I got to the party. I don't know who it was, though—must'a been a charter."

She suspected James was throwing her a tidbit, just enough to get her out of his hair, but not enough to serve as a real clue. "An airplane, huh? What kind of airplane? What color? Did you see any numbers painted on the side?"

"Hey, it was night," he protested. "I couldn't see nothing. Plane looked dark, though, not white. Maybe red? And kinda small, smaller than this one." James gestured at her Cessna 207.

Herman stood by silently, watching Taylor and James trade words. His head bobbed from person to person as though he was at a tennis match. Absently, he hawked another slug of chewing tobacco away.

"Were the plane's wings on the top of the body?" she asked, hoping to goad more information from James. It was like pulling teeth. "Or were the wings by the belly? Did you notice?"

If he really *did* see an airplane.

With a shrug, James grunted. "I don't know, maybe on top, like your plane."

She nodded. "That would probably make it a Cessna.

Did it have a tail wheel, James? Was it sitting on a wheel that hung under its tail?''

He shook his head no, uncertainty washing across his expression. She figured he was realizing he'd said too much, and would clam up soon.

"Okay," she conceded, giving him some slack. "Then it has to be a Cessna, not a Piper Super Cub." But that fact wouldn't be much help. She knotted her eyebrows as she thought about the dozens of Cessnas that called the Bethel airport home. Too many, but at least not all of them were red. That would narrow the search a little.

James interrupted her pondering. "But that plane I saw could have been a charter, not the one with the booze." He glanced at her noncommittally. "I'm just guessing, I only saw it taking off. I didn't see who was flying it."

Taylor's lips pursed, as she looked from Herman, to her Cessna, back to James. The younger man was starting to weasel; she had probably gotten everything she could out of him.

Unable to extract any more facts from James, she turned to the agent. "Okay, Herman, let's get busy unloading this stuff. There's a lot here, and it won't unload itself."

She opened the rear door and clambered into the cabin. But in her rush to get back to her job, she clipped her shin on a case of Spam. "Damn!" she grunted, rubbing her leg. Grumpily, she began slinging cartons of canned sardines and pilot bread toward the door.

In about five minutes, the Cessna was empty. Her job on the ground was done, though the agent's was just beginning. Crammed with boxes, the wheelbarrow listed to the side, but Herman just grasped the handles and set off toward the village. Grabbing the pilot's door, she swung around to look at James. "So, ready to go? Come on, jump in. Other side."

He stepped forward and smiled slightly in acknowledgment. When he parted his torn lips, she saw bloody gaps between his remaining teeth and she flinched. Someone had knocked out a hole the size of a quarter between them.

"Getting drunk doesn't seem like such a great idea the next day, does it?" she asked, rhetorically.

Once on the ground in Bethel, Taylor taxied 96U to the front of the terminal and eased it into its parking slot. Thirty feet away sat TAC's red-and-mustard-gold Cessna 310, with insulated engine covers draped over its twin engine pods. A thin fuzz of frost powdered the neon orange nylon fabric. Farther away a WAT Twin Otter was parked, its propeller blades slowly rotating.

Jumping down to the asphalt, she peered over her shoulder to watch James exit the plane from the right. A *clunk!* ricocheted across the Cessna's body when he slammed the passenger door behind him. His heavy footfalls thumped on the ground as he trudged toward her, and she called out for him to follow her into the terminal.

He stepped in front of the nose of the aircraft to meet her, and she shuddered again at the sight of him. His mashed face still made her stomach churn. She had been cautious during the flight not to look at him unless necessary—his swollen and torn lips made her realize how much pain he must be feeling.

The two of them headed for the terminal. The heavy glass door whooshed as she swung it open and guided him inside. "I bet you'll be glad to see a doctor about your mouth," she said. "It hurts just looking at it." ⎯

James nodded, smiling without parting his lips. He appeared to realize how he looked to Taylor.

"Here's one from Tuntutuliak, Dan," she told the dispatcher upon approaching the ticket counter. "And no, I didn't punch him," she joked, gesturing at James's face. "I never touched him, honest."

After a quick survey of the young man, Dan seemed posed to ask a question about James's frayed appearance, but he checked himself. Instead, he reached down for a ticket receipt and began scribbling on it. "One way from Tuntutuliak, or do you need a return ticket?"

James looked at the form Dan held, and his eyes widened. "I don't have any money," he stuttered. He glanced at Taylor, as though she would come to his rescue.

Dan looked up, interrupting his scrawl, and turned to her, as well. "What's this?" he scowled.

The statement caught her off guard. "I didn't know about this," she said to Dan, and glared at James. "Why didn't you say something before we left the village?" She felt he was taking advantage of her, and she did not care for that. No one had ever whelched on a ticket on one of her flights before. "Did you tell Herman you had money, or what?"

After a few seconds of silence from James that answered her question, she shook her head and shrugged. "Well, I guess he has more to worry about than a ticket, huh?" She pointed at his bruised face, blood caked on the tear around his mouth, and shivered. "Why don't you just give him a break, Dan? There must be a way we can handle this, without getting stiffed. Herman knows this guy, he can probably get him to pay up when he gets home. Why don't we let this slide for a while?" She stared pointedly at the young Yup'ik. "If he doesn't come up with the money when I fly him back to Tunt, I'll just take his beaver hat as payment."

"What if the Tunt flight isn't on your schedule the day he goes back?" Dan asked. "What if you're not even here by then?" He shook his head. "I don't want a beaver hat as a trade for a ticket. I already have one."

"Well, I don't," she stated, and fingered the velvety surface of James's hat. "I'll buy it from him."

James nodded vigorously, his eyes showing gratitude.

"Okay, I'll let him go," Dan agreed. "But if we get stiffed on this, it's coming out of your pay, Taylor."

"Yeah, well . . ." She nudged James. "Go get your mouth fixed. Maybe they'll give you some painkillers. I think you probably need some."

As she watched the thankful James hurry to the front terminal door, she absently leafed through her flight paperwork. Movement to her right captured her attention and she saw Jeff Davidson stride in from the ramp, leading half-a-dozen passengers to the WAT counter. After turning them over to Ray, the dispatcher, he looked across the terminal and caught her eye. "Hey, Taylor," he called, heading in her direction.

She hesitated, then strolled over to meet him in the middle of the room.

"You got time for some lunch before your next departure?" he asked.

She looked over her shoulder at the digital wall clock to give herself some time to think. Was he really trying to be friends? she wondered. Her mind raced. His visit to her apartment the other night had surprised her—not only had he acted platonically; he hadn't even tried to kiss her when he'd left.

He must be lonely out here, she thought. May as well help him. She could run her ideas about the smuggling past him, too—he'd always been a good sounding board. As long as they remained nothing but friends, it might work. "Okay," she consented, "I've got a few minutes." As though on cue, her stomach grumbled noisily.

The two of them turned for the stairs that led to the eatery upstairs.

Three minutes later, they were in line for some grub. "Why's it so crowded in here today?" she asked him as she scanned the room.

He glanced around in turn. People occupied nearly every table. "I don't know. Must be a lot of people waiting for the afternoon jet from Anchorage."

She shrugged, and tugged a folded ten-dollar bill out of her pocket. On her tray she had the daily special, Oriental vegetables and rice. As she stood at the cash register, she noticed the top of a Chun King box sticking out of a garbage can in the kitchen. "So, where do you think this meal came from?" she asked Jeff, pointing at the telltale sign.

"What did you expect?" he replied, grinning. "This *is* Bush Alaska, I haven't seen any Asians out here."

After she paid for her meal, she and Jeff surveyed the room for an empty table. Not until another couple vacated theirs were they able to sit.

Once they'd placed their trays in front of them, both she and Jeff dug into the food greedily. With her mouth full, she mumbled, "I had an odd flight to Tuntutuliak today," and reiterated the story she'd heard from James. When she mentioned that she thought he was withholding on her to protect someone, she waited for a reaction from him. Would Jeff continue to advise her to quit worrying about what was occurring?

No reaction came, though, so she continued. "Somebody's definitely running booze to the villages. I was pretty sure it was going on in Goodnews and Russian, but I wasn't certain until I heard it was happening in Tuntutuliak. Now it's too obvious to blame on coincidence. You got any ideas about who could be behind it?" She poked her fork into her lunch, twirling the tines.

Jeff looked out the window as he pondered. "Hmmm, I don't know. Some of the guys that fly out here are pretty scummy, but I don't know if they'd get into something like that. If they got caught, it could jeopardize their tickets. Without pilot's licenses, they couldn't make a living out here. They're kinda slimy, but not stupid." He laughed.

She rolled her eyes, and dumped more rice into her mouth. "Well, I told you I was going to do some snooping around, so I guess I should start now. That guy from Tunt saw a plane last night, and told me about it. If he was telling me the truth, that may be a place to begin." She took a sip of her Pepsi. "After work, I'm going to check out the flight line. If I spot a plane that matches his description, I'll poke around, see if anything suspicious pops up."

"Are you serious?" Jeff chuckled, shaking his head. "I thought you were kidding when you talked about that the other night. I've never seen your amateur detective side before, but it's kinda cute."

She glared at him, waving her fork at his nose. "Cute?" she glowered. "I'm not trying to be cute! I just don't like the idea of somebody getting booze to the dry villages. You remember what my friend Kittie said. Hearing her story really got to me." A plane taxiing past the window drew a brief glance from her, then she looked back at him. "I'm gonna do something, if I can. I owe it to Kittie."

After taking another gulp of her Pepsi, she wiped her mouth with the back of her hand and shoved her chair back. "I'm gonna look around, even if you think I'm acting stupid. I don't like this." She stood up, arms akimbo. "Stop by tonight, *if* you want to know what I find out. I may surprise you. Anyway, dump my plate for me, will you?"

She marched off, determination in her step.

NINE

By a quarter after four, the sun had begun its trek downward to the horizon. Most of the airplanes were secured for the night, with covers wrapped around their cowlings and draped over their windshields. The bright reds and oranges of the insulated nylon added a subtle dash of color to the monochromatic landscape around the airport.

Very little activity stirred the airfield at that time of the day: with their charges bedded down, most of the pilots had headed home.

Taylor stood alone on the asphalt apron in front of the terminal, snugging down the fasteners on her Cessna's engine cover. After snapping the last buckle, she patted the side of the aircraft's cowling. "I'll see you first thing in the morning. I've got some work to do right now."

Then a wry expression crossed her face and she rolled her eyes. "You're losing it, Taylor," she muttered to herself. "You're talking to your *airplane.*" Shaking her head in exasperation, she trotted toward the terminal to clock out.

Fifteen minutes later, she climbed into her VW Rabbit and maneuvered out of the parking lot. The puffs of her breath iced the inside of her windshield, and she knew the temperature had dropped a few more degrees in the past hour. She was glad she had taken her heavier gloves and her hat that morning.

With dusk spelling the end of the day's flying, she assumed most of the pilots had left the field. That was a good time to do some checking on aircraft without interruption, or so she thought. One hundred feet past the parking lot exit, she turned off the main road and onto the artery that led to the public ramp.

Climbing out of the Rabbit, her feet crunched on the frozen dirt. The small puddles formed between the road's ruts carried a thin rind of ice on their surfaces. While she zipped up her jacket, she surveyed the line of planes and realized she had no idea what to do if she spotted a suspicious airplane.

The sound of Jeff calling her "cute when she played Nancy Drew" echoed in her head, but she silenced it. She didn't care if it seemed stupid, she wanted to find out who was doing the booze-running. She hoped she could somehow end it.

Glancing from side to side as she walked down the flight line, she studied the parked private planes. She was positive that the aircraft seen at Tuntutuliak was privately owned—no one would be stupid enough to use a commercial carrier for illegal activities.

That James guy had said the plane was dark-colored, she remembered, maybe red. Must not have had any bright stripes either, she reasoned, because those would show up, even at dusk. She walked on, hoping that the plane she searched for was not tucked away in a hangar.

Emergency-flasher yellow seemed to be a popular color for the small planes, which reassured her. She had worried about the difficulty of locating the correct red plane amongst dozens, but she hadn't seen any solid red ones so far. White with red stripes, yes, but not solid red.

Then a flash of red caught her eye, halting her in her tracks. Tucked behind a blue-and-white Piper Super Cub sat a grimy red Cessna 172 sporting thick, black stripes. Her heart began to thump. The plane was the color she had been looking for—red with black stripes was pretty dark. Could she have found the right one? This fast?

No telling yet.

Not knowing what she searched for, she stepped over and peered into the plane's windows. She felt like a post-lobotomy Sherlock Holmes: she had no idea what she was doing. What exactly constituted *suspicious*? Boxes containing liquor bottles strewn all over the cabin? Air cargo receipts labeled "Perishable and Fragile, Alcohol"? That would be kind of obvious. Would anyone be stupid enough to leave evidence like that in plain sight?

"What am I looking for?" she murmured out loud, a bit embarrassed by her cluelessness. Cupping her hands around her eyes, she squinted into the cabin. Too dark; she needed some light. Grabbing a penlight from her shirt pocket, she flashed it across the shadowy compartment. A few crinkled aeronautical charts jutted out of a pocket on the far wall, and a gust lock poked through the pilot-side control yoke. Pretty typical stuff; nothing gave her any clues as to what she should be looking for, or looking at.

The beam skated across the front seats, then the instrument panel and the cluster of navigational radios. Nothing odd there. Then she skipped the light over the pilot's headrest to take in the rear of the cabin.

Nothing unusual had shown up so far. She fidgeted a bit, stomping her chilled feet, afraid that she had struck out. Her Nancy Drew adventure was looking like a bust. Boy, was Jeff going to have fun teasing her about it.

Then, wedged in a rear corner, she spied a dark shape: a ragged, ripped tarpaulin draped over a square object. A cardboard corner protruded from one of the rips in the tarp. What the hell was that? she wondered. It had to be a box, but a box of what? Why was it covered?

She tugged on the recessed latch on the pilot's door. No give—it was locked. She couldn't get in. Then she trotted to the opposite side of the plane and tried the passenger-side door. Locked, too.

At that moment, she wished she had taken a friend's

invitation when he'd offered to show her how to jimmy car locks. She hadn't shown any interest at the time, since it had seemed kind of sleazy. She wasn't the type to go for joyrides, and she never locked herself out of her car, so what good would that knowledge be?

"What a fool you were," she whispered to herself. "You want to know how to do that now, don't you?"

From the plane's right side, she shined her penlight on the tarp, looking for a revealing hole. She was hoping that a clue to the box's contents would appear, but nothing did. It *could* contain part of a bootlegger's stash, but there was no way to know.

Pphht! She blew a steamy breath into the cool air, frustrated by her inability to get into the Cessna. She hated being stumped by anything.

Concentrating deeply on her search, the crackle of a truck creeping up the gravel taxiway startled her. Her head shot up abruptly. Then, even before she thought to turn around, a *whack!* signaled someone exiting the truck and slamming its door.

Immediately, her head swiveled. "Damn! You scared me!" she croaked to the approaching man, and nearly tripped over her own feet as she hurriedly stumbled away from the plane. Her face flushed in response to the surprise and her heart began rapping in her chest.

She stared, dumbfounded, at the stranger who'd emerged from the truck. Being discovered while snooping was something she hadn't counted on. How was she going to scam her way out of this? She studied the man's seamed features and wondered if she was looking at the smuggler. Would he realize what she was doing? He could be trouble if he thought she posed a threat.

"What are you doing with my airplane?" the stocky Yup'ik man growled. The visor of a baseball cap cast a shadow over his square face and insulated Carhartt coveralls cocooned his compact body. He wore a stern expression, and his brown eyes seemed to shoot darts at Taylor. He didn't look like someone she would want to confront.

Her mind racing, she attempted to devise a believable

explanation for her presence. "Uh, uh," she stammered. "I was just looking at your plane; somebody told me that you wanted to sell it. I wanted to check it out." That remark seemed pretty lame to her. Would he buy it?

He glared at her, his jaw muscles flexing. "Who told you that? I'm not even thinking about it." The menace in his voice made her flinch, and her heartbeat picked up the pace. He stepped closer and she gulped. "You were trying to get in, weren't you?" he snarled. "Trying to boost the radios or something."

Well, of course she was trying to get in, but she didn't have the slightest interest in the radios. That was the least of her concerns.

She shook her head rapidly, trying to look innocent. It wasn't easy. "No, I wasn't trying to get in," she tried to placate him. "And I couldn't steal the radios, either. I don't even have any tools to do that."

"Then what are you doing here, snooping around?" He stepped closer and her pulse rate rose another notch. She could smell his breath, a ripe combination of garlic and coffee.

Shaking her head, she pleaded, "I told you what I was doing. I'm just looking for a plane to buy." She could feel the hammering of her heart in her eardrum, *tuppita-tup, tuppita-tup.*

"I don't believe you," he sneered. "I don't believe any of you *gussaks.* You're not trying to buy a plane; girls don't fly."

"Yes, yes, I do fly. I work for Tundra Air Charter. See?" She pointed at the TAC patch on her flight jacket, hoping to convince him. "I fly every day, that's why I want to get my own plane. I can't use the charter planes for myself."

Squinting at her with piggy eyes, he didn't appear to buy what she said. "I still don't believe you. Nobody is going to tell you my plane is for sale when it's not. I don't know what you're doing, but I want you outta here. Right now." He frowned and clenched his fists. "Now! Take off!" He pointed down the road, waving his finger.

That was all she needed. "Hey, I'm going, I'm going!" she yelped, and scampered around the nose of the Cessna. Dashing toward her car a hundred feet away, her breath came in gasps as she tripped over the icy ruts on the road.

So much for detecting, she anguished.

Taylor sorted through a pile of laundry she had forgotten in the dryer the night before. The lingering scent of laundry soap filled the air as she rifled through the clothing, her mind miles away from the task at hand. She contemplated the evening's events, baffled by what she had discovered at the airport. She wasn't sure if she had stumbled on the smuggler, or if she had just stumbled over a plane that happened to match the right description. She wasn't even sure she *had* the right description.

But she felt that the Yup'ik man had been too guarded, too angered by her presence.

As she delved into the laundry basket for the mate to a cotton sock, she heard a quiet rapping on her front door. Picking up the sock's twin, she dropped the pair into a bureau and answered the knock.

She opened the door for Jeff, who stood in the hallway, stuffing his gloves into his jacket pocket. "Hi, there," she greeted him, motioning him into her apartment and closing the door behind him. It seemed just like old times, but without the sex that usually concluded his visits. She was actually glad to see him—she needed some feedback about what she'd uncovered.

He obliged her immediately. "You have any fun playing detective today?" He took off his winter-weight jacket and tossed it on the sofa. "Find anything out, Miss Fletcher?"

"Oh, come on, don't tease me. I'm just doing some poking around, helping where I can. Do you like what's happening at the dry villages, people dying?"

"Well, no, I don't, but I don't think we're the ones that should be looking into it. It's not our job." He plopped down on the ratty sofa, crossing his ankles over the coffee table.

She walked over to the refrigerator and poured a glass of orange juice. "That's probably true, but even if the troopers decide to look into those related deaths, I'm not sure they'll get any cooperation. I sure didn't, when I talked to that guy from Tunt." She wiggled the juice pitcher at him, a question in her eyes. When he shook his head no, she shoved the pitcher back into the fridge. "I may as well do the work myself."

"Okay, suit yourself." He shrugged and settled back against the sofa. "So, what did you find out?"

"Well, at first I didn't think I'd find anything," she sniffed. "That James guy was probably playing me for a sucker, feeding me tidbits that weren't worth shit. But now, I think he might have been telling the truth. I spotted a 172 on the public ramp, red with black stripes." She paused, waiting for a positive reaction from Jeff. The flat look in his eyes showed he didn't make the connection. "That fits the description I got from James, remember?"

"Yeah, yeah, okay. I forgot. So you found the villain, huh?" He laughed.

She pursed her lips, annoyed by his attitude. However, she needed to show him she'd gotten some results, so she continued. "Well, I'm not sure what I found. There was something stuffed in the cabin that was covered by a tarp, looked kinda iffy. Could've been just an empty box, but why cover a box unless it has something in it you wanted to hide?" She took a sip of her juice and swirled around the pulp in the glass. "Anyway, I tried to get inside to look at it, but the plane was locked. Then, while I was trying the locks, the owner drives up. I didn't even hear him, he scared the shit out of me. I thought everyone had gone home." The memory of the shock made her shiver. "So, he sees me shining my flashlight inside the airplane and gets pretty pissed. Asks me what I'm doing, snarls at me a little. Then he tells me to get away from the plane, to take off. He was *not* pleased."

"Oh?" Jeff dropped his feet down onto the floor and sat forward, a patronizing smile on his face. "Sounds like something the troopers would want to know. Maybe it's time to retire, let them finish it up. Decide if it's worth looking into. It might not be a clue, like you think. You always did have an active imagination.''

She completely ignored his remark—why did he have to dredge up old stuff? ''There's a problem, though,'' she continued, as though he hadn't spoken. ''The guy was Yup'ik. I can't understand why a Yup'ik would get involved with the very thing his people are fighting. He has to know why some of the villages are dry. How could he justify running booze into them?'' She scowled as she tipped the juice glass up and drained it, then wiped her mouth on her hand.

Jeff crossed his arms over his chest. ''There's unethical people everywhere, Taylor. Not every Yup'ik follows his conscience. If there's money in something, there's always somebody willing to profit from it. Why don't you just talk to the troopers about it? Let them sort it out.''

''No, I don't think I should do that until I'm sure. It would be terrible if I sicced the troopers on somebody for no reason. I'd better do some more checking.''

Her nose crinkled when she added, ''You should have seen that guy from Tuntutuliak. It was almost enough to make me toss my cookies, imagining what that must have felt like when he woke up this morning. It takes a real loser to want to make money on somebody else's suffering like that.''

Jeff shook his head, seemingly disgusted by the idea. ''Let's talk about something else. You got anything good in the fridge?'' They got up from the sofa, and headed to the kitchen. The more things changed, the more they stayed the same.

TEN

Taylor chugged down the five-mile-long road linking Bethel to the airport. The VW Rabbit clattered over the asphalt's frost heaves and motored past the Bethel National Forest—a single, scraggly swamp spruce confined within a square of white picket fence. That spruce was the only tree on the whole west side of the Yukon-Kuskokwim Delta.

She glanced at the rosy tint of the sky to the east and nodded. Looked like a clear day on its way. Good day for flying; she'd get a lot done.

Breaking away from reflections on the good weather, she contemplated a more important issue. She needed to make room somewhere in her workday to do some checking on the airplane she had spotted the previous night, and the Yup'ik man who'd caught her studying it. She had unresolved questions about her discovery.

Finding the plane James described had pleased her. She was glad he hadn't fed her a story. Even so, the fact that the airplane's owner was a Native still bothered her—she couldn't believe a Yup'ik would aggravate a situation that his own people battled. How could he be that greedy, profiting from misery so close to home?

She needed to get more facts, but from where?

"Talk to the ramp rats," she murmured under her breath. "They're like a hotline." She grinned at that solution to the problem, knowing that the cargo handlers and the ramp attendants were the main gossip grapevine at the airport. They always seemed to know details about goings-on at the field, from the names of all the pilots and whom they flew for, to which one was shacked up with a local.

At least, they'd been that way three years ago. Certain things never changed.

With a tug on her car's steering wheel, she pulled into the airport parking lot and slipped her Rabbit into a slot near the terminal. The vehicle wheezed and snorted as she flipped off the ignition. She cursed it as it hiccuped, but realized she couldn't complain. Better not look a gift horse, blah, blah, blah . . . Having the use of a car was a real advantage—calling for a taxi every time she wanted to go anywhere would have frustrated her big time. She wrangled herself out of the front seat of her vehicle and began fastening her heavy down-filled winter jacket. Her breath clouded the air as she wiggled the zipper.

A fingertip from her ragg wool gloves jammed in the teeth of the jacket's zipper as she closed it. "Get out of there!" she yelled at the glove in annoyance, tugging on it. She was impatient with minor snafus like that, feeling as though her zipper and her glove had conspired to ruin the start of her day.

The threads of the knitted fabric tore, severed by the metal edges of the zipper as she jerked on the glove. "Damn!" she swore. "Now look what I've done!" She examined the small hole chewed in it, exasperated.

Still fingering the glove, she walked to the terminal, crunching over the frozen dirt of the lot, and climbed the small staircase at the door.

"Morning, Dan," she greeted the enormous man behind TAC's counter. The sight of his ample girth always made her appreciate LifeLine's fitness policy, which required the pilots to remain trim. If general wisdom didn't prompt her to go to the gym for exercise, the fear of losing her job would.

Dan rubbed his patched eye and glanced up at her.

"Morning, Taylor." He studied her jacket with a raised eyebrow. "Getting ready for winter, huh? I've been hoping it would never come if I ignored it."

She noted his short-sleeved shirt and the light windbreaker hanging nearby, and figured that his extra layers of fat were good insulation. He could get away with ignoring winter's chill, if he so desired.

"Yeah, I thought it was about time for the heavy stuff. I had the sense to pack my expedition parka when I left Anchorage, so when I saw how nippy it looked outside, I dragged it out of my duffel." The sleeve of her coat made a swishing noise as she fingered it, showing its heft. "I don't think I'll need it all day, though. It'll get warmer now that the sun's up. Is it supposed to stay clear for the next ten, twelve hours?"

"Yeah, I guess so," Dan nodded. "On the radio they said it'll stay clear, but that means cold tonight, so don't forget the engine covers when you put the plane to bed."

"Hey, I'm way ahead of you, Dan—I put 'em on last night when I saw the sky. The 310 has had them on for a few days already."

"Okay, good job." He glanced out the glass ramp door where airplanes, bundled in their brightly colored winter garb, stood at the ready. Cracked shards of ice poked up from the small puddles on the asphalt apron, showing the tracks of forklift crossings. He turned back toward Taylor with a frown, seeming to react to the signs of winter's imminent approach. Picking up a form full of scribbles, he handed it to her. "Here's your manifest. No pax, just cargo."

"No passengers, huh?" She peered at the slip of paper as she held it. "Hmmm, Tununak. The coast run. Got any weather from them?"

"Yeah, right here." He grabbed a small notebook with more chicken scratches on it. His haphazard penmanship looked like it came from a busy doctor writing prescriptions. "They're reporting clear, wind out of the north at about fifteen. Piece of cake."

"Okay, can do." She fastened the manifest to the clipboard and smoothed its creases. As she struggled with the clamp, Bob Allum approached and both she and Dan greeted him.

Taylor noticed that Bob's leather flight jacket was similar to the one Taylor had left at home that morning. "Looks like you dressed more sensibly than me today, Bob," she chuckled, looking at his jacket. She could feel the perspiration building inside her heavy coat. The heated terminal hadn't helped matters.

She nodded in the direction of the tie-down ramp. "Is your airplane parked in front of nine-six-uniform? You gonna have to move before I push my ship forward?" First thing in the morning, the pilots had to break out of the previous night's close groupings, where they stood head to tail.

"No, I was the last one in last night, so I put eight-eight-yankee at the end of the line. Nine-six-uniform is in front; you can just taxi straight out."

"Okay, then I better get going." Waving good-bye, she jogged to the ramp door and shoved it open. It swooshed behind her as she walked out into the muted light of sunrise. *Sheesh,* she thought as she scanned the horizon. Nine in the morning and the sun's just coming up.

One of the cargo hold doors was slid open, and she headed for it. Peering into the darkened interior, she surveyed the orderly piles of boxes stacked on wooden pallets. Nobody appeared to be inside the hold, but she heard rustling noises, so she yelled for the invisible worker. "Hey, Keith, you in there?"

A young man appeared from behind a pallet like a sleight of hand. Like most of the cargo handlers, he was barely out of high school. His pock-marked face displayed the scars of a losing battle with acne, and his shaggy hair hung over eyes the color of coffee grounds.

"I need the Tununak load, please," she said. "Is it ready to go yet?"

He pointed at a nearby pallet. "It'll be ready in a sec; I'm working on it now. Goes into nine-six-uniform?"

"Yeah, it's parked at the front of the line, I'll be driving it out pretty quick. I'll meet you out there." She left the cargo hold and ambled over to her Cessna 207. The temperature felt slightly warmer, so she unzipped her coat and stuffed her wool gloves into one of its pockets.

When the ramp handler arrived with the cargo pallet, she pulled her arms out of the coat and slung it aside. Shivering a bit, but certain that exertion would warm her, she bent to tossing boxes in the plane. Years had passed since she'd hoisted cargo like that—that wasn't part of her duties with LifeLine—but her trips to the gym in Anchorage had ensured that she wouldn't miss a beat.

By the time Keith had shoved the last case of Nalley's Chili Con Carne to her, she was dripping with sweat. It would've drowned her if she hadn't shed her down coat.

Sliding the chili carton into place, she dragged a cargo net from the small compartment in the plane's tail section. She strapped it over the load in the cabin and turned to the handler.

"Good job, Keith. Thanks." Taylor felt it was important to acknowledge the aid that the support people provided. Even though flying was the most challenging part of the process, she knew her job would be tougher without their help. She didn't believe she was the star of the show, but rather only one cog in a team effort.

Shifting into forward gear, Keith yelled over the noise of the forklift's motor. "Have a good flight to Tununak." He glanced at the sky and added, "Nice day to fly, not much wind, no clouds. See ya."

She waved at him and looked at the nearby wind sock. A slight fluttering of the sock indicated nothing but a breeze, maybe five knots. It looked good there, but she wondered if it was still blowing only fifteen on the coast.

As Taylor approached the west coast of the Delta, seventy-five miles from Bethel, her 207 bounced under light turbulence. The choppy air rattled the plane, making it ride like a truck traveling down a bumpy country road. She hoped it wouldn't get any worse—she disliked getting her bones dislocated by the forces of Mother Nature.

She flew past the top of a fifteen-hundred-foot hill that bordered the village of Tununak. The settlement clung to the base of that hill, about a half-mile from a twenty-three-hundred-foot gravel runway.

The thirty-five houses making up Tununak looked out onto the Bering Sea, with large Nunivak Island resting on the horizon ten miles away. Taylor remembered a visit to Nunivak years earlier, where she had seen several of the musk oxen that called the island home. She had found the musk oxen interesting, was amused by the odd-looking ungulates shaped like miniature hump-backed bison with upside-down horns.

The boulders covering the rocky beach next to Tununak were smoothed and flattened by the nearly perpetual wash of the surf. If the Yup'iks had been into windsurfing, they would have had a nearly perfect site for it, though peril would have surrounded any return to the beach after a session on the water.

As she neared Tununak's gravel airstrip, she checked the nearby wind sock out of force of habit. It stuck straight out, showing a wind in excess of twenty-five knots. She gaped.

"Twenty-five knots?" she breathed. What happened to the fifteen knots Dan told her to expect? A twenty-five knot wind wasn't a piece of cake—she would have her hands full.

A wind that powerful meant strong turbulence, too, which she was already feeling. The Cessna bucked from side to side as the gusts buffeted it, pushing her against the restraint of her seat belt.

Her next move was to check her airspeed indicator to confirm that the plane was flying below V_a, maneuvering speed. V_a was the airspeed not to be exceeded when caught in turbulence, and she was careful to stay well within that limit.

Lining up with the runway, she glanced down at the

white caps out in the bay. The wind was coming from the north, a direct crosswind. That called for a firm landing, which she prepared for.

She lowered the Cessna's flaps, set the engine controls, and cinched down her seat belt. She was ready to go; it was show time. During landings like the one to come, she definitely earned her pay.

The picture of the runway in her windshield grew larger as she descended to it. Fifteen feet in the air, she eased back on the control yoke to initiate her flare, then guided the plane onto the runway.

With a *thump!* she contacted the ground, the main wheels bearing the force of the impact. Holding the plane in a nose-high attitude, she rolled down the runway on the sturdy main gear, and when she could no longer keep the nose off the ground, she let it sink.

The Cessna decelerated. It was traveling at about forty miles per hour when it hit a soft spot on the runway. Suddenly Taylor heard a *crack!* and felt the airplane's nose dip. Completely out of control, the plane swerved to the side and began skidding through the dirt on its nose. Crackling and popping filled the air as rocks and loose gravel pelted the metal of the cowling.

"Damnnn!" she cursed while she tried to prevent the airplane from going off the runway. Her muscles tightened as she fought both the yoke and the rudder pedals. "Oh, shit!" she screamed, her voice breaking as the Cessna violently smacked the ruts.

The last thing she felt was the forward inertia of a thousand pounds of cargo driving her forward, forcing her against the stranglehold of her shoulder harness.

ELEVEN

When Taylor dared to open her eyes, she found herself wedged up against her shoulder harness, staring at the instrument panel from close range. Her ribs hurt, and the welts on her neck showed where the restraints' webbing had abraded her skin. She tried to ease away from the harness, but realized that the dislodged cargo had driven the seat back up against her torso, preventing her movement.

Well, she couldn't go backward; she might as well go forward.

The seat belt squeezed her abdomen tightly, so she sucked her gut in and undid its clip. After slipping out, she tried to open the pilot's door. It was stuck. "Oh, shit," she muttered.

Bracing her legs against the instrument panel, she leaned against the door and pushed. It creaked but didn't move, so she took a deep breath and shoved harder. Her leg muscles burned as she willed them to move. Then with a *pop!* the door snapped open and she nearly fell backwards out of the cockpit. Only her hand wrapped around the door jamb saved her.

As she wriggled to extricate herself from the suddenly cramped cockpit, she heard the whine of an ATV approaching at full speed. The TAC agent was hurrying over from the unloading area, his vehicle bouncing from rut to rut as he raced down the runway. Undoubtedly he had seen everything, and thought he was dashing to the scene of a fatal accident.

"Taylor, Taylor!" he squeaked when he skidded to a halt. "Are you okay?" He leaped off the ATV and sprinted to the plane.

She finally dropped to the ground from her perch in the cockpit and stood on trembling legs. "Yeah, I'm all right, Walter." She caressed the abrasion on her neck and peered at the Cessna in disbelief. She was confounded—what the hell had just happened?

"I thought you were dead!" Walter yammered. "When the airplane slid off the runway, I was sure you were crushed. . . ." Then the middle-aged Yup'ik man caught her incredulous expression and turned around to see what had grasped her attention. His mirrored sunglasses concealed his eyes, but she could see his head move as he scanned the Cessna.

"Wow . . ." Walter groaned, gesturing at the airplane helplessly. It lay wedged into the dirt at the edge of the airstrip, the nose-wheel strut collapsed and bent back, the tire missing. The propeller was curled up, partially buried in the tundra. A deep furrow indicated the plane's track from the nose impact on the gravel to where it had plowed to a stop.

"Damn! I can't believe this!" Taylor yelled. She surveyed the Cessna, then followed the rut back to its beginning. When she saw the missing nose wheel lying on the ground, she strode over to it. Grunting, she hefted it up and glanced around the adjacent area.

The reflection of sunlight on a piece of metal caught her eye, and she dropped the wheel and walked over to the glint. Bending over, she picked up a heavy bolt, then grabbed its twin, which lay nearby. Neither one was intact—some force had severed them. She squinted. What the hell were they doing there, she wondered, and why had they broken?

Walter walked up behind her. "What are those?" he asked, reaching for one and rolling it in his fingers for inspection.

"I think those are the bolts that hold the nose wheel to the strut. They're broken; that's why it came apart and the wheel fell off." She studied the remaining bolt in her hand, completely baffled. Airplane parts just didn't break under normal operating conditions. "This is weird, Walter. You'd have to land really, really hard to shear these bolts off. But my landing wasn't *that* bad. Kinda rough because of the crosswind, but not hard enough to break these." She shook her head. Then, juggling the bolt in her hand, her eyes panned from one side of the runway to the other. She was looking for the rest of the bolts that matched the first two.

She jogged back to the Cessna, the puffs of her breath visible in the crisp air. "Hey, Walter," she yelled over her shoulder. "Look around for some more of these bolts. There should've been four. If they sheared just like these ones here, I'd have a clue as to what happened. Go see if you can find 'em, okay? I'll check the strut, see if they're still attached there."

However, after five minutes of fruitless searching, neither of them had found the remaining bolts. Walter rejoined Taylor, who stood by the Cessna with a befuddled look on her face. "I didn't find any more bolts," Walter apologized. "I looked all around. You sure there were four to begin with?"

"Of course there were four, Walter. That's the way the nose-wheel fork attaches to the strut. It's been a while since I flew a 207, but I still remember *that*. We should've found all four." She cocked her head, thinking, then shrugged. "Anyway, let's get this cargo out of the plane and loaded in your cart. When we're done, I'll ride back to the village with you and call Bethel, tell them what happened. They'll need to send a plane to get me. This one won't be flying for a long time."

She wasn't eager to own up to the accident, but she

knew she must. Zipping her coat up, she reached for the handle on the rear cabin door and opened it.

Once Taylor and Walter had delivered the cargo to the village store and she had made a sheepish call to Bethel, he drove her back to the airstrip. She needed to evaluate the damage to the Cessna and figure out how it had happened. The *how* still had her dumbfounded.

Walter dropped her off at the strip and turned to head back to the village. With his vehicle in neutral, he revved the engine. "You going to be okay?" he asked. "It's kinda cold out here with the wind blowing."

She pulled up the hood of her parka. "I'll be all right. If I get cold waiting here for my ride, I'll hike back to the village and hang around there. I don't know when someone will be able to break away from the schedule and come get me." Satisfied, he nodded and putted off down the path.

She watched him disappear, then swung around to look at the Cessna. The picture of the plane lying on its nose at the edge of the runway made her shudder. How could she have wrecked her plane that badly? The propeller was ruined, and even more important, the engine was ruined. Just replacing it would easily cost twenty-five thousand dollars. TAC would be struggling for months with its start-up costs; it couldn't afford to repair the damage she'd done.

She couldn't believe the amount of damage to the plane. Her landing hadn't been *that* hard. She knew she'd made rougher landings in the past without the same disastrous result. Why had it happened this time?

The two bolts she'd found were lying on top of one of the main wheels, and she grabbed them. As she examined them, she remembered that the other two were missing.

She looked up. Where *were* the other two bolts? They should have fallen near the first two.

Unless they hadn't been on the assembly in the first place.

She blanched when that thought struck her. Could it be

that the two missing bolts had been removed, on purpose, just to cause an accident?

But why would anyone want that to happen?

She assumed that Tundra Air Charter wasn't monopolizing the available work on the delta. They had just started flying again, for crying out loud. She couldn't imagine another air taxi resorting to sabotaging a TAC plane as a way to get rid of a competitor. There were easier ways to do that. Giving TAC grief could be accomplished without wrecking one of their planes and killing one of their pilots.

And the Cessna's accident could have easily resulted in her death.

Who was that mad at Tundra Air Charter? She paced around the mangled plane, thinking, then stopped and stared at the crushed nose gear. All of the blood drained from her face as she stood there.

What if it was not TAC that was the mark of the sabotage, but her? Maybe her presence in the sabotaged plane wasn't a coincidence, but planned.

That thought was scary.

She bent down distractedly to place the bolts back on the top of the tire, then resumed her pacing. Was someone getting nervous because of her probe into the booze-running? Her mind returned to her visit to the flight line the previous evening. Perhaps the Yup'ik owner of the red Cessna really did have something to hide. He could have wanted to end her snooping, and tampered with her plane so it would crash. Either he hoped for her death or wanted to scare her.

"Oh, damn," she muttered. If sabotage had occurred, she couldn't even save face by claiming the accident wasn't her fault. Nobody else had been in the airplane when she'd landed—she had no eyewitnesses. The only proof she had was the missing bolts.

Frustrated, she plopped down on the main wheel, landing hard on the bolts she had set there. When their metal heads poked her in the butt she yelped, then grabbed them up. She prepared to fling them out onto the neighboring tundra, but caught herself before she did and slipped them into her pocket. She might need them in the future.

Two hours later—after being rescued by Stan Searle—Taylor was approaching Bethel with Stan in his undamaged Cessna. She was relieved. Not only was she nearly back at home base, but her coworker hadn't antagonized her for what he surely believed was her screw-up. She had agonized over how to answer his questions about the wreck—she still didn't know who had caused the crash, so how much could she tell him?—but his questions never came. Once they'd landed in Bethel, he waved her off and busied himself with the cargo for his next flight, a run to Kwethluk. She watched him for a few seconds, then turned away toward the terminal. She was resigned to facing Dan Mackenzie with her report on the Tununak accident, but she didn't know what kind of thrashing she'd get. Even though the accident hadn't really been her fault, she'd have to confess to it anyway. Ugh.

She shoved the heavy glass door open and stepped into the terminal. When she approached the TAC counter, Dan glanced up with an anxious expression on his face.

"Are you okay?" He appeared to be truly concerned about her welfare, which made her feel a little better. He ran his eyes over her, though her heavy down coat covered just about everything from her thighs to her chin. "You were so short with me on the phone that I figured you were in some pain, but didn't want to tell me."

"No, I'm okay. Mostly." She showed him the scrape on her neck. "Got strangled by my shoulder harness when the plane plowed into the dirt."

He stared at her, both concern and relief in his eyes. "How the hell did you crash? When you called, you said you lost your nose gear. You land hard or something?"

She gulped. It was getting really difficult to keep quiet, but she forced out the story she'd manufactured to cover the truth. She didn't know how much she could tell *him*, either.

Dan grimaced as she recited her tall tale, then shook

his head. "It could've been worse, you know. You could've killed yourself. I've heard about guys getting decapitated by major fuckups like yours. All you did was wreck a plane, and that can be replaced. You can't be." He gazed outside at the ramp, then turned back to her with a grin pasted on his face. She could see the laugh lines poking out from behind his patch. "I wish I could've seen the look on your face when you figured you were going to wind up in the muskeg. Hah! I bet you were pissed! That must've been hilarious."

She made a face and looked down at her toes, wishing she could tell him what had *really* caused the accident. Yikes! Now she had to worry about her plane being rigged for a wreck every time she flew. That wouldn't be fun.

Dan chuckled one last time, then tapped the eraser end of his pencil on the counter. "Well, enough jokes, Taylor. You've got some work to do." He handed her the phone book. "Get on the horn. You're going to have to find us a plane to lease until we get nine-six-uniform either repaired or replaced. Maybe what's his name—the dentist—won't be using his 206 this winter and we can use it for a few months. A 206 is a little smaller than a 207, but it'll do in a pinch." He pointed at the phone book. "Plus, ask him if it's set up for winter. If it's not, call the Cessna dealer in Anchorage and have them send everything it'll need on the morning jet."

She was relieved, glad that Dan had taken everything so well. That was a load off her mind. She had other, more important, things to worry about than that. While she searched for the booze smuggler, she would have to look over her shoulder for somebody trying to blow her away.

As she leafed through the phone book for the dentist's listing, she glanced up. The door from the ramp had swung open and Jeff Davidson was walking in at the head of a line of passengers. When he shot a look across the terminal, she anxiously gestured for him to come over and hurried to the middle of the large room. She stood there impatiently, arms akimbo. Once he dropped his manifest on the WAT counter, he sauntered toward her, taking his time.

"Jeff, come on!" she said in a constrained whisper. "This is important!" Finally, he reached her.

He grinned down at her tense figure. "I didn't think you'd want to talk to me, or anyone else, right now."

"What?" She gaped at him. "You know already? I just got back."

"Yeah, well, news travels fast when somebody fucks up. Anyway, I figured you'd need some time to bandage your bruised ego."

"What do you mean, my bruised ego?" she croaked. "You don't think that crash was *my* fault, do you?"

"Oh, come on. You're the talk of the terminal—the news of you breaking your nose wheel off spread like wildfire. None of the other pilots have ever landed hard enough to do that, and they wanted to applaud you for your originality. Boy, when you screw up, you make it something to remember."

A menacing glare lit her face. "Damn it, Jeff, listen to me! It wasn't my fault, I didn't land too hard! Two of the bolts that hold the nose-gear fork on were gone! Nobody could've prevented that crash—somebody sabotaged the ship! I could've been killed. . . ."

He shook his head, his eyebrows raised in doubt. "Sabotage? I don't know, Taylor. I'd say playing detective has gone to your head, turned you a bit paranoid."

"But Jeff, I only found two of the bolts. The other two were missing. I looked everywhere! They probably were removed last night, you know no one checks the bolts on the nose fork during their morning preflight. Believe me, somebody took them off!"

"Oh, give it a break, Taylor. I'm sure they were on this morning; they just got thrown into the tundra when the fork broke off. No wonder you couldn't find them." He sighed and looked away from her. "Every pilot has an excuse for a screw-up; it's human nature. But I would've expected more from you. You never used to do that.''

A virulent snort was her retort. ''Oh, fuck! I can't understand why you don't believe me!'' She spun away from him and stomped off.

TWELVE

Morning start-of-business activity had begun out on the terminal ramp. Yellow forklifts trundled from the cargo warehouses, carrying pallets full of goods to the aircraft dotting the parking apron. Green nylon mail bags peeked out from behind the boxes of canned milk and six-packs of soda pop resting on the pallets.

Pilots busily stripped red-and-orange engine covers off the airplanes and curled up polypropylene tie-down ropes. Several men cleaned the frost off the windshields of their planes—some with plastic ice scrapers, others with credit cards.

A Boeing 737 airliner from Anchorage perched in front of the terminal, blue and green stripes boldly blazoned across its white body. Flight attendants and ground crew members jogged up and down the portable airstair wedged against the plane's rear fuselage. Late-disembarking passengers maneuvered around the workers on the steps.

The faces of people waiting to board the flight filled the terminal windows. A handler drove a baggage tug full of suitcases past them toward the jet's cargo hold.

Taylor Morgan watched another handler drive a load of incoming baggage to the unloading dock, then moved away from the window. On her way to the air cargo office across the terminal, she noticed a man standing near the baggage carousel. He impatiently snapped and unsnapped the fasteners of his blue down vest as he waited. A Western Alaska Transport patch poked out from behind it.

Bill Blaskovich's meaty body spoke of a lack of interest in appearance—his chin sported several days of stubble, his short, greasy hair was unkempt. Muscular forearms peeked out from behind rolled shirt cuffs. One hand held a cigarette to his lips, while the other reached inside his vest to itch a corpulent beer belly.

Blaskovich grabbed two boxes that rolled past on the carousel after a quick scan of their identifying marks. Though the boxes were bulky, he hoisted them up in his arms easily.

As he wrestled with them, Taylor trotted over to him. "Need a hand with that, Bill?" she chirped.

Once she had gotten within a few feet of him, she stopped, her nose crinkling. He desperately needed a bath and a good tooth-brushing. She took a step back from him, hoping it didn't look too obvious. No sense in embarrassing him; he was cantankerous enough as it was.

He glared at her like a major nuisance, and barked a curt "No!" to her offer of help. As he attempted to secure his grasp on the boxes, he turned for the exit, but not fast enough to prevent her brief glance at one of the cartons.

Her eyebrows rose. She noticed both of Blaskovich's boxes were from an Anchorage Cessna parts and service dealer. "Looks like you're fixing one of your planes, Bill. Was it the one you fly? What got broken?"

"Uh . . . Nothing." He looked at the front door, took another step toward it. "These are brake pads—we just needed some replacement brake pads. We don't ding our planes at WAT." Without saying good-bye, he headed for the exit.

She studied his heavy step as he disappeared through the door, then shrugged. Blaskovich was being his usual ill-mannered self, no surprise about that. She had tried to be nice, but she wasn't going to do that anymore. He hadn't even been *civil* to her.

With a snort, she continued to the air cargo office. She had to get the shipment she expected, the winterizing supplies she needed for the Cessna 206. The dentist owner of the plane had agreed to lease it to Tundra Air, since he had no plans to fly it anymore that year now that winter was coming on. Through the glass front door of the terminal, she could see Blaskovich pushing his boxes into the bed of a rusted gray pickup and clambering into its cab. He drove out of the parking lot, a black exhaust cloud in his wake.

She hoped he was heading for home to unpack and bathe. He definitely needed a shower.

The mid-afternoon sun blazed through the terminal windows, reflecting off the shiny metal of the Tundra Air Charter baggage scales. The cherubic faces of two Yup'ik children studied the flight schedule board tacked on a nearby wall, as though planning a trip to a distant village. The kids' mother watched them, sitting stoically on a bench in the middle of the room.

"So, Dan, I'm all done for the day." Taylor leaned on the ticket counter, looking eager. "We got any extras today? I thought I saw some stuff for Kongiganak in the cargo hold—I could take that out."

Plenty of daylight remained to the afternoon, and she wanted to do more flying. With her paycheck based on the number of flights she performed each day, not her clocked hours at the airport, she had to make up for a morning spent working on the leased Cessna.

"Nah, that's gotta wait. Not enough for a trip today and the regular scheduled run tomorrow." He glanced at the wall clock and curled an eyebrow. "It's kinda early, but I don't have anything else, so you may as well call it a day. Go take a nap or something."

"Rats, I only got three hours in today. It's still daylight. You sure you don't have anything else? I wanna fly. . . ."

Dan grinned teasingly and tapped his pencil on the counter. "That's what you get for bending your ship. How'd you expect to do a whole day's flying when you spent all morning getting another one ready to fly in the winter?'' He chuckled, seeming to indicate that he was just jerking her chain.

She didn't see the playfulness in his tone, and scowled. ''Yeah, I guess you're right. I deserved that. Okay, I'll go put that new ship to bed and take off.'' Staring at the floor, she slipped her hands into her gloves and trudged to the exit. The open door let a wash of cool air sneak into the terminal behind her, and she trotted down the staircase toward her plane.

As she knotted the Cessna's tie-down rope, she scanned the ramp. It was nearly deserted. Hers was the only airplane parked for the night, and a WAT Cessna taxiing for take off made up the only other activity on the asphalt apron. She frowned at being done for the day so early.

Tramping to the other wing, she grabbed up its nylon rope. Her gaze traveled down the row of privately owned planes on her left, and her eye paused midway. A van was parked in front of the red-and-black Cessna 172 she had looked at a few nights ago. What was a van doing there?

Hurriedly fastening the second rope, she decided to jog down the row and check things out. Maybe the owner of the plane was preparing it for another booze run that night, and she could catch him red-handed. Wouldn't that be a coup?

As she approached, she slowed her pace. Someone else was there, and it wasn't the Yup'ik man. The suspicious box she'd seen the previous night was there, too, but this time it was resting on the ground with its flaps folded back. It didn't appear too suspicious out in plain sight.

From her vantage point, she saw a metal rod propping the aircraft's cowling up, exposing the engine. Tools were scattered around the top of the nose. A hand-painted sign adorned the side of the van and a large, red, wheeled toolbox poked out from behind its rear bumper.

She squinted at the scene, and a small cloud of steam blossomed as she exhaled slowly. She wasn't looking at the plane's owner, but at a mechanic. Sniffing, her mood darkened for the nth time that day.

Then her spirits brightened. Wait, she thought, maybe the mechanic could give her some information, without the interference of the owner. Yes, maybe this would be even better! She pranced up to the plane.

"Hi, there," she called, peeking around the nose of the Cessna. "What's up?" Her salutation appeared to startle the mechanic who stood next to the cowling, a crescent wrench in his hand.

She smiled at the man looking up from the engine. His tall, lanky frame reminded her of a boy she had had a major crush on in junior high. Like Donny Walters from the eighth grade, he was angular and slender.

As he brushed back a tousle of salt-and-pepper hair, he left a smear of grease on his brow. A pair of oil-spattered Carhartt coveralls cocooned his body. A moustache, something Donny Walters hadn't been able to grow, drooped over his upper lip.

"Hi, miss." A curious look passed across his face, as he glanced at the Tundra Air Charter's patch on her coat. "You need something?"

"Well, sort of." What was she going to say? Obviously, she couldn't come right out and ask if this plane was used for bootlegging. Dumb move. Instead, she decided to use the same story she had told the plane's owner. "I was told this plane was for sale, and I'd like to know some things about it before I buy. I figured a mechanic would know what it's been doing lately, the kind of abuse it gets. I don't want to buy a plane that's been beat up from landing at some of the strips around here."

"Hmmm, I don't blame you. But I didn't know Oscar was selling." The mechanic propped an elbow on the cowling, and leaned thoughtfully against it. "I guess that's why he had that cylinder removed and overhauled, though. Must want this rig in good shape before anyone looks at it."

"He got a cylinder overhauled? One's off?" Her eyes widened. No plane could fly with a missing cylinder, and that meant the aircraft she was looking at could not be the one involved in the recent booze-running.

She glanced at the box on the ground. Sure enough, a chrome cylinder huddled inside, joined by other parts and pieces. "When did he do that?"

"Oh, I don't know. I removed it maybe two, three months ago." He studied the distress on her face and seemed to mistake it for concern about the plane's airworthiness. "But that doesn't make it a bad buy. The cylinder was just out of time ten hours from its TBO. It may be a better buy now, with a zero time cylinder. Everything else is okay, all the radios, the brakes. . . ."

He stared as Taylor shook her head. Without another word, she made a 180-degree turn and trudged away.

"Wait," she heard him say. "Don't leave! It's a good plane, the cylinder overhaul doesn't mean anything. . . ."

Several street lights shone through her apartment window, dappling Taylor's prone figure. Her shoeless feet hung over the end of her couch, her down coat slumped in the corner. The sharp rapping on the door startled her out of her stupor.

Blinking, she struggled to a sitting position and glanced about the room. Once she had her bearings, she stood up and padded to the door in her stockinged feet. The odor of stale sweat clogged her nostrils, and she peered down at her toes. Yecchh. Obviously, she should wash her workout socks more often.

Weather stripping swished over the foyer's linoleum as she let the door swing open. "Oh, hi there," she muttered at Jeff Davidson, while tugging a sock off a sticky foot.

"Oh, hi there?" he retorted. "You sound delighted to see me. I think I'll just turn around and head back home." Crossing his arms, he looked down at her. "Maybe you don't want any company tonight."

"Well, our last talk wasn't too pleasant, if you recall. I don't know if I want to talk to you anymore for a while. Are you going to call me a liar again?"

A remorseful expression clouded his face. "Okay, I apologize. It just sounded sort of improbable at the time."

She stared at him, then yawned and waved him into the

room. Trudging back to the sofa, she plopped down on it. She was still pissed with him for not believing her, but wanted to tell somebody what she'd found out that afternoon. And he was the only one she could talk to about it.

"What are you doing sleeping this early in the evening?" Jeff asked. He ran his eyes over her outfit, taking in the sweat-stained T-shirt and sweatpants. "I don't remember seeing you around the field today—didn't you fly?"

"Yeah, I did fly today, but not much. I spent the beginning of the morning winterizing that 206 we're leasing, then got done with my shortened schedule by mid-afternoon. I felt like shit by the time I left the airport, so I thought I'd go wear myself out at the high school's weight room. I fell asleep when I got home. Your knock woke me up."

He walked across the studio toward the refrigerator and pulled out a carton of milk. "Can I have a glass of this?"

When she nodded yes, he filled a tumbler and took a gulp. Wiping the milk moustache off his lip, he headed back to the couch. "So, why are you in such a foul mood? Not still pissed about Tununak, are you?"

"No, not really. At least not so you'd notice." She tilted her head against the sofa back and sighed. Loudly. "I found something out this afternoon, something about that Cessna 172 I thought was part of the smuggling." She ran through her day's activities, then launched into what she thought was the most significant part of the whole story. "I thought maybe that Yup'ik guy was the one who sabotaged my plane. He might've figured out why I was looking at his 172 and wanted to stop me. . . ." She paused, caught in a memory, then waved her hand and continued. "But that's moot, anyway. He was the only person I could think of that might want to fuck with my Cessna, and now he's out of the picture. I've been real careful to cover my tracks—nobody else knows what I'm doing." Then she looked at Jeff pointedly. "Except you. . . ."

"Yeah, right." He arched his eyebrows, obviously not too alarmed by her subtle accusation. "Obviously, you haven't covered your tracks that well. Somebody else has figured out what's going on." He sat on the other end of the sofa and unzipped his coat. "What about one of your coworkers? They might've overheard you somehow. They'd also know which plane was yours and could've worked it over without anyone noticing. Can you think of anyone who'd do that?"

Shaking her head, she squinted. "I just met them for the first time a week ago. I don't have a fix on any of them." She cupped her chin in her palm and busied herself by picturing her peers at TAC. Nobody had really raised her hackles. Then she brightened. "Well, there is one. Carl Roston. I heard him arguing with Dan Mackenzie the other day, pissed because he didn't get all of the long flights. Said he couldn't make any money on the short ones."

"Ahhh, okay. You think he's having money problems? That'd be good motivation for getting into the booze-running. There's gotta be money in that."

"Yeah, you know there is." She stood and cracked her back. Ooh, that felt good. "I *have* to be on the right track, Jeff, if someone is getting anxious enough to fuck with my plane. Maybe I'll have something to go to the troopers with soon." She headed to the refrigerator, scratching an elbow as she walked. "Anyway, I'm hungry, I'm gonna make a sandwich. You want one?"

Without even getting an answer to her question, she plodded to the kitchen area. Peering into the fridge, she grabbed a plastic-wrapped package. "Bologna," she sighed, staring at the circular slices. "What an appropriate choice. I *feel* like bologna today."

THIRTEEN

"So, there's the Askinuks, Julie, the hills I told you about." Taylor slid the right side of her radio headset back to uncover her ear, then pointed through the Cessna's windshield. A line of twenty-five-hundred foot hills jutted up from the tundra ahead. A dusting of snow colored their tops, adding some white to the gray of the granite.

"Is Chevak behind them?" Julie asked. The teenaged girl unzipped her fashionable down jacket and flipped a hank of black hair over her collar. Her rounded features and dark brown eyes indicated Alaskan Native heritage, though her voice carried no accent other than that of a *cool* fourteen-year-old. English was not a second language for her; she had probably been raised on it.

"No, Chevak isn't behind the hills; it's about fifteen miles in front of us. Don't you see it?" Smiling, Taylor directed Julie's gaze at some dark flecks on the near horizon. "Right there, that group of dots at about eleven o'clock."

"That's it?" Julie gaped, incredulous. "There's nothing there. I thought that was just a bunch of bushes or something, not a town. That's gross!"

Taylor laughed. "I bet when your mom sent you out

to learn about your roots, she never mentioned what it looked like out there. But I wouldn't worry about it, Julie. I bet you'll like it just fine in a few days. Maybe somebody'll take you out hunting, let you get the lay of the land. That'd be fun.''

But then again, she might not like it, Taylor realized. When Julie discovered the absence of running water and television, she might insist on a return to Anchorage.

Taylor pushed the earpiece of her headset back into place. ''Anyway, Julie, I gotta do some things with the airplane right now, so I can't talk. We're getting close to the strip—make sure your belt is tight.''

After cinching down her own seat belt, Taylor glanced out the windows to her right and left, checking for other air traffic in the area. Switching frequencies on her radio, she spoke into the mike. ''Chevak traffic, two-two-sierra is seven to the southeast, landing. . . .''

Five minutes later, the Cessna was bouncing down a rut-strewn strip as it decelerated. Taylor maneuvered around a plane tied near the runway's end and entered the unloading area. Coming to a stop, she scanned the houses nestled nearby and the racks of fish drying in the cool sunshine. A few of the ubiquitous three-wheeled ATVs were parked by the tin-roofed shanties like station wagons by country cottages.

The closest thing to a main drag in Chevak linked the center of the village to the airstrip, and she saw the Tundra Air Charter agent driving his own ATV toward her. As she engaged the Cessna's parking brake and shut the engine down, he swung into the gravel square next to a waiting woman.

The withered Yup'ik woman hobbling toward the plane wore a traditional *kuspuk*, a fur parka covered by a cotton shell. Taylor could see arctic fox fur peeking out from underneath the floral fabric, and the same kind of fur made up the ruff shrouding much of her seamed face.

''That must be Grandmother,'' whispered Julie, squinting at the elfin woman. ''She's so short! She must'a shrunk or something.''

"Yeah, time'll do that to you, Julie."

Once Taylor had jumped down from the pilot's seat, she peered around the Cessna's nose at a sight that had caught her attention during her landing rollout.

A young man was patching a large hole in one of the huts bordering the strip. A three-wheeler sat nearby, its headlight smashed and handlebars twisted.

The crunch of footsteps alerted Taylor to the approach of the TAC agent, and she swung around to meet him. "Morning, Evan," she said. "Got a passenger for you, and some mail. Nothing for the store, though." She helped Julie down from the airplane and nodded at the woman limping toward them. "I bet that's this young lady's grandmother. They've never met before, so we'd better make some introductions."

After the two women traded greetings and tentative hugs, they headed to the village. Once they were out of earshot, Taylor turned to the agent. "So, Evan, tell me what happened over there," she said, pointing at the hole in the shack. "Looks like something ran into that house. It's a mess."

"You're right, something did run into it." Evan peered at her from underneath the brim of his Tundra Air Charter hat. His squat form and the ancient fur parka draped over his shoulders indicated his Yup'ik blood, but the corduroy baseball cap was a complete non sequitur—the gnarled man probably hadn't ever seen a baseball game, or a stadium, for that matter.

Narrowing his gaze, he stared at the young man tacking the patch onto the house's wall. "There was a bad accident last night. That guy, Timmy"—he aimed a knotted finger at the worker—"and his brother Edgar got drunk and went out to race their three-wheelers. Timmy crashed into Edgar, Edgar ran into the house and broke his neck. He had to go to the hospital in Bethel. The health aide thought he might die. The man that owns that plane"—Evan waved across the runway—"flew him in."

"Oh, shit," she cursed. Here it was, again. One more

village with trouble with alcohol. "How'd they get the booze? Chevak's dry, isn't it?"

"Yeah, it is. They got it from a pilot who flew it in." Evan made a snorting noise and blew his nose on his glove.

"A pilot came in with the booze, huh?" Her eyebrows rose and she began to analyze that information, seeing how it fit with the other facts she had. It was the first solid clue she'd gotten.

"Hey, Evan, did you see the pilot that brought in the booze?" She rested a hand on his shoulder casually.

Shaking his head, he pointed at the man working on the house. "I didn't see him, but Timmy was the one who met him at the strip." Evan waved at the young man. "Hey, Timmy! Come over here! Right now, we want to talk to you!"

Timmy laid down his tools and trotted over to the strip. His beaver hat concealed most of his bruised cheek, but the rest of his face left no doubt he'd been in a serious wreck.

"Timmy, tell us about the pilot with the booze," ordered Evan. "You said you knew who he was."

Stubbing the toe of his heavy boot in the frozen dirt, Timmy muttered, "Yeah, I think so."

"You know him?" Taylor asked, attempting to hide the excitement in her voice. "What's his name?" She chewed on her lip as she waited for an answer.

"He never gave his name." Timmy shifted uncomfortably and massaged one of his shoulders. "But I do know him, I've seen him a few times."

"You've seen him more than once?" Taylor gaped at Timmy and eagerly jumped to quiz him. "What does the guy look like? What kind of airplane was he flying?"

Looking like he felt trapped by an authority figure, Timmy stuffed his gloved hands in his jacket pockets. "Well . . . he was fat, big blubber belly like a momma dog. And he flies one of the airplanes that come in with the mail, like you."

"Yeah," Evan interjected. "I've seen him, too. He

comes in on one of the blue-and-white planes with only one motor. He's not very nice, don't say much." Then a chipped-tooth grin spread across his face. "You're a lot nicer than him. I like you better."

Frowning, Taylor ignored the agent's compliment. She was caught up digesting the young man's comment. The smuggler was a Cessna pilot for Western Air Transport, a fat one, according to Timmy. Only one picture flashed across her mind when she heard that, since most of the WAT pilots worked hard enough to stave off excess fat. They weren't Playgirl centerfold material, but not Pillsbury dough boys, either.

There was one exception—she didn't know how Bill Blaskovich could yank the Cessna control yoke back over his impressive girth.

Wiping the concerned scowl off her features, she turned back toward Timmy. "That pilot didn't fly one of the blue-and-white planes last night, did he?"

"No, the pilot came in with another plane. Sorta red." Timmy looked at Evan, then back at Taylor, as though assessing their reaction to his statement.

Taylor squinted, her mind whirling. A red airplane, like the one seen in Tuntutuliak. She was relieved that the clue supplied by James hadn't been false—she had just tracked down the wrong red plane. "Thanks, Timmy, I think I know who that was." She glanced over at the agent, who was half listening and half occupied by looking into the mail sacks. "So, Evan, if you don't have anything for me to take back, I'm gonna leave."

The older Yup'ik man set the green nylon bags next to his ATV and hobbled over. "No, don't got nothing for you today. But when you see that other pilot in the blue-and-white plane, tell him to stay away from here. If we see him again, we'll run him off. We don't want booze in the village."

"Okay, I'll tell him that." Taylor swung around, heading for her Cessna. Murmuring under her breath, she added, "I'll tell him more than that."

• • •

On a break between flights, Taylor found herself wandering into Western Alaska Transport's cargo warehouse. Wooden pallets were scattered about the concrete-floored structure, some full, some empty. Tacked on the corrugated aluminum wall behind every pallet was a colored sign stenciled with a flight number. A forklift was parked in a corner next to a wheeled cart, and a scale occupied another. Partially open bifold doors stretched from one side of the warehouse to the other, letting a narrow horizontal stream of daylight into the dim interior.

The building was nearly empty, with most of the workers outside busy with a Twin Otter. Only one young man, in his early twenties, was left. Long, ash-blond hair trailed down from his head, shielding his face from view.

When her footsteps echoed across the cavernous warehouse, he spun around and peered in her direction. The thick lenses of his glasses magnified his washed-out blue eyes, giving him the appearance of a startled owl. He didn't seem to know who approached. Backlit by the line of sun beneath the door, only the outline of Taylor's body was recognizable, not her features.

"Hi, there, L. T." She stepped up to the pallet he stood by. Last time she'd seen him, he'd been a teenager. My, how time flies. "What's up?" she quipped.

"Oh. Hi, Taylor." He squinted at her. "Haven't seen you for a while. I didn't know who you were for a second, thought you were one of the pilots wondering where his load was." He sat on a stack of canned milk and grabbed up a clipboard with a form attached to it. As he peered at the form, he asked, "What are you doing over here? Need something?"

She pretended to study the boxes piled on the pallet. "Yeah, L. T., I need some info. Me and a couple of the guys are going to play a trick on Blaskovich, get back for something he did a couple of days ago. We don't know where he keeps his plane, but we need to find it so we can mess with it. We figured you'd know, since you ramp rats know everything out here."

L. T. looked up from his perusal of the paperwork, a

gleam in his eyes. "You're gonna screw with his plane? Hah! That'll piss him off, big time. What are you gonna do?"

Her brain scrambled for an answer to the question— she hadn't thought it out that much. "Uh, I don't know if I should tell you. You're not going to let him in on the joke, are you?"

"Not me. He probably deserves whatever you're gonna do. I won't ruin things." Then a sly smile spread across his face. "And if you don't tell me what you're gonna do, I'm not gonna tell you anything."

"Well . . ." She had drawn a blank. Then she remembered a stunt a friend's little brother had pulled on him, and jumped on it. "We're going to smear STP over the control yoke, make it all sticky. That should be a real mess to clean up. It'll be like honey, all goopy. He'll have to get it off before he flies."

"Ooh, that'll do it. He hates cleaning anything. Every Cessna he flies comes back looking like a pigpen. I don't know how he gets them so dirty." L. T. sniggered, shaking his head. "I wish I could see his face when he grabs the yoke and gets that stuff all over his hands. Wheeyoo! That'll be funny." He chortled in amusement.

"So, where's the plane?" she pressed. "We can't do anything unless we know where it is." She looked at L. T. questioningly.

"Yeah, okay. It's in a hangar down by the end of three-six. Corrugated metal, like this building, painted beige."

She nodded, her mind already focusing on the hangar he described. She knew where it was; she had taxied past it every time she'd taken off from Runway 36. "Thanks, L. T. That's what we needed to know." She turned toward the warehouse door, and paused. Over her shoulder, she said, "Make sure that *nobody* hears about this, okay? Especially Blaskovich. I don't want him to get wind of this from someone else before we can take care of his plane."

"Okay, will do. Tell me when you do it, would'ja?"

"Yup, I will." She trotted off, and stopped again. "Hey, L. T.—what do your initials stand for? I've always wondered why you don't use your full name.''

''Are you kidding?'' he scoffed. ''Would you answer to a name like Leopold Thucydides Alderman? I'd rather be shot!''

Taylor narrowed her eyes, and cocked an eyebrow. ''Yeah, I see what you mean. I'd probably sprain my tongue saying it.''

FOURTEEN

Taylor straddled a chair near the window in the terminal café, staring through the thermal glass at the tie-down ramp below. She clasped her second mug of hot chocolate with both hands, sniffing at the ribbons of steam that wafted through her fingers. Periodically, she took a tentative sip of the scalding liquid.

During the past half hour, the activity on the ramp had slowed considerably. By that time, virtually all of the aircraft had been secured for the night, their engine covers adding a splash of color to the dim light of dusk. As she surveyed the scene, a lone blue-and-white Cessna pulled off Runway 36 to taxi to its parking spot. It was the last of the air-taxi planes to return to home base, and once its pilot had tied it down and left, the ramp was empty.

Satisfied that everyone had left for the night, she drained her mug and pushed away from the table. Now that she knew where Blaskovich kept his plane, she wanted to examine it, but had been waiting for the airport to clear for the night. She didn't want any company during her mission.

Furtive glances made on her trip down the stairs assured her that nobody else remained in the terminal. She didn't see anyone but a janitor sweeping the floor.

The sun had slunk down the western horizon, and nothing but shafts of white from floodlights broke the darkness outside. Scattered clouds blocked most of the faint light from the pallid moon peeking over the Alaska Range.

The terminal's floods guided her across the ramp. The absence of light dulled all the colors around her: red and mustard-gold dissolved into gray and white; blue dissolved into black. The white from the previous night's spare dusting of snow had faded to silver. Pulling a penlight from her shirt pocket, she swept it across her path, picking up the tire marks left in the snow by airplanes and vehicles.

She tromped down the road paralleling Runway 18, and scanned the aircraft that lined it. Small hangars dotted the area behind the aircraft, some housing mechanics' shops, some shielding planes from the elements. A larger building in their midst served as office and maintenance facility for Yup'ik Air.

When she approached the beige metal structure L. T. Alderman had described she halted, then ducked behind the body of a plane. A quick intake of breath swelled her lungs—Blaskovich's rusted gray truck was parked right next to the building. He had to be inside; she realized she'd better get out of there before he saw her.

But wait a second, she thought. Shouldn't she just wait for him to leave, then go look around inside? He could be doing something incriminating right then, and she might discover what it was. She could gain useful information that way.

However, she couldn't wait in the chill of the evening forever. She'd freeze her butt off. Stamping her feet to warm them, she blew on her hands.

When the noise of a door opening startled her, she tried to melt into the plane's fuselage. She couldn't let Blaskovich find her—there was no telling what he'd do.

From her vantage point, she saw him slam the hangar door and trudge to his pickup. Muttering to himself and sucking on a cigarette, he climbed into the cab and keyed the ignition. After some coughing and sputtering from the pickup, he motored bumpily down the rutted road. He headed to the south and the terminal, not to the north and the town—apparently, he wasn't going home.

And, he hadn't locked the hangar door.

A burst of adrenaline shot through Taylor's body when she realized her chance had come. Of course, his absence wouldn't give her much time—who knew when he'd return—but all she had to do was dash inside and hide somewhere. She'd be stowed when he got back, and upon his final departure he'd unknowingly lock her inside. Then she could take her own sweet time in looking around the hangar. Pretty slick idea.

The gray truck wasn't even around the corner before she sprinted for the hangar. The sound of her feet striking the frozen ground ricocheted in the cool air, and her excited breathing launched steamy smoke signals from her nostrils. She threw the door open and leaped into the room, stumbling over the raised threshold.

Swinging the door closed behind her, she immediately stopped. The interior of the building was pitch black. Flicking her penlight on, she shined it around the room in search for a light switch. Spotting one near the entrance, she flipped it up and bathed the room in one-hundred-watt incandescence.

Wow. The hangar looked like a pack rat's den. A massive collection of useless junk enveloped Blaskovich's plane, a four-place Cessna 172 painted two contrasting shades of red and burgundy. Three empty five-gallon jugs smeared with dry house paint sat next to a wrecked ten-speed bicycle with its chain dangling from a pedal. Stuffing poked out of holes in the upholstery of a recliner that supported several broken window panes. A child's playpen full of toys occupied a corner. The only clear area on the floor was a path leading from the plane to the front door of the hangar.

Agape, she stared at the jungle. The effluvium of moldy, discarded items wafted across the stagnant air. When she recognized a few aircraft parts and a set of

Piper tires, she realized that a plane other than Blaskovich's had occupied the hangar at one time.

Then she broke away from her scan and set to finding
a hiding place. First things first.

She quickly discarded the idea of climbing inside one
of the scattered boxes. None was big enough to hold a
human body, not even a body as slender as hers.

A set of tall metal lockers attracted her attention—
maybe she could stand inside one of those. However, even
those were packed with junk. In the first one she inves-
tigated she found a big heap of old scuba equipment.

Thinking about the assembled crud, she was startled by
the crunching of truck tires outside. Then, the sounds of
a second pair of tires. "Damn!" she whispered, frantically
scanning the hangar. Blaskovich had left only three
minutes earlier. Where the hell had he gone? And who
was with him?

Her eyes darted from one wall to the other, but nothing
stuck out as a hiding place. *Quick, find something!* she
screamed silently. Her pulse pounded in her ears, her muscles tensed.

Then she focused on the Cessna, and her heart leaped.
That had to be it! It was the only hiding place she had
spotted.

As vehicle doors slammed outside, she leaped at the
plane and scrambled into its cabin. She clawed her way
over the rear passenger seats, and fell headfirst into the
narrow crevice behind them. With a yank, she jerked the
plastic bulkhead cover off, the snaps on its edge popping
as they tore away. Removing the cover exposed the airplane's tail section, where she could hide. The metal cables running through it scraped her face and snagged on
her clothing as she wedged herself into the tiny tunnel,
but she could do nothing but wince quietly.

She could not reposition the bulkhead cover from
where she lay; all she could do was hope that no one
noticed it was dislodged. Unconsciously, she held her
breath as she waited for someone to open the hangar door.

Her heart hammered so loudly in her chest, she *knew* it could be heard by someone nearby.

When the door was shoved to the side with a *clunk!,* she tensed and squirmed even farther into the narrow cubbyhole. She had to stifle a gasp when a cable dragged over her earlobe and abraded her cheekbone. Pain washed over her, making her face throb.

Even buried in the Cessna fuselage, she could hear a pair of voices discussing something as they entered the hangar. The men's words were muffled, and the conversation was broken, but she was sure only two people had entered.

"I . . . stuff   out   of . . . tonight . . . wait . . . house." Then there was a pause, as though the speaker was looking at something. "I thought . . . off . . . when I left." Another pause. "Anyway . . . out of here."

"Rush?"

"Worried . . . bad feeling about Chevak . . . afraid that kid . . . booze . . . mouth shut. . . . If he's caught . . . implicates me . . . any evidence in the hangar . . . prove . . . nothing . . . tie me . . . smuggling."

"Why . . . ?"

"Because you . . . deliveries . . . seen you. The troopers . . . search your house. I'd be . . . first one . . . after."

Ten seconds passed, then more words. "Okay . . . where?"

A cardboard box grating across the floor followed the last muffled remark. Then there was a grunt, succeeded by a heavy clomping of boots. Seconds later, the lights were flipped off, enveloping her in inky darkness. The door banged shut.

Taylor sucked in a lung full of air, the first she had taken for minutes. She finally noticed the aching of her ribs, and felt the awkwardness of her position. Her muscles were as tight as violin strings. Purposefully, she commanded her limbs to relax and tried to lessen the sting of the metal cables grating on her cheek.

Gingerly, she eased out of her cramped quarters. Her butt waggled in the air as she edged hind-end-first over the rear seat backs. Finally, she could clamber out the cabin door and drop down to the concrete floor. Her knees trembled and she balanced herself on the plane's door-frame.

That had been a close call. If the men hadn't taken their time exiting their vehicles, they would have discovered her, still hanging halfway out of the Cessna. She gulped, conjuring up pictures of bodily injury, or worse, if they had found her.

But who were they? Certainly, one of them had to be Bill Blaskovich; he had just been in the hangar. She was fairly sure that most of the conversation had come from him, but she wasn't sure at all who the other man was. The inflections in his speech were somewhat familiar, but he hadn't said enough for her to recognize the voice. Even her sharp ears, tuned to pick up the nuances in garbled radio talk, hadn't discerned anything. The metal surrounding her broke the words up like the enemy jamming a radio message.

But even with half of their speech blocked out, she had gotten the gist of their conversation—they'd been talking about removing something incriminating from the hangar. The words booze, Chevak, and smuggling told her she had found the party responsible for the illegal activities.

Unfortunately, the damning evidence of their involvement had just left the hangar in their possession.

She couldn't believe she had been so close to it, but hadn't seen it during her quick scan of the hangar. Damn! If the pack-rat owner of the hangar hadn't amassed such a collection of junk, she might have spotted it. Then she really would've had the goods on Blaskovich.

She stomped over to turn the light on again, blowing her bangs off her forehead with a *phhmph!* She would have to comb the hangar to persuade herself that she hadn't missed anything else. Maybe they had forgotten some other telltale item. Grinding her teeth, she headed back to the Cessna. "May as well start here," she grumbled.

The interior of the plane was dirty, but standard for its

ilk. Plastic upholstery on the seats, gray-blue mud-daubed carpet on the floor, a smoke-stained white headliner on the ceiling. She clawed through the contents of the wall pocket next to the pilot's seat, finding nothing but a couple of maps and an encyclopedic handbook for Alaskan aviators. Digging through the small compartment in front of the forward passenger seat, she uncovered a pair of scratched sunglasses and a roll of lemon Life Savers. Big friggin' deal.

Poking into the rear of the cabin, she saw a ratty engine cover thrown over one of the aft passenger seats. She figured it was used for wintertime overnight stays away from the hangar, but wondered where Blaskovich went on those occasions. Did he go as far as Anchorage, through the Alaska Range? The pockets behind the front seats yielded nothing suspicious, either—just an unused airsick bag.

As she snapped the plastic bulkhead back into position, a faint glimmer in the corner caught her eye. Wedged in between the right-side seat runner and the door was an *ulu*, a semicircular knife of Alaskan Native origin. That particular *ulu* was chiseled out of a large flake of stone with a wooden handle attached to its spine.

What was that knife doing in Blaskovich's plane? she wondered. She knew the *ulu* was an all-purpose implement used by Eskimos for everything from skinning a beaver to dicing a frozen hunk of seal meat—why did a white man have one in his Cessna? She couldn't think of any application it would serve in the airplane. Her upper lip curled as she examined the hefty *ulu*, then she tossed it back where she had found it.

It didn't seem important. Maybe he just carried a link of reindeer sausage with him when he flew, as a snack, and used the *ulu* to cut small morsels. She had done that herself on occasion, when she had missed breakfast and wouldn't eat again until dinner. The sausage wasn't greasy, didn't need cooking before eating, and fit perfectly in a map compartment. Perfect finger food for a pilot.

She crawled out of the Cessna, disappointed by finding

nothing untoward inside. Painstakingly, she poked in all
of the boxes scattered about the hangar. She even cleared
the metal lockers, rifled through their contents, and re-
packed them. Nothing. The most interesting item she uncovered was a stack of well-thumbed issues of *Playboy*.

Fifteen minutes later she was done, with nothing to
show for her efforts. It was frustrating, knowing that the
damning evidence had been right there.

She desperately needed some additional evidence to
present to the authorities if she wanted to support her
story. Nonetheless, she decided to go to the State Troopers
with what she had. It would just be her word on what she
had heard, but surely that would be enough. The conversation *had* been significant. Certainly they would see the
merit in her claims, and maybe arrest Blaskovich that very
night. They had ways to pull the information out of him
concerning who had the evidence that would prove her
case.

FIFTEEN

The VW Rabbit hummed as Taylor sped down the road from the airport to town. Not even the bumpy ride over the frost heaves dotting the asphalt could derail her thoughts. Her eyes were glazed and she drove on autopilot, not really *seeing* anything. She blew her breath out the side of her mouth as she drove to prevent it from freezing on the windshield.

What was she going to tell the troopers? she wondered. "That plane inside the hangar had to be the same red plane from Tuntutuliak," she murmured into the chill air. "I'll have to tell them about that. That's the key."

Still organizing her "evidence" she swung into a small gravel parking lot in front of a wooden building. The large blue-and-gold decal covering the front door was an enlarged version of the Alaska State Troopers' logo emblazoned on the two vehicles in the lot. Short pilings supported the small building, leaving about a four-foot gap between the ground and its floor. Through a window, she could see lights shining and a man bent over what appeared to be an administrative desk.

While parking her car, she smiled at the stilts propping up the office. She was remembering her reaction when she had first seen similar scenes all over Bethel. She had been brand-new in town at the time, and the pilings had amazed her. "What's with all of these buildings with legs?" she'd asked Jeff Davidson, who was more familiar with Bethel. "They somebody's idea of a joke?"

He'd shaken his head. "Not at all. The houses have to be elevated to prevent them from sinking into the ground."

"But why would they sink? It's not swampy out here."

Laughing, he'd stubbed his boot on the solid surface. "It's the permafrost, Taylor. Couple feet down, the dirt's permanently frozen. If the buildings sat right on it, their weight'd thaw the permafrost and the floors would buckle when the ground turned into goo. The solution's those pilings—they keep the houses off the ground."

Still chuckling at herself, she clambered out of her vehicle and took the wooden stairs two at a time. Then she paused on the last step, a bit nervous about approaching someone with her story. She wasn't in law enforcement; she wasn't even a private eye. Would a trooper listen to her?

Her previous confidence was eroding, and all she could think of was Jeff's Nancy Drew jokes. Maybe a professional law officer would think the same thing, and see her as nothing but a police dilettante. A *cop groupie.*

Then she set her jaw, lifted her chin, and marched into the building. She hadn't been imagining the accidents in the villages. People were dying because alcohol was making its way to the dry villages. It *was* a crime. The troopers would see that.

The door squeaked as it swung shut behind her. She scanned the room, taking in the muted gray-green walls reminiscent of offices at the Air Force base in Anchorage. A utility-grade carpet—heather gray, of course—covered the floor. She wondered how they kept it clean during the spring flood of the neighboring Kuskokwim River. Did the troopers have to take their boots off after returning from wading in the Bethel mud?

"May I help you?" the man behind the desk asked, setting down an official-looking manual. His plump form strained against the buttons of his uniform. He had combed several strands of nondescript hair over his shiny pate in a last-gasp attempt to resemble a man who wasn't balding.

"Yes, Officer,"—she glanced at the name tag on his shirt—"Officer Lawrence. My name is Taylor Morgan, and I would like to talk to somebody."

"Regarding what?" He gazed at her solicitously in an expression he surely *thought* spoke of efficiency and competence. But to Taylor, he looked as if he hoped she was selling Girl Scout cookies.

"I have evidence of a serious crime I want to share with the troopers." She set her features, trying to look formidable, someone with something important to say. Kind of hard for someone her size.

Officer Lawrence's eyebrows rose. Perhaps civilians rarely dropped by with "hot tips." Especially women. "Well, it's rather late, miss. Officer Pedersen is the only one here right now." He glanced down a short hallway behind him. "I'll see if he can talk to you, though. What was your name again?"

"Taylor Morgan." She nervously shifted from one foot to the other as Lawrence dialed another office. She could hear the phone ring from the other side of the building, and listened as he announced her presence.

"Go on down." He pointed over his shoulder and swung a gate open to admit her to the inner part of the office.

As she walked down the hall, she gazed at photos tacked on the wall. In one, a trooper stood next to a blue-and-gold Super Cub parked in Quinhagak, and in another two troopers held armfuls of walrus tusks and beamed smugly for the photographer.

A few more steps took her to an office, where she peeked around the doorknob. Three desks filled the cluttered room, and a bulletin board full of memos and an out-of-date calendar was tacked on the wall. The calendar was still turned to December of the previous year. She wondered about that, until she saw the picture that corresponded to that month—a striking photo of a moonrise over the Alaska range.

She shrugged. If *she* had liked the picture for December that much, she would have cut it out and framed it, not left it in the calendar.

A man looked up from one of the desks, as he leafed through some paperwork in a file. The earpieces of his wire-frame glasses seemed to underline two squares of gray at his temples, and the rest of his coarse dark hair was oiled back from his receding hairline. His trooper's uniform was creased so sharply, it could have cut cheese. Either he hadn't done much work that day, or he used industrial-strength starch when he ironed his pants. He stood when she stepped into the office, and offered a hand to shake. "I'm Officer Pedersen," he boomed in a deep baritone.

That voice surprised her. The man's slight, wiry frame didn't appear to be the kind of body able to generate such volume. "What can I do for you?" he asked politely. "Officer Lawrence said you had some information about a problem."

"Yes, I do." She pulled over a chair and sat. "I've learned of a serious crime. I'm a pilot for Tundra Air Charter, and during my flying in the last week I've noticed some disturbing things." She proceeded to detail what she had seen and learned about the booze-running, emphasizing the deaths related to it. However, she left out the possible sabotage of her plane—even though she was sure of it, it could be easily disproven and make the rest of her story less credible.

He nodded as she spoke, often asking for clarification on a point, a subtle smile spreading across his face as she grew more and more excited during her recitation.

Finally she finished: "And I'm sure Bill Blaskovich and another man were trying to hide the evidence of their activities."

"Uh-huh." He steepled his fingers and flexed the tips. "You say that you never got Blaskovich's name from anyone? And you never saw the *contraband* in the han-

gar? You're just guessing about it, based on a description
that fit Blaskovich and what you overheard?'' He frowned
and cocked his head. ''You know, that's not much to base
an investigation on. We have a lot of work as it is, in-
vestigating crimes with concrete leads.''

''What?'' She shook her head in confusion. ''I figured
you'd listen to my story, even without hearing his name.
But you won't? I mean, we're talking about deaths here,
not just routine alcohol abuse. The decription fit him to a
tee.''

''Well, yes. I understand that.'' His gaze narrowed, and
he drummed his fingertips on the blotter in front of him.
''You said you fly for Tundra Air? And the guy you suspect flies for Western Alaska Transport? Aren't you com-
petitors?''

She nodded vigorously, then her nod slowed when she
realized the implication of his question. A flush crept up
her cheekbones.

''Y-you are going to look into th-this,'' she stammered.
''Aren't you? I mean, this is serious!''

He reached across his desk and patted her arm. ''Yes,
yes, we'll check into it. But we're kinda shorthanded right
now, may not be able to get to it for a bit.''

''You don't think I made the story up, do you? I swear,
it'll check out.'' Her worried tone made her words sound
rather suspect, and she realized that wasn't helpful.
''Can't you do anything about this tonight? I mean,
they're probably stashing the evidence right now!''

''Perhaps. But we're going to have to wait until tomorrow, at the earliest, before we can begin any kind of
an investigation. We're not going to arrest someone just
because he seemed to fit a description. You're relying
heavily on eavesdropping as a basis for your claim, and
we'll need more. The best I can tell you is that we'll look
into it.''

She lowered her eyes and picked at a hole in the upholstery of the chair she was sitting on. This was not
turning out the way she had envisioned. Looking up, she
asked, ''Do you think you can get to it ASAP?''

"I hope so. But what you gave me isn't much to work with. We'll have to get our own sources. You'll just have to be patient. I'm sorry you're disappointed, but—"

Before he had finished his remark, she was rising from her chair. Scowling, she said, "I'm going to keep on this guy. If you can't get involved, I'll get the evidence you need."

"Miss, I don't think that's a good idea. You'd be interfering with our handling of the affair, might even wreck it. Plus, you could get hurt."

She snorted, crossing her arms with a defiant look etched across her face. "I can take care of myself, Officer. And I know I'll find something to convince you to listen to me."

Sighing, he shook his head. He looked kind of frustrated. "We *are* going to look into it, miss, but we're not going to arrest anyone tonight. . . ."

Ignoring his attempt to placate her, she swung around and marched out the door. The calendar's pages rustled as she blew past. Without even a brief glance at the framed photos on the hallway walls, she stomped past the startled Officer Lawrence and headed for the headquarters' front door.

The cool night air washed into the room when she opened the door, and the glass rattled as she slammed it closed behind her.

Taylor's teeth chattered as her VW Rabbit lurched down the side road leading away from the State Troopers' office. With every bump, her grip on the steering wheel tightened. The vehicle's heater spewed nothing but cold air into the cab, so she swore at it and flipped the switch.

Four minutes later, she pulled into the third slot of a four-car lot and switched off the vehicle's ignition. Scanning the nearby aluminum-sided fourplex, she noted a light shining out of the upper left apartment. Good, that meant Jeff was still awake. She glanced at her watch, holding it up to the porch light, and read Mickey Mouse's hands. It was only nine-thirty, but she had worried that a hard day had prompted him to retire early.

Hesitantly, she swung her legs out of the car door. What would she tell Jeff? Her strikeout with the troopers embarrassed her. Well, she amended, she didn't really strike out; they just didn't share her excitement for her story. Rather than tell him about that, she should start with the conversation she had overheard while wedged into the tail cone of Blaskovich's Cessna. That was important stuff.

Setting her face in a determined expression, she slid off the seat and headed to the fourplex's stairway. As she started to climb the flight of steps, she saw the profile of some two-thousand-gallon tanks huddled on the ground behind the building: a water tank and a septic tank.

Just like her first sight of permafrost, her introduction to tanks like that had surprised her. A lot. Jeff had explained their necessity—no water or sewer lines could be placed beneath the frozen soil, so every house had receptacles for incoming clean water and outgoing waste water. She had shuddered when wondering if the identical tanks ever became mixed up.

Shaking her head at that memory, she trotted up the remaining stairs and entered the foyer. Another flight of steps stood between her and Jeff's upper-level unit, and she bounded up them. The closer she got, the more excited she became. She had forgotten her disappointing visit to the troopers' office, and was eager to tell him of her breakthrough in her search. She *could* make a difference.

After rapping on his door, she impatiently shoved her hands into her coat pockets. Thirty seconds passed, and she knocked again. Ten more seconds went by—another knock.

"Just a second, just a second," came the reply. "Let me get my pants on." Twenty more seconds elapsed, then Jeff pulled the door open. A pair of Jockey briefs peeked out from his unbuttoned Levi's.

"Did you know it was me, or do you expose yourself to everyone who comes to your door?" She marched past him after eyeing his belly button and shrugged out of her coat. Tossing it on the couch, she glanced about the living room. Nothing about his living quarters had changed, except the location. But the same half-empty glass of cola and the same ripped bag of chips were parked on a coffee table in front of the same tattered sofa.

The poorly appointed room screamed *bachelor* with its lack of any homey touches on the walls and abundance of clutter on the floor. Magazines papered the carpet, joined by three weeks worth of the *Anchorage Daily News,* Sunday edition. A box of pretzels was propped against the thirteen-inch color television perched on the top of a large cardboard box. The box had an address scrawled on its side: Jeff Davidson, c/o Western Alaska Transport, Bethel, Alaska.

"So, I told you I'd find something out. And I did. Tonight," she bragged, plopping down next to her discarded coat. "That'll teach you to underestimate a woman. I was fairly sure Blaskovich was involved before, but now I'm convinced." She crossed her arms and began detailing the steps she took to find the cantankerous man's plane, her entry into the hangar and her inspired idea to hide in the Cessna's tail. Jeff sat down next to her, a resigned look on his face.

"I knew he was coming back," she continued, ignoring his expression, "but I didn't know when. He almost caught me, him and that other guy I heard with him."

A quizzical expression crossed his face. "I thought only one guy was doing this," he said. "Where'd the other one come from? You know who it was?"

"Well, Blaskovich was doing most of the talking, so I couldn't figure out who the second guy was. I *had* thought Bill was doing this by himself, but he must have gotten some help. Like I've been thinking all along, he's not smart enough to plan something like this." She laced her fingers behind her head, sinking further onto the couch. "I think they were talking about taking something from the hangar that would tie Bill to the smuggling, and he sounded worried. Said, 'Chevak something.' Then I heard one of them shove a box toward the door and carry it out.'' She released her head, and began fumbling with a lace on her boot. ''I was pissed because they took it with them. It was there the whole time, and I didn't see it. I still don't know what it was. Damn!''

''Hmmm . . .'' Jeff nodded. ''So, you must have gone to the troopers with that information. What did they say?''

She glanced down at her lap. Here was the part she wanted to forget. ''They weren't too excited. I suppose it was just my word against Bill's. I didn't have anything concrete. No photos or recordings or wiretaps or anything. This isn't *Law and Order*.''

''So, they're not going to do anything?'' Jeff asked. Leaning back on the sofa, he tilted his head and stared at her.

She got a hurt look in her eyes. ''They said they would check into it, but it wasn't going to be a top priority. Without any corroborating evidence, they couldn't put it at the top of the list. I think they just figured I didn't like somebody at the airport and wanted to get him into trouble. I couldn't support what I was saying.'' She sniffed, and poked at a cuticle. ''Shit, I haven't been back here long enough to get that pissed at somebody.''

She leaned forward. ''So, what are we going to do? I told the troopers that I was going to continue looking into the situation. They didn't like that.''

''I don't like that, either. Why don't you just lay off? You're going to get yourself in trouble if you keep poking around.'' He rubbed his eyes and blinked in rapid succession. ''I can see you want to do something, but I wish you'd consider your own safety.''

''Well, I'm a big girl. I'll handle this on my own.'' She stood, and grabbed her coat. ''I'm leaving, got a phone call to make. To somebody that believes I'm smart enough to figure this out.''

She stomped to the door and exited without stifling the sound of its slamming.

SIXTEEN

Around noon the next day, Taylor Morgan stood at the end of the terminal café serving line, the toe of one boot tapping on the floor behind her heel. In her hands she grasped a triangular cardboard sign emblazoned with a colorful slogan: "NEW!!! The meatless veggie burger!" The ingredient list had caught her eye, and as she scanned the text she nodded. The veggie burger included whole grains like rice and oats, blended with spices. It sounded like a tasty, healthy blend.

Setting the veggie burger propaganda back on the counter, she slid her tray down the bar toward the front of the grill. "Hey, Myron," she called out to the twenty-something Yup'ik fry cook attending to a sizzling hamburger. "These new, these veggie burgers? Look good."

"Yeah, those veggie burgers are new," Myron confirmed. "We're trying them out, see if people will buy 'em." He flipped the burger over with a practiced hand and swung around toward her. A chef's hat covered his closely cropped black hair, and a grease-dotted apron hung over his torso. The faded creases on his denim shirt and pants showed they were favorites of his, as were his well-worn Nikes. His facial features—round face, dark eyes, flat nose—were the only part of his appearance that showed his Alaskan Native heritage.

"Well, count me in," she requested. "I want to see if they taste as good as they look in the ad." She pointed at the vegetable array near the grill. "Fry up some of those onions to go with it, too, and put all of the rest of the veggies on the side. Plus, I'll take some mayo. Ketchup's on the table, isn't it?"

While Myron cooked her veggie burger, her ear tuned into the sounds of conversations between the other diners. She couldn't discern particular words, but did get a feel for the voices behind the words. Sidling up to the bins full of ice and cold soft drinks, she pretended to study the selection, a blank expression on her face. Her eyes didn't move, not even to blink.

The echo of the stranger's voice she had heard in Blaskovich's hangar still rang in her ears. She wished she'd heard more—the intonation and cadence had seemed familiar, probably speech she'd overheard at the airport. She'd assumed the voice had been that of a pilot, since that's mostly whom she talked to each day, but it would be stupid to exclude all others.

"Here you go, lady," Myron's musical tone broke through her preoccupation with the speech of others. "One veggie burger with fried onions, veggies on the side. Pay up front and let me know how you like it, okay?"

"Will do, Myron." She knew the voice she searched for was not his, or that of *any* Alaskan Native. The guttural quality of a Yup'ik accent would be easy for her to pick out anywhere.

After paying for her lunch, she headed for the window tables. Maneuvering through the clusters of diners, her ears picked up some of the conversations, but none of the sounds caught her attention.

She waved at L. T. Alderman and a companion across the room, and set her tray down at a table for four. Tossing her coat on one chair, she pulled its twin out and plopped down in front of her veggie burger.

Glancing around the café, she began dressing her burger: first came the lettuce, then the tomato and pickles. Lastly, she threw a jalapeño on the mixture and slapped the mayonnaise-smothered bun on top of the mess. Midway through her first bite she yelped, and began fanning her mouth vigorously. The ensuing gulp of Pepsi didn't improve the situation, either, with the carbonation adding its own sharp tingle to the hot pepper. She felt as though she'd chugged a beaker of hydrochloric acid.

"Damn!" she scolded herself. "Why did I put that pepper in there? I *never* eat peppers!" Grabbing her napkin, she wiped her watering eyes.

With her back to the café entrance, she didn't see Jeff Davidson approach, but when he sagged down into a chair across the table she shot him a curious look. His face was haggard and drawn, and lines were etched into his forehead.

"You look like you got kicked in the balls, Jeff. What's wrong?" She studied his expression with concern. "You were out flying this morning, weren't you? Something get screwed up?"

He exhaled deeply and fingered the silverware arranged upon his paper placemat. "We lost a plane today," he muttered, and glanced across the room toward the windows.

"What? Did you say someone went down?"

"Yeah, that's what I said." The strength of his voice increased as though her inability to hear angered him. "Happened this morning."

"*What* happened this morning? Engine failure, or what?" Visions of a Twin Otter losing an engine on its climb-out from a village strip, and caroming over the neighboring tundra, made her flinch. No pilot liked hearing about aircraft accidents, no matter how minor—they realized it could have been them. "Are the pilots okay? They didn't get hurt, did they? Any passengers?"

"It wasn't pilots, plural, it was pilot, singular. A Cessna went down, not a Twin Otter." His eyes met hers, and she could see his Adam's apple bob as he swallowed.

"Oh, no." Once she learned a single-engine Cessna had crashed, the picture flashing across her mind became much more gruesome. "So, emergency dead-stick landing, huh? Pancaked down on the tundra?" She distractedly shoved a wandering pickle back into position underneath the burger bun. "How'd you find the plane so fast? Was somebody flying past, or did the pilot radio base?"

"Hank and I were returning from a run up the Yukon," he croaked, "and we picked up an ELT when I flipped past one-twenty-one-five. We called back to Bethel to report it and found out Blaskovich was overdue on his flight to Scammon Bay."

"Blaskovich?" Her gaze narrowed. Even though he was behind the booze-smuggling, and she hated him for that, she hadn't wanted him injured in a crash. She couldn't wish that on anyone. She gulped. "He hit hard enough to activate his ELT? He's all right, isn't he?"

"I don't know." Jeff shook his head slowly. "We were landing here when the National Guard copter took off to check on the ELT signal. I haven't heard what they found."

"Why didn't you guys look around on your way home? You knew Bill would be somewhere around that side of the Delta. I would've thought you'd try to locate the wreck. You know, shortening the search could've saved his life if he was in trouble."

"Yes, of course I know that. We just couldn't do anything. That part of the Delta was socked in, clouds down to the ground. We couldn't see anything." He reached out to grab his napkin, beginning to shred it as he stared glassy-eyed at nothing. "You know, if he got caught in that weather . . ."

The clunking of heavy boots interrupted his musing. Hank Seymour approached the table, his face as drawn as Jeff's. The chair creaked as he settled his stout frame and arranged his long legs. His rugged plaid wool jacket combined with his hefty physique to make him look like a young Paul Bunyan. Nothing but the Western Alaska

Transport logo on his baseball cap indicated that his actual profession was pilot, not lumberjack.

"The Guard helicopter radioed in a few minutes ago," Hank muttered. "Post headquarters called us with what they found." His eyes swung from Jeff to Taylor, then down to the tabletop. "Looks like Blaskovich screwed up for the last time."

A groan from Jeff filled the air and he buried his head in his hands. Taylor saw his stricken look and took over the conversation. "What happened?" she asked. "Mechanical malfunction, or what?"

Hank's brow furrowed and he exhaled loudly. "They're just guessing—nobody'll know for sure until the NTSB's done—but they flew through the same crap we stayed out of to get to the crash site. He musta got caught in it, and got nailed trying to get out." He shivered, though the room was not cold. "They said it didn't look too bad—they figured they'd find a survivor when they landed—but looking inside the cockpit told 'em no."

"Oh, God." Jeff unconsciously encircled Taylor's hand with his, and glanced at her with an odd expression. "What'd they find?"

Hank didn't reply for a minute, then suddenly shrugged. "I guess he didn't have his cargo net secured. The whole damn load shifted forward when he hit the ground. Pretty messy, pieces of him were plastered all over the panel." He adjusted the bill of his cap nervously.

"Unnnhhh, you didn't need to say that." Taylor grimaced. A vivid image of the crash site hit her like a fist and her gut spasmed. The same thing could've happened to her in Tununak—*she* could've been lying beneath a bloody mound of cargo. She squirmed in her seat.

Then another thought surfaced. Blaskovich's crash was just too coincidental. The previous night, she had heard him talking about the bootlegging, and the next day he's dead. Was his *accident* like her *accident* in Tununak? Had someone decided he was the weak link in the scheme?

Hank Seymour's throaty cough interrupted her contemplation. "Well, that's the news," he intoned, standing and shoving his beefy hands into his jacket pockets. "Looks like we'll be taking some extras to pick up the slack. Should I plan on a late night?" His expression became distant when Jeff nodded, and he scratched his chin half-heartedly. "Tough way to earn some overtime." He walked off, a faraway look in his eyes.

Taylor stared at Jeff, dumbfounded, as Hank disappeared. "Damn! He's not too concerned about what happened to Blaskovich, is he? We're the ones that shouldn't care about Bill's death, knowing what we do about him, but both of us are more upset than *he* was." She stared at the retreating Hank and made a face. "I'd hope to get more of a response from him if *I* clocked out some day after an accident. Jeez!"

"Well, don't be too hard on him. Something's distracting him, has been ever since we figured out that ELT was from Blaskovich's plane. Maybe the crash is bothering him more than he's willing to show, and he hides it by acting cool. Like it's beneath him to feel bad."

"I hope so. I can't believe he's such a cold fish, but maybe he's worrying about something else. I wonder what could preoccupy him enough to block out a crash like Blaskovich's." She wrinkled her nose. "Well, I guess he's caught in the ozone layer somewhere. Anyway, if Bill's killed himself, I wonder how that'll effect the booze-running?"

Jeff's eyebrows knurled and he straightened in his chair. "I don't know. What do you think?"

"I'm not sure." She pressed her fingers into a vee in front of her lips. "If the other guy in this is smart, he'll realize that someone will start going through Blaskovich's stuff. If there's incriminating shit in his house or his plane, and if the other guy couldn't get rid of it, I'd think he'd want to keep a low profile for some time. Maybe he'd want to make a hasty exit from Bethel, get out of the picture."

She peered at the sloppy remains of her burger—lettuce and onions oozed out from beneath the bun. Poking at it, she declared, "I don't think I can eat this now. I may not be able to eat anything for days." She pushed back her chair and stood. "I think I'll go check all of the straps on my cargo net before my next flight. Seems like a good idea, all things considered."

SEVENTEEN

A middle-aged Yup'ik woman and a child perched on the two mid-cabin seats of Taylor's Cessna, the youngster wriggling restlessly under the confines of his seat belt. "We'll be landing at Kipnuk in about ten minutes," she called over her shoulder, reassuring the twitching boy. She was fairly sure that a full bladder prompted his squirming.

As one-half of her mind dealt with an antsy child that had to pee, the other half analyzed her talk with Jeff and Hank. She had been so engrossed in the talk, she had neglected to note the tone of Hank's *voice*. Everyone should be suspect, she reasoned, and she couldn't exclude Hank just because he seemed friendly and likable. Thinking back on it, she tried to recreate the sound of his voice, comparing it to the fragments of the stranger's voice.

She wasn't certain if the deliveries matched, but it made sense that they would. The mystery voice had been familiar, and the young copilot's voice was familiar, too. Hank's apparent preoccupation when he supplied the news about Blaskovich fit the puzzle, as well. If he *had* been the second voice in the hangar, he certainly would be worrying about something else.

Pieces were starting to fall together. Hmmm.

But what about Hank's involvement? Could he have been ruthless enough to stage Blaskovich's accident? It didn't make sense. He seemed like a nice guy. But she hadn't known him for more than a week, and outward appearances could fool you.

Then she focused on her approach to the Native village of Kipnuk, five miles ahead of the Cessna. It was time to attend to other things. The short, rutted gravel strips on the Delta didn't forgive the pilot who got distracted by other matters.

Reaching down for the throttle, she eased it back to commence her prelanding checklist.

Seven minutes later, the Cessna bumped and thudded down the airstrip at Kipnuk. The village of approximately one hundred people sat nearby on the coast of Kuskokwim Bay. Several skin-sided boats, called *oomiaks,* rested on the rocky shoreline. A nasty breeze nipped at the wind sock at the end of the strip.

The small houses of Kipnuk huddled together, as though brooding over their isolation and the bite of the north wind. A wide path connected the settlement to the airstrip—the Tundra Air Charter agent guided an ATV through its ruts, followed by a pair of village women on foot. The three-wheeler putted up to the approaching Cessna, and the driver applied the brake.

After the propeller swung to a halt, Taylor jumped out and opened the cabin door, shoving it against the stiff breeze. The young boy clambered around her and bounded out of the plane, fumbling frantically with the zipper of his pants. He relieved himself unceremoniously in the low scrub next to the airstrip. Taylor was thankful that he had succeeded in holding himself until they had reached Kipnuk.

A youngish Yup'ik man, perhaps in his late twenties, hopped off the parked ATV and strutted over to her. Self-importance added bounce to his gait. She grinned and held out a hand to shake as he neared. "Hi there, I'm Taylor Morgan. You must be the new agent. They told me about you before I left Bethel."

"My name's David Paul. I'm pleased to meet you." The young man's proper recitation of a conventional salutation made her chuckle. Obviously, he had been practicing the greeting.

The Delta's rural standard, a beaver hat, covered David's pelt of black hair, though his stocky body was enveloped by an urban-issue Army-Navy Surplus store jacket and white rubber bunny boots.

"Well, David, it's nice to meet you." She reached into the back of the cabin and extracted a single mail bag. Holding it out, she confessed, "That's all I've got for you today. You got anything to go back?"

"No, nothing." He shook his head and glanced inside the airplane as though looking for more, regardless of what she had said. "Is it always like this, nothing in or out?"

"Well, I haven't flown this route for some time, but things probably haven't changed much. Most of the time, I'd guess it'll be like this—kinda light—but once in a while there'll be a load for the store. Then you'd have more." She swung the cockpit door open and waved at David as he turned to mount his ATV.

Without warning, a young boy of twelve or thirteen scampered around David and dashed toward Taylor, puffing as he skidded to a stop.

"Slow down, slow down, little guy," she cautioned him. "What's the hurry?" She lowered her foot from the step, shifting her weight to the ground as she looked at him. "Where'd you come from? I didn't see you run up."

He smiled in reply and shoved something at her with pride in his eyes. "Here," he stammered. "Will this work? I took it from my grandfather's shed. He's a seal hunter."

She stared down at his outstretched hand, where he clutched an old bone harpoon point, the kind the Natives had used in the past before steel points had become available.

"What's this?" she asked, confused, turning the point over in her hand. Why was he trying to give it to her?

"It's a harpoon point, old one. Really old." He peered at her as though he couldn't believe she was so stupid that she didn't know what he had given her.

"I know what it is," she retorted. "I just don't know why you're giving it to me." She was perplexed—in the past she'd been approached by villagers wanting to sell their hand-woven grass baskets, but never by someone with tools like this. This was weird.

"It's for trade," the boy said. "Don't you have any of the stuff with you today?" He looked around her toward the plane. Then realization seemed to flicker in his eyes— he squinted at her suspiciously and glanced at the distinctive logo on the Cessna's tail. Uncertainty clouded his features. "Aren't . . . aren't you one of the pilots trading booze for old stuff?"

She gaped at him, the disbelief obvious in her expression. Trading for liquor? Why would he think she would exchange booze for something as useless as an old harpoon point? "I don't want to trade anything for booze. Who told you I would?"

"Uh . . . uh, I thought you were one . . . one of the pilots that were . . ." He sidled away from her in retreat. "Never mind," he said. Grabbing the point out of her hand, he jammed it into his pocket and darted off toward the village. He passed the startled David Paul and continued his dash for his house as though a bear was close on his heels.

"What the hell . . ." she muttered. Staring at the running youngster in amazement, she yelled at the disappearing back of the agent. "David, David, come back! I need to talk to you!" Perhaps he could enlighten her on the odd behavior of the boy, tell her what was happening. "David, David!" she clamored.

The agent's pace never slackened; he obviously hadn't heard her screams. Maybe the flaps of his beaver hat sound-proofed his ears, or maybe he was ignoring her. "Oh, shit," she groused, arms akimbo as she glared at his departing form. "Who the hell did that kid think he was talking to?"

Hiking herself up into the Cessna, she plopped down in the pilot's seat and fastened her shoulder harness. As she fumbled with the seat belt, her mind was spinning.

Once she'd set the parking brake, Taylor jumped down from her plane and onto the asphalt of the Bethel airport. Snapping up a thick polypropylene rope, she began to secure her plane for the night. In a matter of minutes, the wing ropes were fastened and she was dragging the engine cover out of the rear cabin.

The awkward bulk of the nylon cover obscured her view, and she accidentally knocked her aluminum clipboard from its position on the plane's wheel. "Oh, damn!" she cursed, throwing the insulated cover across the engine, then stooping down to retrieve the flight manifest forms that had fluttered free.

While attempting to wipe the snow off the paper without smearing the ink, she glanced up to see Jeff Davidson jogging toward her. "Hi, there!" she called out as she straightened.

"Hi," he answered. "Don't have much time to talk, heading up the Kuskokwim. Kwethluk, Akiachak, Tuluksak and back."

"Aren't those Cessna runs? Why's a Twin Otter taking those?" she asked. Jeff's expression answered her question instantly, and she bit her lip. "Oh, yeah." She was surprised it had been so easy to forget the morning's events. She glanced down at her clipboard, then back up to meet his gaze. "I heard something fairly surprising just now, when I was unloading in Kipnuk. Has to do with the booze-running."

Jeff's gaze narrowed and he looked over his shoulder. The cargo handlers appeared finished with his airplane, and Hank was trotting down the terminal steps. "Make it fast, looks like we're going to be ready to go in a second." He turned back to focus on her. "What did you hear?"

Taylor condensed the encounter with the Kipnuk boy

for him, adding her belief that Blaskovich had been using the booze for barter.

"Nah, why would he do that? He wouldn't want to barter, just get some quick cash." He shook his head in doubt. "Anyway, why'd the kid think you were in the deal with Bill?"

"I don't know. He must have gotten only part of the story, figured that all the pilots around here were in on it. That's all I could come up with." Her eyes clouded over, as she considered the idea. "I figured Bill wanted cash, too. Why would he want old stuff? The kid was very specific about that—he said the harpoon point was *really old,* that it came from his grandfather's things."

"That's just too weird, Taylor. The kid must've gotten his story really screwed up. I can't believe that Bill would've tried to trade; he had to be after the cash."

She shrugged. "Yeah, maybe you're right. I may be seeing too much in this. Anyway, the kid was only about twelve. What would he want with booze?" She raised the zipper on her coat to the level of her chin.

She sighed in exasperation—she'd convinced herself that she'd really discovered a new twist to the story. "Well, at least we don't have to worry about it anymore. I hate to sound like there was something good about Bill's death, but maybe the booze-running will slow down or quit now. If his partner has any sense, he'll get lost." She nodded, trying to look sure, but she still felt that something was missing. Perhaps not all of the pieces of the puzzle were on the table.

EIGHTEEN

The leading edge of a weather front had traveled twenty-five miles north by nightfall, and by midnight it was menacing Bethel. The accompanying sheet of clouds loomed over the tundra and the day's partly cloudy sky had become a gloomy, low overcast. The dense stratus hung only twenty-five hundred feet above the snow-covered ground.

The clouds threatened trouble, and at 1:22 A.M. the threat became reality. Heavy flakes tumbled to the ground, adding to the previous layer of snow.

The window in Taylor's studio apartment overlooked the dreamy, white scene—flakes dropped silently onto the pane and melted, streaking the glass with slender rivulets. Oblivious to the snow, she stirred under the covers.

She didn't wake, though, trapped in the grip of a disturbing nightmare. It played across her subconscious like the previews of coming attractions—scenes flashed across her mind in Technicolor, and she couldn't look away.

In dream shot one, she saw herself standing next to Tundra Air Charter's twin-engine Cessna, surrounded by a pack of dark arctic wolves. The beasts snapped and growled at her as she attempted to shield a white-clad woman crouching behind her.

Shot 2: The camera cut from her protective stance to what the other woman guarded. A man wrapped in an army surplus blanket lay unconscious in the snow next to the two women, as the wolves slunk toward him.

Shot 3: The pack magically doubled in size, with one half of the pack attacking Taylor while the other half began shredding the blanket shrouding the man. The other woman screamed as the wolves snarled, and Taylor wailed, "I can't stop them! I can't stop them!"

Shot 4: The indifferent eye of the camera panned across the wolf pack as it galloped off, the blackest wolf dragging the man through snow drifts with its strong jaws. Taylor heard herself ululating in despair as the wolves dashed away.

With a start, she jerked her eyes open. Her pulse raced. She felt the *THUMP-a-ta-THUMP-a-ta-THUMP* of her heart ricocheting across her chest. Her breath rasped in her throat and the clammy patina of sweat on her forehead chilled her as it evaporated.

She felt quite alone, lying in her bed while she curbed her racing heart. Once she had cleared the residue of the nightmare from her head, she attempted to fall back to sleep. "Forget it," she mouthed to herself. "Just relax, it's nothing." Plumping her pillow, she nestled into it.

Several hours later, the strident *bbrringg!* from the telephone jolted Taylor from her slumber. Bright red digits on the clock radio flashed 2:37 . . . 2:37 . . . 2:37 as she pulled the phone to her mouth.

"Hello," she mumbled. "What is it?"

"Good evening, I'm sorry I woke you. This is the public health hospital. We just got a call from Kwigillingok. There's been a beating, and the health aide needs a medevac. The victim is alive, but he'll die if we don't get him to the hospital. He's seriously injured."

Those words set Taylor's heart to hammering. It felt just like she'd returned to Anchorage and was taking the call as a LifeLine pilot, but the unfamiliar surroundings around her told her that wasn't true. She was still in Bethel. No high-tech King Air awaited her at the airport, no copilot, no flight nurses. All she'd have tonight would be a twin-engine Cessna 310. A lot more low-tech.

Dan Mackenzie had warned her to be ready for a medevac call on top of her charter duties, since the emergency flights were doled out to whatever operator had available airplanes.

Taylor shot a glance at the window, then frowned.

The street light outside illuminated fat snowflakes spilling to the ground. A groan slipped out of her mouth. "I don't know," she hesitated. "It doesn't look too good out there."

"This is a life-or-death situation. . . ." The tone of the nurse's voice carried all the weight of the desperate situation.

"Okay, okay, I'm on my way. I'll see what I can do." She cradled the phone and looked out the window again. "This is fucking *déjà vu*," she murmured, staring in disbelief out the window.

The Quinhagak medevac had involved nearly identical weather. But even as images from that dangerous flight flashed across her mind, she recognized that on that particular night she had something that bettered the odds of her success. She might be able to pull this one off without scaring herself to death.

No rain mingled with the snow that evening, and if she stayed out of the clouds, most likely she wouldn't have to deal with the deadly threat of icing. All that compromised her safety on this flight was the dark of the night and the heaviness of the snowfall.

Like that wasn't much to worry about.

"Shit!" she cursed. "Why doesn't this happen during the days when it's dead calm and clear?"

She yanked the covers off and shivered in the cool air. With one hand, she grabbed her pants from a wrinkled heap by the bed and jumped into them. Stuffing her arms into a chamois-cloth shirt, she tucked the tails into her jeans and stomped across the room in search of her socks. Nabbing them up from the floor, she glared at the weather over her shoulder.

By the time she had tugged on her moon boots and wriggled into her expedition parka, she was mentally ready to tackle the medevac. With tension knotting her shoulders, she stepped out of the room and shut the door behind her. In a few minutes the whine of the VW Rabbit filled the air as it pulled out of the parking lot into the slowly falling snow.

Taylor trotted into the dimly lit terminal, her face pinked by the cold air. Her heart hammered, fired by her determination. As she approached the Tundra Air Charter counter, nothing but the dust on its faux-cedar Formica top caught her gaze. Everything had been packed away for the night.

A keychain dangled from her hand. A dozen keys were attached to a brass oval with the official-looking inscription, CAPTAIN'S OFFICE—S.S.TITANIC. An engraved whale's tooth swung from the metal ring next to the keys for her car, her apartment, and many other keys.

Thumbing through the keys, she applied one to a wide, deep drawer. Two radios and a telephone nestled inside. She pulled the telephone out of the drawer, scanning the list of phone numbers taped on its side. Her index finger traced down the smeared paper and halted at the listing for the village of Kwigillingok, called "Kwig" for short.

She dialed the number for the Kwig agent. After just one ring, the phone was answered. "Hello?" grunted a voice colored by the intonations of a Yup'ik man.

"Hi, this is Tundra Air. I'm coming in for a medevac tonight and I need you to do some stuff for me so I can land there." Like it or not, she was going to have to ask for some aid. Her stomach churned—she didn't enjoy sounding helpless.

"Okay, what you need?" the agent asked.

She made a wry face. "First, I need you to get the plow driver out of bed and get him to take a few runs down the airstrip. I don't want to get hung up in the new snow. Can you take care of that?''

"No, can't do that," the man confessed. "The driver forgot to put oil in the truck and it quit running yesterday. Somebody's comin' tomorrow on the big plane to fix it.''

"Oh, shit!" she exclaimed. She certainly didn't need snowdrift trouble tonight. The situation was difficult enough as it was. "How much snow do you have out there?''

"I dunno," the agent said matter-of-factly. "Haven't been outside tonight.''

"Well, shit. Go check. Hurry, I'll wait.''

The phone clicked and she groaned in response—the man had misunderstood her and hung up.

"Damn!" she swore. "I was going to wait *on the line!* Isn't this guy awake?''

She dialed again. The phone rang twenty times before the agent returned from his reconnaissance trip. "Hello?'' he said curiously, as though the call could have been somebody else.

"I can't believe you did that," she admonished the man. Then she realized scolding him wouldn't help—she had to get to Kwig quickly, and had no time to waste. "What's the snow depth?''

"Looks like about five inches. We got three the other day, two fell tonight.''

Several seconds passed without a word from her. Drumming her fingertips on the counter, she studied the tracks they left on the dusty counter. "Okay, I think the airplane can handle that.'' She hoped she was right about that, and wasn't overestimating things because of her anxiety. "Here's the next thing I need. Can you get about six guys from the village to go out to the strip?'' She outlined her idea for the agent, who agreed to haul the men out of bed. After another minute of discussion, she hung up the phone and slipped it back into its cubicle.

She knew that taking off in five inches of snow was going to take everything the Cessna had, plus some luck, but she had made her decision and wouldn't back down.

She knew some people called that obstinacy, but she reassured herself by calling it tenacity.

Walking to the glass terminal door, she looked outside. Her stare at the ramp didn't reassure her. The light over the door beamed down on flakes dropping on the ground incessantly.

NINETEEN

With the wings cleared of snow and the engine covers stuffed into their storage compartments, Taylor taxied the twin-engine Cessna toward the runway and contacted ground control. With no other aircraft moving on the airfield, her communication with the controller was brief and informal.

"Bethel tower, five-four-niner-five-yankee is heading south, need a special."

"Five-four-niner-five-yankee, Bethel. Yeah, you *definitely* need a special, they're calling the visibility a mile. If it drops any more, we'll go IFR. You're scooting out right under the wire. You're out late, got a medevac?"

The chattiness of the man comforted her for some reason. Maybe it made the flight seem more routine, less dangerous. She knew a conversation like that would've been unusual somewhere like Chicago's O'hare field, but not in Bethel. Controllers in the small Alaskan towns were familiar enough with the pilots who flew there to talk fraternally. Plus, he was the only one in the tower that late, and he was probably lonely.

"Affirm', Bethel," she replied. "Gotta get going a-sap." She wanted to get moving right away. With every minute, the snow depth increased and diminished the likelihood of a successful conclusion to her flight.

"Roger, niner-five-yankee. Winds calm, altimeter two-niner-oh-two, cleared out of Class D airspace, maintain special VFR conditions while within and report exiting. Cleared for takeoff, Runway one-eight. Good luck."

"Roger, niner-five-yankee is rolling." Immediately, she taxied onto the active runway and paused, steadying herself. She could feel the pulse throbbing in her neck. A second later, she eased the throttles forward—the twin engines of the Cessna 310 roared in harmony as the red-and-gold fuselage lifted from the snowy runway and disappeared into the storm.

Ten minutes later, well on her way, Taylor peered out the side window of her aircraft. Nothing appeared but snowflakes zipping past the red-and-green glow of the wingtips' nav lights.

Squinting hard, she forced herself to concentrate on the panel in front of her. Mistakes were life-threatening in weather like this. She scanned the circular instruments scattered across the panel, checking and double-checking everything. Her gaze shifted from left to right, top to bottom—airspeed, attitude indicator, altimeter, turn coordinator, directional gyro, vertical speed. Even though she was legally following visual flight rules, the snow precluded relying on her own eyes for navigation.

She made slight corrections whenever the gauges displayed any shift from the correct flight path. Her methodical watch of the airplane was monotonous and tiring, but she had to do everything perfectly. Her life depended on it.

By the time her Global Positioning System instrument showed a mere five miles between her position and the village of Kwigillingok, nothing had come into view. That was no surprise to her—the visibility at Bethel had only been one mile, and she doubted it was any better the farther she got into the storm. She had to trust the gauges. Unable to see through the snow, she had no way to verify what they were telling her.

She descended from two thousand feet to one thousand feet in preparation for landing. Flicking the Cessna's landing lights on, she hoped to identify herself to the TAC agent waiting at the strip. Inhaling deeply, she licked her dry lips.

Two miles from the landing site, she picked up the faint twinkle of several lights. Rapidly, she dashed through the pre-landing routine: gear . . . flaps . . . fuel . . . prop . . . gauges. Her fingers felt wet on the cool steel of the controls as she manipulated them.

Upon nearing the flickering yellow glow, she felt relief. The agent had come through for her. The lights were flames blazing from fifty-five gallon fuel drums positioned on the dark runway. She lined up with the hazy shimmer illuminating the night sky.

A reduction to the engine power started her final descent. The first of the fuel drums grew in size, shining in the darkness. "Come on, baby, come on!" she encouraged herself. "Piece of cake!" The heartbeat thumping in her ears urged her on like war drums, and she ached from the tension in her muscles.

The upcoming landing wouldn't be like anything she had ever experienced. She didn't know what to expect, and her rasping breath marked that fact like an exclamation point. Still using partial guidance from the flight instruments, she dove toward the runway.

Fifteen feet in the air and fifty feet down the runway, she eased the nose up, flaring for landing. "Damn!" she cursed. "This is it. You better have it set up right." God, was she scared!

Seconds later . . . *plumph!*

The Cessna sank awkwardly onto the cushion of new snow. It decelerated quickly, throwing her sharply against her shoulder harness. Her gaze widened—she had made it to the ground in one piece. It felt almost anticlimatic.

But not even the safe landing comforted her. The ordeal wasn't over—it was just starting.

The loading area appeared on her left, and she coaxed the plane through the drifts toward it. She sighed in relief

as she shut down the engines and ran a hand through her
hair. Even the chill of the nighttime air hadn't prevented
her from sweating, and her bangs were sticky. But she
had no time to relax, or congratulate herself. She was up
and out of her seat in a flash, shoving the door open and
shouting at the people standing nearby.

"Where's the guy that's injured?" she yelled. "Get
him in here, let's go!"

Several men dashed off toward a nearby house, appearing a minute later carrying a blanketed man. A be-
spectacled health aide, fortyish, trotted at his side, gasping
from the exertion her plump body never got.

Two of the men lifted the injured patient into the plane,
with the older woman scrambling behind. "Come on,
come on," she shouted at Taylor. "He's hemorrhaging,
there's no time!" As soon as she and the battered man
were on board, Taylor had the plane running again and
taxiing to the runway.

Once she had it centered on the strip, Taylor thrust the
throttle levers forward to begin her takeoff run. Her heartbeat had slowed slightly during her time on the ground,
but when the aircraft began to crunch through the snow
berms, her pulse shot up again.

The engines screamed as the plane fought through the
new snow. She was asking for everything the engines
could give her, but the plane was not accelerating fast
enough to lift off. It seemed to inch forward, growling as
it toiled.

She had been afraid of that. The Cessna couldn't handle
the depth of the snow. A surge of adrenaline burst through
her body. Without using her wits and skills, the plane
wouldn't get off the ground—nothing but the mood of the
fates would stand between success and failure then.

When the runway end emerged from the blackness
ahead, the Cessna still had not reached flying speed.
Damn, what could she do to get the plane in the air? It
wasn't going fast enough!

In an effort more reflexive than planned, Taylor
wrenched the control yoke back, forcing the nose of the

plane up into a takeoff attitude. The stall warning horn
shrieked in her ears as the plane wallowed in the air, its
wheels dragging in the snow. *Bbreeeeeeeeeee!* the horn
shrilled, its squalling blasting her ears.

Every part of her brain screamed at her as she ordered
the plane to fly, to do something every bit of her pilot
training told her was wrong. As the Cessna lumbered over
the end of the runway, it staggered across the tundra beyond, a foot in the air. *BBreeee—bbbb—bbrreeeeeeeeee!*
wailed the alarm.

She prayed the stunt she was pulling would work, because she couldn't see any other escape. She had committed herself. Her eyes darted back and forth from the
airspeed indicator down to the ground shooting past,
merely feet below. Her pulse throbbed in her neck, her
eyes were glazed with fright.

The airspeed needle still wavered below the proper
mark, even after breaking out of the snow. To further aid
the plane's acceleration, she grabbed a lever on the panel
and flipped it up. An electric motor whined as it retracted
the landing gear, and she heard a sturdy *clunk!* as doors
snapped shut beneath the wheels.

Almost instantly, the airspeed needle began to creep to
a safe level. Much too slowly to please her, but at least
it was moving. The stall warning horn yelped less insis-
tently, then ceased its clamor completely.

With the excitement waning, the rest of the world came
into focus for Taylor. Unwittingly, she had been holding
her breath for the past few minutes, and her lungs burned
in their need for oxygen. She gulped deep draughts of air
to fill them.

As she dragged the plane away from the snow-covered
muskeg, she finally heard the pounding of her heart. The
percussionist for an orchestra could have been practicing
next to her for all she knew. That forced her to recognize
the jeopardy in which she'd placed herself and her passengers, and she didn't like that, not one bit.

"Jesus!" she stammered. "That was too fucking
close." She glanced over her shoulder at the people be-

hind her as her hands trembled at the controls.

The white-faced health aide clutched the blanket wrapped around the injured man to steady herself. "I don't know much about planes," she whispered, "but I'd say we were *this* close to hitting something. Am I right? And was that some kind of danger signal I heard?" She pushed her glasses up on her nose, the lenses steamed by her worried breathing. "That scared the hell out of me— I've never heard anything like that before."

"Yeah, it scared the hell out of me, too." Taylor looked away. She didn't want to tell the aide how right she had been about the takeoff. No use in frightening her any more that night—the injured man lying on the floor still needed care. "But we're okay now," she stressed. "It's just a short flight back to Bethel. You can relax and look after your patient. How's he doing?"

"He's still unconscious, and his breathing's kind of shallow, but at least he *is* breathing." The aide used a corner of the blanket to wipe her patient's bruised forehead. Looking about the poorly lit cabin, she asked, "How will you find your way back to Bethel in this snow? I can't see anything." Her face panned from dark windows on her right to dark windows on her left, her eyes as wide as a scared deer.

"Don't worry," Taylor reassured the woman. "This is the easiest part of the flight. All I do is follow my nav instruments. Soon we'll see the lights of town, but even if we didn't, my gauges would take me straight to the airport." She craned her head to look down on the seemingly lifeless man, her gaze narrowing at the disturbing sight. "How'd he get beaten up? Some fight? An argument?"

The other woman nodded. With a blood-streaked hand, she pushed her bangs off her forehead. "Yeah, sort of. Thomas here was attacked by another villager because he wanted some alcohol and the other guy wouldn't give it to him without payment. Thomas had bought some from him earlier, but ran out of money to buy more. Oogruk, the dealer, wouldn't take an IOU for the booze."

Booze? Taylor shivered instinctively, blinking rapidly. She'd thought that the booze-running had stopped with Blaskovich no longer involved, and that his death was likely to cause an end to the operation. But if that was the case, what had been going on in Kwigillingok? And who was behind it? The whole situation—a refusal to deal in alcohol and the following beating from an angry former customer—sounded exactly like what had occurred in Quinhagak.

Taylor wore a pained expression as she contemplated that new question. "This Oogruk guy, is he smuggling the booze into Kwig himself?" She hoped it was that easy, only one person implicated who was not part of the Blaskovich puzzle.

"I don't know," the other woman shrugged. "Thomas *couldn't* tell me anything, and nobody else *would*." The aide stroked the man's swollen cheek and moved the blanket around him. "But it musta just come in tonight. The trouble always starts right after it hits town."

Taylor squinted out the window, contemplating the snowflakes whipping past as she thought. "I'll go to the troopers tomorrow, tell them what happened tonight. They can check into it."

"Well, I hope someone brings a stop to this business. It's ruining too many lives." Distaste wrinkled her brow. "Booze. Hell of way to die, fighting over that damn stuff."

"No, this guy's not going to die." Taylor shook her head vehemently. "I'll get him to Bethel in time. We're almost there already." She peered at the GPS display in front of her and read off the distance to Bethel. Twelve miles.

In a few minutes, the lights of the town glimmered in the near distance. The heavy snowfall had tapered off to a light flurry, exposing the town to her view, and the relief on her face was evident.

But so was the stress.

Fatigue had encircled her within its strong grasp, along with anger. She was mad. Somehow, the alcohol trafficking was continuing, and now a man had almost died fighting over it. Who was responsible?

Her hand quivering in exhaustion, she tuned in the Bethel control tower on the radio. "Bethel, this is five-four-niner-five-yankee, niner south for landing. We need an ambulance to meet us at the ramp."

"Five-four-niner-five-yankee, Bethel, you're cleared for a straight-in approach to Runway three-six, wind calm, altimeter two-niner-three-zero. I'll notify the hospital." The controller paused for a moment, then added, "Glad you made it back okay."

"Yeah, so am I," she murmured to herself. She exhaled loudly and shut her eyes for a second.

Then she looked up. As she continued toward Bethel, she began to set the airplane up for the landing. The red beams of the visual approach situation indicators glowed at her in the distance—VASI lights had never seemed so friendly to her before.

TWENTY

By four A.M., Taylor was home. After throwing her winter gear in the corner and talking briefly on the phone to a somnolent Dan Mackenzie, she shedded the rest of her clothes and buried herself under the covers. But before she allowed herself to doze, she turned back to examining the night's events again.

If Oogruk was Kwig's booze supplier, she wondered, where was he getting it? Bringing it in himself, hidden in personal baggage on the scheduled run to the settlement? She realized that happened more frequently than anyone liked to admit—she didn't know how many disguised bottles of whiskey she'd unwittingly delivered to dry villages on her own flights.

Had Oogruk heard of Blaskovich's booze-running operation and decided to take over the Kwigillingok dealing upon Bill's death? A calculated move like that would be unusual, but odder things had happened when huge profits came into focus.

She continued to consider the problem until her thoughts became fragmented and vague, and she felt herself struggling to stay awake. The last image that flashed across her mind was that of a walrus, an *oogruk,* hugging a number of brown glass bottles to his massive, wrinkled chest.

With a sore forearm, Taylor tugged the terminal door open. Once she had released the handle, she stared at her hand in surprise. Had she clamped her fingers on the twin Cessna's control yoke that hard last night? Her eyebrows danced above puzzled eyes as she trudged toward the Tundra Air Charter counter. Maneuvering around two youngsters playing on the floor with marbles, she noted a woman dividing her attention between them and a magazine.

Dan Mackenzie flipped his head up from his own reading material when the clonking of her boots reached his ears.

"Morning, Dan." She leaned over the Formica countertop, her gloved fingers reaching for a clipboard with N4696U scrawled on its clasp.

"Morning? It's afternoon, Taylor!" Dan twisted his wrist to expose his watch, making a *snuff!* noise of mock irritation. "You're keeping banker's hours."

"Hey, you didn't tell me when I had to get up." She shrugged without any emotion.

Dan studied her closely, reclining against the back of his chair. The coils under the Naugahyde seat squeaked when his weighty bulk shifted. "Those late medevac calls really beat you up, huh? I don't envy you. But that's what you get for having medevac experience. If you weren't here another one of the twin pilots would get them." He hefted himself out of the chair and stepped to the counter. "Anyway, have any trouble with the snow? I glanced out the window when you called before you left—it didn't look too hot."

The lecture she had given herself for taking that flight still rang in her ears, prompting a gulp from her. "No, the snow wasn't a problem," she lied. "I needed a special to get out of Bethel—visibility was only a mile—but it got better farther south and it had just about quit by the time I got back."

''Why was the medevac call made? The hospital didn't give me any details other than 'who' and 'where.' ''

She didn't want to talk about that, either. Better play that down, she resolved. ''Some guy got beat up, had to go to the hospital. Health aide called for a medevac.''

''Beat up? Musta been a real thrashing, if he needed a medevac. A fight, huh?''

''Yeah. Somebody wasn't happy about something.'' She didn't see any need to elaborate on that statement. The more she kept to herself about the booze smuggling, the better. She still remembered the sabotage to her plane and the fact that one of her coworkers could have done it. ''Anyway, Dan, what's left for me to do? I'm ready to go; all I gotta do is my run-up.''

''Okay, let's see.'' He leafed through the manifests piled on one corner of the counter. ''We got some extras, stuff to go upriver. Looks like Alaska Commercial got a big shipment in from Anchorburg, headed for''—he squinted at the paperwork in his hand—''Kwethluk and Tuluksak. You can take that. I've already divvied up your schedule for the day, didn't know when you'd get in.''

''All right, I'll go hustle up a load. See ya later.'' Zipping her down parka and sliding her clipboard off the counter, she tromped to the ramp door. She felt relieved by her return to her ordinary, daily work—she could concentrate on the mundane and allow herself to forget the past twelve hours.

After returning from her flight upriver, Taylor left her Cessna for the warmth of the terminal. Stomping the snow off her boots, she stood by the closing door and fiddled with her cargo manifest. With the colored copies separated, she walked over to deliver them to Dan.

Midway through the hand-off, she saw Jeff Davidson walking over from the WAT counter. ''Hey, Taylor, Dan,'' he greeted them. ''Heard you got a medevac last night, Taylor. Musta been a bear with that snow.''

She shook her head subtly, attempting to warn him not to counter her story. She'd told Dan she hadn't had any difficulty. When Jeff noted her signal his eyebrows rose, but he stopped talking.

"Yeah, I had to sweep a coupla inches off the wings before I left," she told Dan, hoping it would reassure him. She could tell he was wondering why her story didn't match Jeff's. "That's part of why I was so tired this morning. I really appreciated the chance to sleep in."

As she tried to cover her butt, she saw a man reach the bottom of the stairs across the terminal and turn toward them. His long, gangly stride seemed slow, but brought him to their sides in seconds.

"Hey, Storch. What's up?" Dan asked, when the man stepped to the counter.

Allan Storch towered over the others in his thickly soled work boots. Even in his bare feet, he had to look down on most people. A wraith-like six-foot-nine-inch frame had earned him the nickname "the Stork," though nobody called him that to his face. As a briefer for the federal government's Flight Service Station, he was well-known by the dispatchers at the local air-taxi operations.

"I got a question for you, Dan," he drawled, flipping his jacket collar up in preparation to walk outdoors. His slow and easy speech matched his slow and easy gait— both his voice and his walk dragged like a seventy-eight RPM record played at forty-five speed. "I thought that tubby guy . . . what's his name? The one who drove the Cessnas for WAT?"

"You mean Blaskovich?" Dan asked.

"Yeah, Blaskovich," Storch confirmed. "I thought he bit the big one the other day." The tall man's choice of words seemed rather inappropriate—he didn't seem too distraught about Bill's death.

"Well, he did." Dan caught Taylor's wrinkle of disgust and grinned. "I don't think I would have picked quite that phrase to comment on it, but why do you ask?"

"Didn't he own a plane out here?"

"Yeah, he did," Dan corroborated. "I think it was a red-and-burgundy 172. An old one."

"Yeah . . ." Storch murmured. "I saw it leaving last

night, around dusk. I didn't have my radio tuned to the tower—didn't hear the pilot's call—so I didn't recognize his voice. Couldn't figure out who was flying the plane. You guys have any idea?''

His comment made Taylor squirm and glance at her feet. So, Blaskovich's plane *had* been flying last night. The trouble in Kwig had happened last night, too. Too coincidental.

Someone was still using Blaskovich's airplane to deliver booze to the villages, she thought, even without him around. Must've been his coconspirator flying, lending credence to her feeling that the voice Taylor had overheard talking to him was that of another pilot.

Without noticing her studied look, Dan shrugged his shoulders at Storch. ''I don't know who would be flying the Cessna so soon after Bill's death. For that matter, I don't really care. Blaskovich's old news and I don't want to talk about it. I wasn't a fan of his.''

''Who was?'' Taylor agreed, abandoning her thoughts. ''I've always been pleasant to him, but I never got anything but surly back. I finally gave up.''

Storch turned to leave. ''Well, I just thought it was odd. I figured that they couldn't have found a buyer for the plane just a couple of days after the guy died. I thought maybe you guys would know who was flying it. Maybe WAT was just leasing it to Blaskovich and would want to know if someone else was flying it.

''Anyway,'' he muttered, ''I guess it's not big deal.'' The lengthy stalk of his body lumbered off, waving at the three as he left.

Taylor waited about thirty seconds, then zipped her coat. ''Come on, Jeff,'' she hissed, gesturing urgently toward the ramp door. ''Follow me out for a second, I gotta check on the load for the next flight.'' The two of them walked across the terminal, Jeff looking down at her curiously as she nudged him.

''What are you doing?'' he protested. ''I don't want to go look at your airplane. I have a flight coming up, too.''

''I don't want you to look at some stupid load, I wanted

to talk to you about who was flying Blaskovich's plane last night. Any ideas? Who were his friends?''

''Friends? I have no idea. I didn't think he had any.'' Jeff poked his hands into his pockets and glanced out the window. He saw his copilot, Ryan Briody, trot down the airstair of a Twin Otter and swing over toward them. ''Hey, I better get going. Talk to you later.''

She nodded, and thought about what Storch had said. Looked like she had to make a visit to the troopers' headquarters that night.

TWENTY-ONE

The powder-blue VW Rabbit whined into the parking lot of the Alaska State Troopers headquarters. Taylor could see that a snowplow had been at work there, clearing the previous night's snowfall. The foot-tall berms rimming the area were nothing but the initial indicator of winter's arrival—by the end of the season, they might hit a height of four or five feet. As she clambered out of the driver's seat, she could see the chalky marks left on the gravel by the snowplow blade.

During her walk to the office, she stuffed her gloves into a pocket of her down coat. Her cheeks were flushed from the cold, her jaw had a determined set to it. She had decided she wouldn't leave without a firm commitment from the troopers to look into the booze-running. Now that she had more evidence—another *pilot* was involved with Blaskovich—she wouldn't back off.

Knocking the snow off her boots, she trotted up the steps leading to the front door.

A gust of cold air blew into the room when she shoved the door open. She glanced about her, absorbing the orderly snugness of the office. It looked so *official*. Officer Lawrence sat behind the raised dispatch desk, right where she'd seen him the last time she'd visited, displaying the same ingratiating look on his face. "May I help you, miss?" he asked politely.

Then he peered at her more closely and his features shifted from cordial to chilly. "Aren't you the pilot that came in here recently to talk to Officer Pedersen?" When she nodded, his brow creased. "Yeah, I thought so. What do you want now?"

She squinted at him, taken aback by his tone. "I need to talk to Officer Pedersen again," she replied. "I have more information for him." She stood up tall, trying to look imposing, like a person with something important to say. Hopefully, her voice carried some weight, too.

Officer Lawrence eyed her as though sizing up her resolution, and tapped the eraser-end of a pencil on the desk top. "Officer Pedersen isn't here, so you're out of luck. Give me your name again and tell me what you wanted, I'll take a message. He can call you." The man's potbelly rammed up against the desk's top when he leaned over to grab a notepad. After smoothing the resulting wrinkle in his uniform shirt, he poised his pencil to write.

Taylor didn't want to leave a message and give the troopers a chance to ignore her—what she had to say needed to be said soon, and acted upon soon. "When is Officer Pedersen due back? I really need to talk to him, this can't wait." She didn't understand why Lawrence seemed so hostile about her appearance at his office.

"I don't know when he'll be back," Lawrence stated flatly. "He had to leave the office to check on something. Just leave a message, he'll get back to you."

She bristled when she heard that. It was an unimaginative excuse and she could see his rather obvious air of condescension.

"Well, why don't you just make a guess at when he'll return?" she snapped. "I'll come back then and talk to him. . . ."

At the same time she started to get visibly annoyed, the door swung open and Officer Pedersen entered. As he stamped his snowy boots on a black rubber welcome mat, he glanced up to see who the visitor was. His air changed from curious to cool when he focused on Taylor, and his features took on a tint of distaste. "Oh, it's you," he growled.

She turned to speak to Pedersen, but his lackluster recognition brought her up short. Both of the men had acted irritated with her. What had she done? Her glance darted from one officer to the other and back.

"Officer Pedersen," she hesitated, "I need to talk to you again. I've got some more facts on the alcohol trafficking." She dropped her hands to her sides from where they had gripped the top of the desk, and stared at him uncertainly.

"I hope it's better than what you gave me before." He frowned and gestured toward his back office. "I don't like wasting my time, and the state's money, in chasing leads that take us nowhere."

She flinched at his words. What did he mean? Was he saying that the information she had given him was no good? How could that be? Her gaze trailed down the wall to the runner on the floor as she followed Pedersen down the hallway.

Once in the rear office, Pedersen lowered himself into his chair and began rearranging the paperwork on his desk. Taylor entered the room behind him and halted. He continued to organize his things as though she wasn't even there. She eyed the chair in front of the desk, took one step toward it, then decided to remain standing. Perhaps that would give her a slight advantage, her speaking to the officer from above him.

Pedersen cleared his throat and leaned back in his chair. His expression looked dubious. "You know, Miss Morgan, I checked up on what you told me the last time you came in. I was disappointed."

"Disappointed? Why?" Her gaze clouded—the information she had given him had been sketchy, but it should've been a good start.

He thumbed through some papers abstractedly. "I flew out to Chevak to talk to your 'informant.' Not only did he not support your story, he denied ever seeing you.

Who's lying here, you or him?'' He glared and pointed at the chair as though ordering her to sit.

So much for her advantage.

"Going out to Chevak cost the state some big bucks,'' he continued, "and I don't like spending the state's money without getting anything for it. You're a pilot, you know that flying out to one of the villages isn't cheap, even with a state airplane.'' He started counting on his fingers to emphasize his point. "First, not only does the state have to pay for gas, they have to pay me for my time flying the plane out there. Second, they have all of the additional expenses of stationing a plane out here to begin with—''

"Yeah, yeah, I know,'' she interrupted. Shaking her head, she contemplated the fact that the Chevak man had lied about talking to her. Did someone get to him, urge him to change his story somehow? Now that he hadn't confirmed her story, how could she assure Pedersen she was trustworthy? "What about that damaged shack by the strip? I told you how that happened. That would confirm what I said, I know *that* couldn't be hidden.''

"Well, I remembered what you said, so I asked the man about it. He did admit responsibility for hitting the shack, but he had a different tale about *why*. He said his three-wheeler had a sticky throttle and it got away from him. Before he could get it slowed down, he hit a bump and fell off. Without him steering, it hit the building. Simple as that.''

She gaped at the officer, amazed by the altered story. "You didn't believe him, did you? He's sure not going to tell a trooper about getting drunk in a dry village. He's no idiot.'' She twisted uncomfortably in her chair. "Obviously, somebody convinced him to cover. Can't you see that?''

The trooper shrugged. "Well, it's not that I believed him completely. But his story varies so much with yours that it's going to take more to prove what's true. Anyway, the trafficking is probably done with, isn't it? The pilot you told me about is dead. I heard about it from the National Guard when they picked up his body. It appears he got caught in the weather and spun in." He glanced at the photo clipping on the bulletin board, then back at Taylor. "I'm sure you know that, so why are you continuing to pursue this? He's not going to get prosecuted if he's dead."

"Well, yeah, I *do* know he's dead, but the trafficking is still going on. I told you someone else came into the hangar with him the other night. That guy's probably the one that's still bootlegging the booze."

"You said you weren't sure who it was, though. The conversation wasn't too clear, you said. Have you had a sudden revelation?"

Taylor blushed when she heard the sarcasm in his voice. "Well, no, but the smuggling is still going on. *Someone* is doing it. I think it's another pilot."

Pedersen looked skeptical, so she decided to pull out the big guns. "Would you be more likely to listen to me if I said my life has been threatened, and that Bill Blaskovich's death might not have been an accident, but a murder?" She saw his eyebrows shoot up. Even though she couldn't prove either statement, she needed to take advantage of his piqued interest. She began to recite the details about the sabotage in Tununak and Blaskovich's crash, then ceded into the Kwigillingok medevac and the Cessna 172 sighting.

"Hmmm," he murmured. "Those smuggling details are new, but there's no more support for them than the other ones. However, the possibility of murder and the threat to your life does alter the picture. All of your allegations should be looked into." He drummed his fingers on the blotter on his desk, then traced the doodles on one corner. "Maybe we can talk to the air traffic controller on duty the night the Cessna was spotted and see if he recognized a voice. If we're lucky, he'll remember who it was. Then, we could check into the specifics of the two crashes, find out if they really were accidental or something else." He grabbed a pencil and pulled a small notebook out of his shirt pocket. Licking the lead of the pencil, he poised to write. "I need that source name from you again, the one that saw the Cessna. If time permits, and I think it will, I'll go out to the airport and talk to some people."

Nodding in delight, she rattled off the name Pedersen needed. After he scribbled it down, he flipped his notebook closed and stuffed it back into his pocket. "Thank you. I'll check into this."

When Taylor pushed her key into the apartment's lock, she could hear the bleat of her phone. Pulling her gloves off, she darted across the room and grabbed the phone from its cradle. In her haste, she jerked the receiver off its perch and the telephone crashed to the floor. "Real good, Taylor," she cursed.

Retrieving it from the floor, she snapped, "Hello!" into the mouthpiece.

"That's not much of a greeting for the bearer of good tidings," Dan Mackenzie objected. "I'm not interrupting anything, am I? You all caught up in some steamy romance novel or something?" He sniggered.

"Oh, cut it out, Dan. I haven't been away from Steve *that* long." What was he accusing her of? The slime. "The phone just fell on the floor, nearly hit my foot. You must have heard it hit."

"Sure did. It almost blew my ear off. People will stop calling you if you break their eardrums every time you pick up the phone."

"Well, it wasn't my fault. I was just coming through the door when you called, and I had to race over to answer it. I thought it was a medevac or something. Anyway, what's up?"

"Well, our boss called me from Anchorage a few minutes ago. Looks like he bought a new plane for us to replace the one you creamed, and you have to go get it."

Her eyebrows shot up. "Why doesn't he fly it out himself? He's right there and he has to get out here some way. I would think he wouldn't trust me with any airplane after what happened to nine-six-uniform."

"Well, you're partially right, but he does have a reason for farming the flight out. The plane's a Cessna 185 and he hasn't ever flown any tail draggers."

She nodded, Dan's answer made sense. Not every pilot had flown a tail dragger, an airplane with a wheel hanging down below the tail. The different wheel configuration made for trickier handling on the ground, and a pilot had to get used to the feel. "But why did you pick me to go get it?"

"You're the only one that has any appreciable tail-dragger time. Remember, you told me your dad taught you to fly his 185."

"Yeah, right." She had forgotten discussing that with Dan years ago. He must have an amazing memory, she thought. "So, when do I leave?"

"Tomorrow. I've got a seat on the jet to Anchorage for you." Dan continued to give her directions, telling her where the Cessna was, what the arrangements were for picking it up, and when her flight would leave Bethel the next day.

Once she had hung up on Dan, she ambled over to the sofa with a smile on her face. What a treat, she thought, as she flopped on the sofa and shed a boot. A company-paid flight to see Steve. Well, not a long one—just over-night—but she only had a couple of days left in Bethel, and a single sleepover at his house would hold her until then.

She reached for the phone and dialed.

TWENTY-TWO

Wen Taylor's clock radio blasted music in her ear at half past six, she swatted the snooze button and rolled over again. "Leave me alone," she croaked, not ready to rise and shine. She'd manage to catch the Anchorage jet even if she snoozed a bit more, so she pulled the bedspread over her head and crawled into a fetal position.

However, she had gotten too conditioned to early starts, and after an hour of fidgeting under the covers, she rose. Within five minutes, she had the radio back on and had begun packing for her trip. She hadn't really unpacked her big duffel bag when she'd arrived in Bethel, so repacking only consisted of setting some things aside to go in a backpack. Of course, she could swing by her Upper Hillside cabin for a change of clothes when she got into Anchorage, but she anticipated spending the night at Steve's and doubted she'd want to race home in the morning before she left for Bethel.

Wriggling to a loud rendition of "Can't Get No Satisfaction" on KYUK, she rummaged through the duffel and extracted a pair of ragg wool socks. She studied the holes in the toes, then shrugged and stuffed them into the backpack. An aquamarine cotton turtleneck followed the socks, along with a thermal knit top. She stared at the knapsack for a second, then peered into the duffel, trying to decide if she had everything she needed for her trip.

Nodding, she stepped back and grinned. ''All right, packed and ready to go!'' she called out to the empty room, holding her arms up in a victory salute. ''Anchorage, here I come!'' She fastened the clip on the pack and tossed it on the bed.

Then she paused, and marched back to the duffel. With a swipe, she grabbed a pair of white cotton bikinis. ''Underwear,'' she muttered. ''Don't forget underwear.''

As she stowed the underwear, she could imagine her mother asking her, ''Are those clean? What if you were in an accident?'' In all likelihood, almost everyone's mom had spoken similar words at one time or another.

Once she'd added the bikinis to the other items, she walked to the foyer closet for her cold weather gear. Reaching for her moon boots, she wedged a foot into one while contemplating what she'd do in Anchorage that night.

Steve would be meeting her at the airport when she arrived—providing he didn't get called for a medevac— and he'd mentioned needing to find a gift for his mom's birthday. Maybe they could go downtown to the Fifth Avenue Mall, do some shopping, get dinner at a Thai restaurant, head back to his condo, and . . .

Well, she wouldn't let her imagination run away. More than a week had passed since she'd seen him, and her anticipation would be hard enough to deal with as it was.

With her backpack slung over a shoulder, she stepped into the hallway. As she zipped her parka and locked her door, a noxious smell assaulted her nose—apparently, someone had lost his or her lunch outside her door last night and hadn't bothered to deodorize the area. Or even *clean* the area. Stepping gingerly around the eau de upchuck, she headed for the parking lot door. She wasn't going to miss *this* place when she left.

● ● ●

Taylor swung her car into the terminal lot, parking in the row nearest the front door. She grabbed her backpack and exited her car, a big smile on her face. Going to Anchorage, she thought. Going to see Steve. Going to get—

Then she shook her head, surprised by her need to connect with him—she hadn't been gone *that* long. Maybe she just wanted to talk to him about getting close to finding the booze runner. She was kind of proud of that, stepping in to help in a bad situation. In the several times she'd called him, she'd never mentioned what she'd been doing, afraid of alarming him unnecessarily. But maybe, when the time was right, she'd tell him.

When she stepped into the terminal, she was surprised to see Jeff Davidson and Ryan Briody, his copilot, marching over to the Western Alaska Transport ticket counter. Determined looks were etched on their faces. The WAT dispatcher, Ray Evans, sat there on his tall stool, back to the approaching pilots, shoulder cradling the phone. He appeared to be finishing a call.

Curious, she trotted over. It looked like she'd hear something interesting.

Setting the phone back on its receiver, Ray turned around and noticed Jeff and Ryan standing in front of the counter. "Hi, guys. You got a short rest until the Kwig-Kong flight. You gonna head up for coffee?"

Jeff shook his head, then spied Taylor approaching. Beckoning with his head as though to say, "Come on over here, and listen to this," he replied to the dispatcher: "Well, we may as well go up for coffee, Ray, because we're not going to Kwig today. Or Kong, or anyplace else, for that matter."

Ray laughed, bewildered. "What's this?" he asked. "You're not going to fly? I'm used to pilots bailing out in bad weather, but the skies are only overcast today. That shouldn't mean cancelling a flight. Is this mutiny, or what?"

"Uh-uh, no mutiny," Jeff declared. "We got a problem, and I don't think I wanna fly the ship assigned to us anymore until it's fixed."

His eyes widening, Ray bent forward. "What kind of problem? I haven't gotten any squawks written up." He looked pointedly at the clipboard Jeff had placed on the counter.

Jeff frowned. "This has been going on for a few days, Ray, but didn't get written up." He shuffled awkwardly, clearing his throat. "I don't like having to do this, but I'm going to ground this ship. We keep getting an intermittent over-temp warning light. If I can't trust it, it's no good to me. I don't want to be worrying about whether it's telling me the truth."

"Oh, come on, Jeff," Ray protested. "What's the big deal if you've got a light blinking on once in a while? Just turn it off!"

Gaping at Ray, Jeff shook his head. "Are you kidding? It's more serious than that. The book says an over-temp light malfunction is a grounding squawk." He glanced at Taylor. "Tell him what that means," he growled. "I know you do the same thing with the King Airs."

She screwed up her face, not wanting to become caught in the middle of an argument between the two men. She didn't even work for the same company. "Well, that light monitors the temp of the main Ni-Cad battery," she muttered, glaring at Jeff. "You definitely don't want that battery to overheat." She shrugged, with a that's-all-you-get-from-me expression directed at him.

He took the conversation back, determined to prove his point to Ray. "Hey, Hank Seymour's seen Ni-Cads overheat enough to melt through the floor, go through the control cables. *Poof!* No rudder or elevators." He crossed his arms tightly. "How'd you like to make a landing with no rudder or elevators, just a trim wheel and differential power?"

Ray's face whitened as Jeff spoke. "Shit, I know enough about airplanes to know that'd be wild," he stammered. "That'd be like braking a car by raising the hood to catch the air."

"Yeah, about like that," Jeff said sarcastically. "And hey, it gets better! If it really gets overheated, you have a thermal runaway, and the battery goes up like Hiroshima! And guess what it takes with it?'' He paused dramatically. ''You got it . . . the rear fuselage! The whole fucking tail'd get vaporized! If you're lucky, you'd have enough left for a *controlled* crash.'' He looked at Ryan, who nodded vigorously.

Taylor shivered at the same time, the image of a crippled Twin Otter spiraling down to the ground in her mind's eye. She could almost hear the shrieks of the trapped passengers inside, aware that they were plummeting to their deaths.

''Sounds like fun, huh?'' Jeff leaned over the counter, pointing at Ray. ''That's why I don't want to fly that ship until the problem is solved. There's something wrong with the system and we gotta find it. Better call somebody from Anchorage.''

Troubled, Ray glanced back and forth among the three pilots, unsure of what to do. He tilted his head and stared across the terminal for a few seconds, then appeared to make a decision. He reached for the phone and dialed. ''I'm gonna call Mr. Bergeron,'' he said, ''see what he wants to do before I get my ass in a sling. I wanna get this approved.''

Taylor looked at Jeff, raising her eyebrows. He shrugged.

With the phone up to his ear, Ray waited for someone to answer, all the while drumming his fingers on the counter. A faint *bring . . . bring . . . bring* could be heard as the phone rang, then a *click* when it was picked up.

''Good morning, Mr. Bergeron?'' Ray said, his voice oozing politeness and deference. ''How was your vacation, sir? . . . Yes, sir, I'm sure the Mexican Riviera is nice when it starts getting cold here. . . . Yes. . . . Yes, I know. . . . Well, we've got a small problem with one of the Twin Otters out here. We need a mechanic from Anchorage to come out and look at it.'' Ray took a minute to describe the trouble to WAT's owner, alternating ''Yes, sir,'' with ''No, sir,'' and ''I see, of course.'' His fingers continued their drumming as he spoke. Then he said, ''Yes, sir, you're certainly right. I'll let them know.'' He set the phone down in its receptacle.

Ray smiled at Jeff. ''Mr. Bergeron says okay, take the ship to Anchorage.''

Jeff gawked at Ray. ''What? I *said* I wouldn't fly it around *here*. No way am I gonna take it four hundred miles away over a fucking mountain range!''

Ray shrugged. ''Well, Bergeron said it'd take too long to get a mechanic out here, not to mention the cost. He doesn't want the airplane sitting on the ground waiting for a mechanic, so he figured we could fly it to Anchorage and find a wrench there. Less time, less money.''

''So, who's gonna take it in?'' Jeff quizzed him. ''*I* won't do it, and I doubt that you could get any copilots for that flight, either. Would you go, Ryan?''

''No way,'' Ryan vehemently replied. ''I like my butt just fine the way it is, don't wanna let a Ni-Cad rearrange it for me.''

''Well, you wouldn't need a copilot, anyway,'' Ray persisted. ''This would be Part 91—you could go alone.''

''Ray, just because it's not a scheduled flight, it's not any safer. You're not gonna find anybody who'd risk their butt like that and ignore the rules.''

As they argued, the ramp door opened and Ken Mayshak walked into the terminal. Ken, one of WAT's captains, was a former air force aviator. His closely cropped steel-gray hair was a throwback from his days as a military flight instructor, as were his regimented gait and cut-to-the-chase style of speaking. The navy-blue winterweight flight jacket draped over his trim form sent the same message.

Mayshak marched up to the counter and plopped his clipboard next to Jeff's. ''What's next, Ray?''

Ray glanced at a paper in front of him. ''You got Marshall-Russian next. They've got six in Marshall that want to go to Russian for a potlatch. It's somebody's hundredth birthday.'' One eyebrow raised, he stared at the older man. ''Before you go, Ken, I got a question for you.'' He detailed the situation for him, and finished up by asking him if he wanted to fly the plane into Anchorage.

Mayshak glanced at the three pilots surrounding him with an incredulous expression. He turned back to Ray. "Are you nuts? You know there's something wrong with the battery and the generator, and you want to fly it with *no over-temp warning light?* Not this guy! That's a grounding squawk, you can't fly the ship without an over-temp light."

"Oh, shit!" Ray exclaimed, glaring furiously at Jeff. "Who's left to ask? All of my captains said no, and I gotta get the ship to town! Bergeron will kick my ass if it's stuck on the ground until a mechanic comes out. That'll take a week!"

"Hey, I ain't flying it," Jeff affirmed, and he and Ryan walked off, heading for the stairs to the café. "Come on, Taylor," he said.

Ken Mayshak looked askance at them, and turned for the ramp exit.

Taylor lifted her wrist, pulling her parka sleeve off her watch. "Hey, I can't go get coffee. They're probably starting to board the flight to Anchorage; I need to check in. I'll see you in a few days." She swiveled toward the terminal's single gate.

"Hey, whoa," Jeff murmured. "Why're you going to town?" Arms akimbo, he leered at her. "You on hormone overload or something? Gotta go see the stud?"

"Nooo. . . ." she retorted, blushing painfully. Talk about awkward—having a past lover tease her about a present one. She couldn't believe she'd told him about Steve. Bad move. Undoubtedly, Jeff knew how eager she was to get home, since he had firsthand knowledge of her sexual appetite. "No," she repeated. "This isn't pleasure, I'm working. Gotta go get a 185, ferry it back out here."

Jeff barked, "Hah! Don't tell me you're not already planning for tonight, 'cuz I know you are!"

"Oh, fuck off," she snapped, and wheeled away for the gate.

TWENTY-THREE

A white Boeing 737 with blue-and-green stripes on its fuselage lounged on the ramp, as a steady stream of passengers climbed the airstair attached to its belly like an umbilical cord. At a window seat inside the jet, Taylor contorted her body to tighten her seat belt over her bulky down parka. Eventually it became evident that the parka had to come off to make room for the belt, so she stood up and stripped down to her heavy sweater.

Once properly situated, she glanced around, watching people stroll down the aisle between coach and first class. Some were Yup'iks, some were Caucasians—undoubtedly, most of them were traveling to Anchorage for services unavailable in Bethel.

Flight attendants stood by the jet's entrance, directing last-minute boarders to their seats. Taylor smiled contentedly at the sight of them performing their duties. It would be nice to be nothing but a passenger on an aircraft for a change.

A minute later a subtle *thump!* signaled the closure of the cabin door and the engines began a throaty whine when they ignited. Gazing out her window, she saw the jet ease away from the terminal, slowly moving past strands of sunlight checkering the snow-covered tarmac.

The previous night's low overcast was breaking up and the white snow reflected the golden streamers. The red lenses of the flashlights held by a ramp attendant added a dot of color to the gold and white.

In a matter of minutes, the jet was lumbering down the runway, accelerating for takeoff. Taylor delighted in the feel of being pushed back against the seat by the thrust of the engines—she wished she had that much power under her command.

Ten minutes later, her eardrums stopped popping. The Fasten Seat Belts sign flicked off, and flight attendants began moving about the cabin. She squirmed down in her seat and started a daydream.

One of the uniformed servers interrupted her reverie by stopping at her row with the beverage cart. "Would you like a snack?" the attendant asked, offering the ubiquitous bag of nuts.

"Yeah, thanks," she nodded, taking the nuts. "And pour me a 7UP, please." The flight attendant plunked ice cubes and soda into a glass and reached across the seats to hand Taylor her drink. After receiving a thank you, the All-American-looking man wheeled the cart down the aisle to the next row.

She smiled, pleased to see a man performing a job formerly relegated to buxom blonds that said things like, "I'm Tina, fly me to Las Vegas!" on the TV ads.

After a gulp of her 7UP, Taylor shivered as the carbonation bubbled up into her nose. She attempted to subdue the tingle by popping one nut in her mouth, then another.

With a handful of nuts crunching between her teeth, she looked down at the terrain below. A panoply of white, dappled by charcoal gray, spread to the horizon. The jet was crossing the Alaska Range, and the grandeur of the mountains beneath the white belly of the Boeing 737 nearly took her breath away.

Their angular beauty impressed her—the view from the window of the Boeing could have been a *National Geographic* centerfold. She felt lucky because she didn't have to flip through a magazine to see such wonderful sights—all of Alaska offered itself up to admiration at any time.

She had flown through the Alaska Range on numerous occasions on medevacs with LifeLine, but looked forward to getting another one-on-one view of the craggy slopes. As dramatic as the Range looked from a jet cruising at thirty thousand feet, it was infinitely more so from inside a small plane at five thousand. When she ferried the new Cessna back to the Yukon-Kuskokwim Delta she'd fly through Merrill Pass, one of only three routes through the mountains.

Even as she appreciated the mountains, she realized that the spectacular and elegant Alaska Range had a dark side. Its magnificence hid menace. She had heard of pilots lulled into complacency by the range's beauty, only to come face-to-face with its unforgiving nature. The Alaska Range brooked no mistakes.

As she stared at the blue-and-white glaciers passing below the jet, she contemplated the hazards of the range. Shivering, she wondered what it would be like to freeze or starve to death, trapped alive within the crumpled body of a wrecked airplane. It made her shudder.

Finally she tore her gaze away from the terrain. She would give herself nightmares that evening if she didn't think about something else. Snatching a magazine from the seat pocket, she leafed through it, only occasionally allowing her stare to wander back to the mountains.

Forty-five minutes later, after the soft drinks had been taken away, the Fasten Seat Belts sign flashed on and the jet began its descent into the Anchorage bowl. The rugged tops of the Alaska Range shrank to a less threatening size as the aircraft left them behind.

As the Boeing 737 taxied to the jetway, Taylor allowed herself to think of the night ahead, something she hadn't permitted herself to do during the flight to Anchorage, since a flight attendant was likely to question her if she started squirming in her seat. But Steve was only about a minute away now, so it seemed all right.

While Mr. All-American warned the passengers to re-main seated until the jet reached the jetway, she struggled to extract her backpack from beneath the seat ahead of her. A tingle of excitement washed over her body.

What's with you? she asked herself silently. *You act like you haven't been home for years. Sheesh!* Then she cut herself some slack. She probably missed Steve and Anchorage so much because seeing the bad side of the Y-K Delta was getting to her—seeing it, and being unable to do anything about it. She hoped that when she returned to Bethel, she'd find that the troopers had arrested some-one for the booze-running.

Strolling down the jetway, she peeked around the gate to catch a glimpse of Steve, but didn't see anybody fa-miliar. Well, he was probably sitting in one of the chairs, waiting for her.

She emerged from the confines of the jetway into Con-course B, and scanned the thin crowd cooling their heels as the passengers filed into the terminal. In one corner, she saw several men reaching out to shake the hand of a returning friend or coworker. Next to them, a Yup'ik woman attempted to hug her husband as she wrestled with two adorable elves wearing tiny *kuspuks*. Most of the other debarking travelers had connected with their loved ones, but she still hadn't. Where was Steve?

Hiking her backpack higher on her shoulder, she sur-veyed the room. Nobody there for her. The last of the passengers were leaving, and the gate agent had just closed the door to the jetway. She better go. He must've been called out for a medevac, probably wouldn't be home until late that night.

Or maybe not until she'd left for Bethel tomorrow.

With a last glance, she shuffled toward the bank of phones on the wall. She'd call LifeLine, see if anyone could come pick her up, take her back to her car. It wasn't too far, but she didn't feel like challenging the wild driv-ers on Old International Airport Road during her walk back to the hangar. Once the snow fell, the plows that cleared the road left little in the way of sidewalk for a person to navigate. It was either walk on the pavement, or drive—no in between.

As she trudged over to the phones, she heard running footsteps and a voice. "Taylor, Taylor!" Steve yelled as he dashed around the corner. The fabric of his blue Nomex flight suit fluttered as he ran—obviously, he had come directly from work. Breathing hard, he screeched to a halt in front of her and planted a juicy kiss on her lips.

After a five-second lip-lock—prolonged by her—he broke free. "Whew, I'm glad I caught you. I just got back to town from the slope with a burn victim. Ran over here as soon as I got the ship in the hangar."

Shifting her backpack to her other shoulder, she encircled his waist and tugged him down the hall. "I'm glad you caught me, too. I thought you'd got called out. That'd shoot my plans to hell."

He swung an arm around her. "You got plans for me, huh? Well, I'm still on duty until six, but let's see what we can do. Why don't we drive back to the hangar; I want to get out of this monkey suit."

"I'd like to get you out of that monkey suit, too," she growled at him.

"Oh no, looks like I'm in trouble," he laughed. "One week away from civilization and you turn into an animal."

TWENTY-FOUR

Steve's Camaro merged into the light traffic on Sixth Avenue. Taylor craned her head to catch a glimpse of the changing horizon of Anchorage, noting several new stores in just three blocks. Two of the three shops were tourist traps, advertising souvenirs and T-shirts.

Swinging left onto B Street, Steve took another left into the big parking garage connected to the Fifth Avenue Mall via a skyway. In minutes—after leaving the car and dodging incoming traffic—he and Taylor were swallowed by the three-story mall. Like every time she'd ever gone there, new shops had sprung up like ant colonies.

"A birthday present for your mom, huh?" she asked him as they strolled down the first-floor arcade. "What does she like?"

"Oh, I don't know," he shrugged. "That's why you're here. What do you gals like? Perfume? Scarves?"

"Ugh, that's not very imaginative. Let's just look around, see if something catches your eye. Or mine." She scanned the store windows as they wandered around, and her eyes were drawn to a colorful display of kites. Kites of various shapes and fabrics dangled from wires like pieces of an ornate mobile. Bright red-and-orange nylon competed with metallic Mylar for the consideration of shoppers, and an elaborate dragon soared over the ordinary box and diamond forms.

She stopped and studied the merchandise, turning back to him after a few moments. "Your mom's not into kites, is she? Think she'd like something unique like that? That's not your typical gift for a mom—shows imagination."

"Naw," he chuckled. "The only imagination that would show is how the hell I came up with an idea like that. My mom's definitely not into kites. She's not even into going outside unless it's downtown to go shopping. We'd better find something else."

They continued. Next to the kite store, another window arrangement caught Taylor's attention—she halted again to peer at several display cases holding artwork.

Baleen scrimshaw perched on the small pedestals scattered about one of the cases, surrounded by animal forms sculpted from materials only used by Alaskan Natives. A rearing ivory polar bear seemed to menace a greenish-gray soapstone seal, and a spirit mask made from a walrus vertebra appeared to be witnessing the fight.

Then Taylor's attention was drawn to a small sign in the window. It read, Biggest Selection Of Native Artifacts In Anchorage! "That sounds kinda interesting, Steve. Does your mom collect any artifacts? That's kinda neat stuff. It'd make a wonderful gift."

Beckoning for him to follow, she stepped into the store. They approached a wiry man who was bent over one of the display cases. Taylor cleared her throat. "Excuse me, sir. I saw your sign about artifacts. Could you tell me where they are?" She pointed at the sign that had caught her eye.

"Ah, yes. The artifacts." The man stood up, fingering his pencil-thin moustache. A strand of his slicked-back black hair had fallen down over his Coke-bottle-top glasses, and he pushed it into place. "You know, we have an extensive selection of artifacts from the Yukon-Kuskokwim Delta in southwest Alaska. Let me show you." He scooted around the corner of the case and walked to one side of the store. Undoubtedly he thought he had a couple of live ones in hand.

With a puzzled expression, Taylor shot Steve a look, then followed the man. "Did you say these are from the Yukon-Kuskokwim Delta?" she asked.

"Yes. Are you familiar with that region of Alaska?"

"Yeah, I w—" She stopped herself in mid-word. Her pursed lips told Steve not to say anything more. "I've heard about it," she amended. "Haven't been there, though. If you've got some artifacts from there, I'd sure like to see them."

"Here we are." He led them to a case near the rear of the store. "Tourists really like these items. It allows them to take a part of ancient Alaska home with them. Where are you folks from?" He unlocked the display case as he spoke, and drew out an *ulu*. The stone *ulu* was battered and chipped, with nicks and scratches on its wooden handle.

Taylor ignored his question. "Ooh, that looks really old," she exclaimed, turning it over in her hand. "How old?"

Smugly, he said, "Hard to tell, but probably more than a hundred years old."

"That old, huh? I guess that's why it's so beat up." She peered at the *ulu* skeptically, drawing the blade's edge over her thumb.

The man seemed to interpret her gesture as dissatisfaction, and he frowned. He turned to Steve, as though to get approval from the one *really* in charge of the purse strings. "Well, these *are* Native artifacts," he stammered. "Of course they're gonna be beat up. This piece has probably been in the ground for an extensive time." He took the *ulu* from her and nestled it back into the velvet lining of the case. He extracted another item and handed it to her. "Look at this harpoon point. It's certainly several hundred years old."

Looking up from the point, she nodded at it. "Where'd you get this? You go out there and dig around yourself?"

"No, I'm the store owner," he sniffed. "I don't have

time to do that." He puffed up as though he felt his position was vastly important. "I have connections on the Delta, you know. I got these artifacts from a man who works in a town in the area these came from. He's a pilot, and he flies into all of the villages out there. The Natives sell these to him and he brings them into Anchorage for me."

She almost froze when he said that, and her heart started to beat faster. She didn't even trust herself to glance Steve's way, afraid that her excitement would show.

The store owner didn't notice her abrupt expression shift, and continued his spiel. His eyelids drooped in a conspiratorial way, and he leaned closer to her. "Keep this under your hat, ma'am, but I think the Natives do some grave robbing to get these."

Hefting the harpoon point, she looked at the man with a solemn face. "I may want to buy one of these artifacts." She set the point down and reached for her wallet. "How much are we talking about?"

Surprised, his eyes widened. He'd thought Steve held the moneybags. Promptly, he changed course. "Well, remember, ma'am, the Natives robbed graves to find these. They don't want to part with them for pennies. Jack said he has to deal out some serious money to—"

"Jack? The pilot's name is Jack?" Taylor interrupted. She gaped at the store owner for a split second before she thought to conceal her shock. She hoped Steve wouldn't blurt something out when he caught her facial expression.

The man looked at her in bewilderment, appearing to have seen her sudden start. "Yeah, his name is Jack. Do you know him?"

"Uh, maybe," she fudged. "I had a friend named Jack that moved out to Bethel. He wasn't a pilot last time I saw him, though. What does this guy look like?"

The store owner's description of Jack-the-pilot fit Jack Shumock to a tee. "So, is that your friend?" he asked.

"Nah, it isn't. I didn't think he'd become a pilot anyway. He usually got airsick in planes."

"Oh, well. Whatever." He gazed at the harpoon point she had placed on the counter, then glanced back up at her face, as though reading her to see how high he could jack up the price. "I'll make you a deal, ma'am. That harpoon point you were holding, I'll give you that for twenty-five hundred dollars. That's a bargain, an artifact like that for less than five thousand dollars."

"Twenty-five hundred dollars?" she squawked. "There's no way I could pay that!" She returned her money to her wallet, and shoved it into her rear pocket.

"Now, now, ma'am. That's not an extraordinary price to pay for something that's a relic from ancient times. Think about it. It's a piece of history." He winked, as though he was making her a deal she couldn't refuse.

"Well, I can't pay that. Thank you for your time." She stomped out of the store, leaving the store owner gazing up at Steve as though he thought he could get the tall man to buy something instead.

Tugging on his jacket, Taylor pulled Steve down the hall away from the store. "What the hell are you doing?" he protested, trying to wrest his sleeve away from her grip. "And what the hell was going on in there?"

She continued to drag him toward a bench next to the wall. Once they had reached it, she forced him down on it like she was teaching a dog *Sit!* He gaped at her. She was coming unglued.

"I got it figured out, Steve. I know what they're doing," she yelped, then lowered her voice to a whisper to disguise her words. "It's been driving me nuts. . . ." She sketched the story of the alcohol trafficking on the Y-K Delta, her involvement in stopping it, and the odd things that had happened. As she spoke of the sabotage of her Cessna, his face got whiter and whiter and the skin over his cheekbones tightened.

"Why didn't you say something?" he growled. "If I'd known, I'd of—"

"That's exactly *why* I didn't say anything. I didn't want you to worry. I'm a big girl, I can cover my tail. . . ." When he tried to say something else, she held her hand over his lips to hush him. "Wait a second, let me finish. This'll make sense pretty quick." She adjusted her seat on the bench and fiddled with her parka zipper. "I finally had everything unraveled, but I couldn't explain why they were doing it. They had no motive, as Perry Mason says. There couldn't be that much money in bootlegging out there, not enough to warrant felonies. And murder sure is a felony."

His face clouded at the second mention of murder, but eased as he decided to let her talk. "But why did you get so excited when you saw the things in that store? I thought you were going to split a gut holding it in."

"Maybe it'll make more sense when I remind you that the store owner was showing off his native artifacts from the *Y-K Delta*."

"So?" he shrugged. "I know you used to work there, and you're out there now, but who cares?"

She raised her eyebrows, a satisfied gleam in her eyes. "When he said he had artifacts from the Y-K Delta, it *really* caught my attention. I've done enough reading about Alaskan archaeology to know there's no artifacts on the Delta; the villages there are too new. Plus, the rivers change course so much that any artifacts would get washed away, and nobody would find them. Plus, there's permafrost—nobody's burying stuff in the ground out *there*. I could see that this guy was bullshitting me, big time. He didn't know that I've worked out there, that I know more about the Delta than your average souvenir shopper. That's why I wanted to keep you quiet."

Steve's gaze narrowed and he shook his head. "Okay, so he was bullshitting you. That's not a crime."

"Well, it isn't. But when he said how he got a hold of those artifacts, I paid attention. Remember, he was bragging about his connections out there, telling us 'a pilot buys the artifacts from the Natives' and brings them in. He said the guy's name is Jack." Taylor beamed, proud of herself for solving the rest of the puzzle.

"Ahhh." Steve was getting it. "This 'pilot named Jack' is the Jack Shumock you told me about, right? So who cares if he's able to con some Anchorage shop owner into buying junk that he calls artifacts?''

Taylor arched an eyebrow. ''Jack has to be the other man involved in the bootlegging. Remember when I told you about that kid in Kipnuk who tried to trade a harpoon point for some booze? And I didn't understand what he was doing?''

''Yeah, I remember,'' he nodded.

''Well, that's what Shumock was doing. Telling the Natives that he'd trade alcohol for old junk they found around the village. I think Blaskovich was doing the same thing. Anyway, once they got a stash, Shumock would sell the junk to this guy in Anchorage. Either Shumock told the store owner that they were genuine artifacts that had been stolen from graves, or he cut the guy into the scam. One or both of them is getting a lot of money for worthless cast-off crap. See?''

Steve smiled, comprehension dawning in his eyes. ''Yeah, I get it.'' He leaned back against the wall. ''So, what are you going to do about it? Anything?''

''I'll do plenty when I get back to Bethel. The troopers are already checking into the booze smuggling, and when I tell them about the sale of those 'artifacts,' they'll have more to work with. That may give them enough to go after Shumock.''

Taylor drew in a deep breath and propped her elbows on her knees. ''All of a sudden, I'm starving. Amazing how exhausting conversation can be, you know? You want to go get some Thai food for dinner?''

TWENTY-FIVE

At seven o'clock the next morning, Taylor nuzzled Steve awake. "Hey big guy, I gotta leave in a few hours. Interested in one for the road? I've got another week or so in Bethel before I come home, you know. . . ."

Opening his eyes, he yawned and tucked her under his arm. "Oh, yeah?" he murmured into her rumpled hair. "A whole week? Then I guess it's the least I can do, service a lonely woman."

Her head jerked up from his chest where it lay, and she grabbed a pillow. "Who do you think you are, God's gift to horny women?" she teased, whacking him with the pillow, then trying to suffocate him. As she held the cushion over his head, she nipped at his chest and he strained against her hold halfheartedly. When she began to tongue his nipple, he put his full strength into the struggle.

"Now you're gonna get it," he said in a mock-snarl, and flipped her over onto her back. With most of his weight on her, he fastened his lips to her mouth and held her down as he kissed her.

Just as she wrapped one leg around him, a *wheep-wheep . . . wheep-wheep . . . wheep-wheep* sound tore into the air, and they both froze. "Oh, damn," she groaned.

"Talk about *coitus interruptus*. Do you think they planned that?"

"Well, it doesn't matter if they did. I still have to go." He rolled off her and grabbed his pager to check the message on it. Sitting up, he reached for the phone on the nightstand and dialed a number. After a minute of talking to the medevac dispatcher at the Cook Inlet Medical Center, he cradled the phone and flopped back on the bed.

"Sorry, duty calls. Somebody chopped his hand off in Cold Bay—gotta go get him." Chucking her under the chin, he stood and started dressing. As he stepped into a pair of well-worn Levi's, his eyebrows rose apologetically and he shrugged. "I guess you'll have to take a cab to the airport. You got enough money?" When she nodded, he grabbed a navy-blue turtleneck and pulled it over his head. "You be careful flying back, don't take any chances. You got that? Merrill Pass isn't anywhere you wanna go down." He tucked the sweater into his jeans and began the search for his socks. Over his shoulder he said, "And when you get back to Bethel, talk to the troopers right away. Now that you've got something for them to work with, quit with your poking around. You've done enough, maybe too much. Okay?"

"Yes, Mom," she lipped. "I'll watch it." She snuggled under the covers and tugged them up to her chin. "I'll probably be home in a week or so, give or take. Depends on when that other pilot can break away, make it out to Bethel."

"Okay, I'll be waiting. Why don't you give me a call tonight once you're back on the ground?" He leaned down and gave her a slow, leisurely kiss. "And remember where we left off this morning, okay?"

She saw him walk to the living room, then heard him grab his coat and slam the door as he left. Sighing, she rose and padded toward the shower. "Oh, well," she muttered. "Only one more week."

The cloudless sky above the city of Anchorage allowed rays of sunshine to poke over the tops of the Chugach

Mountains, which formed a balustrade around the city. Their forty-five hundred to sixty-five hundred foot peaks stood tall, preventing the march of civilization into the wilderness.

Anchorage International Airport sat twenty-five miles west of the hills in the triangle formed by the confluence of Cook Inlet and Turnagain Arm. A tall concrete column jutted up from the middle of the field and supported an air traffic control tower.

Taylor Morgan occupied the pilot's seat of a Cessna 185 that was located in one of the aircraft parking areas near the tower. Head cocked, she listened intently to a special radio recording that gave her information about current weather and airport conditions.

After taking note of the information, she switched radio frequencies. Next call went to departure control for an identifying *squawk* number, then ground control for directions to taxi for takeoff. Finally, she found herself half a mile away from where she'd started, speaking to the tower as she sat near an active runway.

"Anchorage, three-two-quebec holding short of three-two," she transmitted.

"Three-two-quebec," replied the controller, "continue to hold short, traffic is a 727 departing three-two."

Blue-and-green stripes and a smiling Eskimo face flashed past as an Alaska Airlines jet thundered down the runway she faced. Three minutes after the Boeing 727 lifted off, the tower called back, clearing her for takeoff.

"And contact departure control upon reaching two thousand feet," the melodious male voice concluded.

She tightened her seat belt and shoulder harness and sank deeper into the seat cushion. Ready to go, she eased the throttle ahead—the plane began to accelerate, lining up with the runway centerline. With a smooth gesture, she pushed the throttle full forward. Her heartbeat raced to match the surge from the engine, and the roar of the propeller hammered in her ears.

"Mmmm," Taylor murmured. "This is almost better than sex!"

The Cessna climbed out from the runway, carrying her across the murky gray waters of Cook Inlet. As the plane broke through five hundred feet, she peered over the tree-tops on the northern edge of the inlet and spotted a familiar landmark, Mount Susitna.

Native legend said that the mountain was really a slumbering woman waiting for the return of her lover. The similarity between the hill and the profile of a prone figure had earned it the nickname of the Sleeping Lady.

Shifting her gaze to the left, Taylor studied a sight that displayed Alaska's diversity. Her view of oil-drilling platforms piercing the gray water of the inlet jerked her away from the romance of myths and back into the modern world. She studied the silhouette of an experimental platform called the Monopod, which stood like an egret on its single leg next to other, more conventional, rigs.

Twenty minutes later, Taylor approached the eastern slopes of the Alaska Range. Over her right shoulder, she could see the massive profile of Mount McKinley, North America's tallest promontory. Even though the peak stood two hundred miles to the north, the clear day made it easy to spot.

More obvious than McKinley was the dome of the Mount Spurr volcano that guarded the entrance to Merrill Pass. She recalled the day in the recent past when Spurr had erupted and flung a plume of ash and stones sixty thousand feet into the atmosphere. The volcanic fallout had rained down on Anchorage, eighty miles away, coating the town with a layer of the gritty residue.

As a lifelong resident of Alaska, volcanic eruptions didn't alarm Taylor. Her home state sat on the northern edge of the Ring of Fire, a string of volcanoes that dotted the Pacific Ocean's rim. Several active volcanoes fumed within two hundred miles of Anchorage—Mount Redoubt and Mount Augustine had joined Spurr in the group of volcanoes that had erupted in the past decade.

The sight of Spurr generated memories of Redoubt's week-long series of eruptions, the most spectacular involving a Boeing 747 which accidentally flew through the volcano's ash plume. The engines flamed out and quit, and the jet fell more than ten thousand feet before the panicked flight crew could restart them and limp back to safety.

Troubling thoughts of frantic passengers flitted about her mind as she envisioned the ordeal. Then she turned back to the hills ahead of her, focusing on images of beautiful, snow-covered terrain to drive away the reflections on disaster and destruction.

Grabbing the candy bar she'd taken from Steve's house, she bit into it, trying to let peanuts and caramel distract her.

TWENTY-SIX

By noon, Merrill Pass had ensconced Taylor within its steep walls. The Alaska Range crowded around her, and the path through the mountains became tougher to follow. She paid strict attention to her navigation through the pass, recognizing the trouble that a wandering mind could cause.

Directly ahead of her lay a segment of Merrill Pass that seemed to be an aircraft graveyard. A forty-five degree dogleg near the summit held the carcasses of several light planes that had crashed in poor weather. Pieces of red and silver aluminum poked up from above the snow-covered slope like memorial markers.

The clear sky minimized the difficulties the pass could pose that day; but even so, Taylor felt subtle stabs of apprehension. The weather didn't bother her, but something still nagged at her. She shrugged, puzzled by the odd sensation she was trying to stifle.

By the time she had crossed the summit, Taylor had allowed herself to relax somewhat. Undoubtedly her active imagination had provoked her restlessness, she assumed—lingering on images of volcanic eruptions and airline near-disasters would make anyone become flus-

tered. She squirmed in her seat and ordered herself to pay
attention to the flight.

Enjoying her view of the staggeringly beautiful hills,
she studied the drifted snow below her. As she panned
across the slopes, a flash of sunlight glinted off white-
and-blue paint. She stiffened.

"What the hell?" she whispered.

Her gaze widened when she recognized the random collection of painted stripes for what it was: a battered Western Alaska Transport Twin Otter resting in a
snow-covered field, a gigantic boulder crouching by the
plane's side like a lion guarding its fresh kill.

From sixty-five hundred feet, a thousand feet above the
crushed heap of aluminum, she wasn't too sure of what
it was she was seeing. Was it a smoldering heap, or a
largely intact aircraft? And what was it doing out here?
Pushing the control yoke forward, she dropped down to
get a closer look. The pounding of her heart doubled as
she approached the wreck.

The Twin Otter's mangled fuselage lay belly-down in
the snow. Gaping holes dotted the rear structure, the pro-
truding shreds of metal indicating an inner explosion.
Squinting at the wreckage, she recognized the identifica-
tion numbers on its side and gasped. It was the airplane
Jeff Davidson had been flying, the one with the potentially
lethal mechanical problem. He had refused to fly it into
Anchorage the previous day—had he changed his mind
for some reason? Had he encountered the very disaster
he'd predicted? Was he down there?

A burst of adrenaline hit her system. Regardless who
was trapped in the heap of charred aluminum, she had to
call for help, somebody to land at the crash site and rescue
any survivors.

But as she reached to dial in a emergency frequency
on her radio, she froze.

The Cessna 185 only had a very-high-frequency radio
installed in it, and that meant the radio waves would only
travel on a line-of-sight path between the two senders. The
only way she could use her VHF radio to talk to anyone

at a distance would be if another aircraft was passing by and picked up her call, or if she climbed to about ten thousand feet, above the mountains, where the signals would travel farther.

Flicking to 123.45—the commercial aviation chat line—she attempted to raise an airliner flying overhead, maybe on the way to Tokyo. They could relay a message to the state troopers who could send a helicopter and medics. Even though they'd be an hour away, they could make the save.

"Anybody on twenty-three-forty-five, three-two-quebec has an emergency," she transmitted, waiting for a matching call from a Fed Ex freighter or a United 747 heading for the Far East.

But no reply.

She tried again. "Aircraft on twenty-three-forty-five, Cessna four-two-three-two-quebec has an emergency, aircraft down in Merrill Pass. I need help."

Still nobody replied to her distress call.

"Damn!" she cursed. Where was everyone? There were always jets up there. Where'd they go?

Frantic, she tried 122.9, a frequency used by aviators flying to the Far Side, the western edge of the Alaska Range, but again nobody returned her panicked transmission. "Damn, where the hell is everyone? Doesn't anybody fly out here during the winter?"

As she circled the wreckage for a closer look, trying at the same time to decide if she should initiate a climb to a higher altitude, she peered down at the crushed nose cone and squinted. To her amazement, she saw a limp figure fastened into the pilot's seat by the shoulder harness. A WAT winter-weight jacket was draped around his shoulders, and a familiar cap shielded his face.

"Oh, God," she yelped. "It's Jeff!" The adrenaline surges pulsed across her body once more.

Without even thinking twice, she pulled the control yoke back to her chest and initiated a climbing turn to return to the crash site. She didn't have time to climb to ten thousand feet; Jeff needed her right away. A rescue chopper would be hours away, surely, and he may not have that many minutes left on this earth if he didn't get immediate help.

While the plane swung into the turn, hundreds of pictures flashed through her mind in a matter of seconds. Images of the good times she and Jeff had had together, keeping each other cozy during the long, cold nights on the Y-K Delta. She remembered the days she'd battled a virulent head cold, when he'd catered to her with chicken soup and hot-water bottles. Memories of the intimate sport they'd enjoyed—the laughs, the dreams they'd shared— made her quiver.

But in those short seconds, she also focused on the bad times: their eventual antagonistic breakup, the insults, the vindictive taunts aimed at each other. Their volcanic final fight had been turbulent. Could she risk her life to save this man? The one who had put her through hell?

And she *would* be risking her life. Her first quick pass over the field had showed her the rescue would be fraught with hazards. The field was small. Massive boulders encompassed it. Obstacles could hide under the coating of snow.

But she never hesitated. Jeff's behavior toward her since her return to Bethel showed that he had put the past behind him—shouldn't she do the same? He might have survived the crash. Could she live with herself if she left him to die in the cold?

She couldn't.

Taking a deep breath, she stared at the treacherous terrain below as she circled the wreckage a second time. Ruts dug through the snow by the Twin Otter's landing gear exposed stones camouflaged by the recent snowfall. There had to be other buried rocks, but where were they?

If the Cessna touched down on an unseen obstacle, the plane could be torn apart. She shuddered in response to that image. Jeff's fate could befall her as well, with her own body as brutalized as his must be.

Did she want to die like that?

TWENTY-SEVEN

Sweeping around the peaks surrounding Merrill Pass, Taylor's Cessna arched smoothly back to the alpine field.

During the descent to the wrecked Twin Otter, she contemplated the situation. "How am I gonna do this?" she muttered out loud. "Think, lady, think!" She felt like a college student staring at the toughest test she'd ever faced.

Edging the throttle back, she reduced her speed and cruised over the crash site again, slowly, giving herself more time to examine things. Looking at the field, she grimaced.

The field jutted out from the side of a mountain—the upper level sloped moderately then leveled off into a shallow plateau before it angled sharply down into a steep cliff.

The ruts left by the Twin Otter showed a snow depth of nearly a foot. She believed the Cessna 185 could handle that much snow for takeoff with two people on board, but she wasn't certain, and that bothered her. Her guess on what the plane could handle had to be dead-on; *dead* being the operative word.

It was obvious that she had to avoid the other aircraft's

tracks, which had exposed several large rocks. Certainly others existed, but she'd just have to take her chances with *them*. She decided to stay near the middle of the field, hoping to avoid most of the rocks.

Her hands quivered nervously as she reduced the power to nearly idle. A slow touchdown was imperative—she wanted to minimize contact between the plane's wheel-skis and the rocks.

Quickly, she ran down a mental list of techniques for short takeoffs and landings. Her knowledge of STOL procedures could be the one factor that could guarantee her safety that day. She had never performed a touch-down so critical.

With a sweaty grip on the control yoke, she finalized the preparations for landing. She had no more time to assure herself that she'd planned correctly. Either she would make it and live to see another day, or she wouldn't. It was that simple.

The picture of the field grew enormous in the Cessna's windshield, like an image on a big-screen TV. The *THUMPataTHUMPataTHUMPata* of her heart chattered in her ears. She was committed—she couldn't back down.

"This is it," she muttered as she gnawed on her lower lip. Flicking her bangs off her forehead, she felt the perspiration sticking to her fingertips, and wiped them on a pant leg.

The Cessna seemed to hang in the air over the snow-covered field, then slid downward toward it. Fifty feet . . . forty feet . . . thirty feet . . . twenty feet . . .

Then, *SSSCCCRRREEE!*

The shriek of the stall warning horn blasted through the cabin. Its shrill sound startled her, prompting a burst of adrenaline to hit her system like an atomic bomb. "Shit!" she cursed, nearly ready to lose control of her bladder.

Ten feet . . . five feet . . .

As the plane dropped to within inches of the snow, the glare of the midday sun glanced off a hidden rock—its profile jutted out in bas-relief. "Damn!" she yelled, jerking the control yoke to the right.

The Cessna lurched to the side, the edge of a wheel-ski slicing past the rock with a grinding noise. She sucked in her breath, anticipating the plane's subsequent flip. Surely, she'd be tossed about the cockpit like a tetherball. She grabbed the yoke with both hands and shut her eyes, knowing the wreck was imminent.

"Daammn itttt!" she screamed, as the plane skidded sideways past the boulder and planted its skis in the snow. The Cessna thumped over a second rock, continuing to decelerate. The end of the field neared as the skis rattled over smaller rocks.

"Oh, no! Don't do it!" she pleaded. Her body tensed, ready for the crash. . . .

But the plane slid to a stop, intact.

With a heavy exhalation of breath, Taylor sank back against the seat. Staring wild-eyed out the windshield, she felt her pulse hammer in her veins. Its *thup-thup-thup-thup* was strangely comforting. Leaning forward, she rested her forehead on the yoke.

Finally she stepped out of the Cessna on weak legs. Trying to calm herself, she began to chant, "You're okay, you're okay, you made it, you're okay. . . ." She couldn't believe she was in one piece.

Then she saw the *other* plane. Two hundred feet away sat the Twin Otter fuselage, pieces of the fractured nose cone scattered around it.

The enormous boulder it had nicked seemed to strain toward the maimed fuselage like a carrion vulture reaching for a stricken animal. The shocking sight had Taylor trembling in seconds—a similar scene could have included her!

She floundered through the snow toward the De-Havilland, still pumped up by the adrenaline coursing through her body. She had no idea what she would find when she reached the aircraft—she hoped Jeff was alive, but the state of the wreck made it seem unlikely. She squinted at it—if she had risked her own life, only to find him slipping away or already gone, she would have been devastated.

When she reached the front of the fuselage, she stopped in her tracks. Her gut twisted in repulsion when she scanned the scene. Yawning holes in the tail section near the baggage compartment made the plane look as though it had been in a war zone.

Nothing of the nose cone and instrument panel remained on the plane—the Twin Otter looked as though its face had been ripped off.

The main and nose gear were mutilated, torn apart by the force of slamming past the buried rocks. The aircraft lay on its naked belly. Red streams of hydraulic fluid had squirted across the field, leaving tracks like blood across the pristine snow.

A body hung motionless from the cockpit bulkhead, still strapped to his seat. The bill of his hat shrouded his face. Screaming, ''Jeff, Jeff!'' she struggled through the drifts to his side, then stopped abruptly.

It wasn't Jeff. The figure wore his hat, but it wasn't him.

Gaping, she focused on the face of Jack Shumock.

''What the hell . . .'' she breathed. Looking closer, she choked back a throat full of stomach acid. Blood and gashes colored his face in a grotesque patchwork, and his head looked like the leftover steak given to the family dog.

She studied his closed eyes, then reached up to feel his carotid artery for a pulse. Nothing. Her touch on his throat connected with stiff, icy skin.

''What are you doing here?'' she whispered to his lifeless body. Had Ray Evans talked him into flying the plane to Anchorage in Jeff's place? she wondered. Maybe with a bribe that persuaded him to ignore the danger?

Stepping back, she mulled over the question, then turned to return to her Cessna. She felt vaguely uneasy as a witness to his death. Surely, the last seconds of his life had been terrifying. True, he had been a real predator, profiting on the misery of others, but she couldn't cheer over his grisly end.

But before she had taken a single step, a strong arm

encircled her neck in a choke hold. "Aggghhh!" she gurgled, clawing at the nylon sleeve wrapped around her throat. "Damn you, let go!" she croaked at the unseen enemy.

Jerking and struggling, she tried to break out of his grasp, but she couldn't free herself. His lock on her windpipe made colored lights dance across her eyes, and she pummeled his forearms with all of her waning strength.

As the blackness surrounded her, she desperately grabbed at his crotch, clutching his balls with fingers like claws.

"Unnnhhhh!" A groan of pain shot from his mouth, and his grip on her neck loosened. With his weight crushing her, they fell in a pile on the snow-covered ground. Instinctively, he reached to protect his balls with one arm, flailing with the other to reconnect with her throat.

She could barely move with the man's entire body smothering her, but she got one leg disentangled. With him spread-eagled over her, she strained to release an arm. Her free hand groped in the snow ahead, searching for a weapon, for anything. When her fingers encompassed a palm-sized rock, she swung it over her shoulder toward his head, where it impacted the side of his skull with a sickening *thud!*

Instantaneously, she felt his muscles go limp. "Oh God, I killed him!" she cried, scrambling in the snow to escape. Grunting as she shoved his immobile frame off her, she struggled to stand, then peered down at the man who'd nearly ended her life. Confusion wracked her brain—she couldn't believe who lay beneath her.

"Jeff!" she exclaimed.

TWENTY-EIGHT

"**M**y God," she stammered. "You tried to fucking kill me!"

What had he been thinking? Had he mistaken her for someone else, someone trying to kill *him?* And what was he doing here in Merrill Pass, in an airplane with Jack Shumock?

Then her confusion lifted. It became startlingly clear. Jeff and Jack had been together because they were both involved in the booze-running, and both of them saw the need to flee upcoming prosecution. The malfunctioning Twin Otter gave them the perfect excuse to get out of Bethel without raising any suspicions. Undoubtedly, they had no intention of delivering the plane to a mechanic— for all she knew, they had planned to fly past Anchorage and continue to Canada, or beyond.

And both of them knew the troopers were closing in on the smuggling because she had trusted Jeff, and told him everything she'd done.

Shuddering, she realized that Jeff had probably orchestrated the sabotaged flight to Tununak. He knew everything she knew, and most certainly wanted to scare her. He may have planned Blaskovich's fatal mishap as well.

"Damn," she cursed. "How could I have missed all

the clues?'' How could she have let old feelings for Jeff cloud her reasoning? His arrival at her front door a week ago had corresponded with her first discovery of the bootlegging, and that couldn't have been coincidence. Surely, he was just sniffing around to determine what she knew. How could she have failed to recognize that? Every time she'd crowed about the discoveries she'd made, he'd used the information to his advantage. He knew every step taken in the investigation of the illegal activity.

And so had Shumock.

Staring narrowly at his prone body, she reached down to check for a pulse. "If I'm lucky, he'll be dead. Fucking slimeball.'' Then she caught herself—if he died, *she'd* be charged with murder. She was the one that smacked him with the rock. Nobody would believe self-defense—she had no witnesses.

She couldn't even leave him in Merrill Pass to die of his injuries. If he survived in the cold long enough to be spotted by Search and Rescue, he could swear that *she* had left him there awaiting his death. Once again, the troopers would haul her in on a murder rap.

No question about it, she would have to get him out of there. The creep—she couldn't let him die.

But how the hell would she do that? She didn't even know how to get him into the Cessna.

After ten minutes of gut-busting exertion, she had been able to wedge Jeff into her plane. Cautiously, she double-checked his bonds—if he regained consciousness and broke free, the results could be disastrous.

But with him safely hog-tied on the cabin floor of the plane, she repinned its door onto its frame. A grin stretched across her face.

She felt ordinately proud of herself. Getting a well-built adult man, an *unconscious* well-built adult man, into the airplane had not been easy. But she had scrounged around the wreckage for items that would serve her in dragging him to the Cessna.

Still breathing heavily, she opened the pilot's door and

clambered into the left front seat, the only one remaining in the plane. She glanced over her shoulder and tensed when she saw him stir against his bonds. That wasn't good—she still had to complete a difficult takeoff and couldn't afford any interference from him.

Suddenly, his eyes jerked open, fury emerging from them when he looked at his restraints. "What the hell!" he cursed. He strained against the seat belt webbing wrapped tautly around his limbs. Then he focused on her hands at the plane's controls. "What are you trying to do, Taylor? You won't be able to fly out of here, there's no way you could handle it! I know your flying, you're not good enough!" He flopped around on the floor like a hooked salmon. "Don't try to take off! You're gonna fucking kill me! When I get out of this mess, I'm going to wring your scrawny neck!"

"Oh, shut the hell up, Jeff! You already tried that. If you're smart you'll see it wouldn't be wise to distract me right now." Scanning the straps trussing his hands, she nodded. There was no way he could get loose. "Just relax, sweetie. That's all you can do, no sense in thrashing around."

She swung around to face forward again, and fastened her shoulder harness. She had no idea what she would face during the takeoff, but she was going to secure her belt. Tightly.

"You better hope you're wrong about me, Jeff," she laughed, her voice cracking with uncertainty. "My skill is the only thing between you and a nasty death. Remember that." She started the plane and sat for a moment, collecting herself.

Grunts and thuds reverberated in the cabin as Jeff grappled with the straps binding him. "Let me go!" he shrieked. "I don't want to die! Let me go!"

She extinguished any thoughts of the man tied behind her and stared at the drop-off cliff ahead. Regardless of her cocky words, she was terrified. If the plane wasn't in the air by the time she went over the edge, a downhill plunge to death awaited. That thought actually comforted her, knowing that the end would be swift. Hitting the boulders at the cliff's base would bring an instantaneous end, no suffering.

With that fatalistic reflection floating about in her head, she reached out to the flight controls. Her hand trembled as she forced herself to push the throttle full forward. The voice of the Continental IO-520 gathered to a throaty scream that drowned out the pounding in her ears. She released the brakes. It was show time. From the rear of the cabin, Jeff screamed in terror. "Don't do it! Abort, abort! You can't handle it, we're gonna die. . . ."

The Cessna 185 slid down the slope, gaining speed every second. Twenty knots . . . twenty-five knots . . . thirty knots . . .

It reached the midpoint of the clear area.

Thirty-five knots . . . forty knots . . . forty-five knots . . . fifty knots . . .

The plane neared the end of the field where the massive boulders menaced, filling the forward view. Instinctively, Taylor yanked the plane into the air to clear them. A silent cry caught in her throat as the plane shot into the sky.

The gigantic boulders seemed to stretch up and grab at the air to block the plane's passage. The Cessna staggered up and over them, and lanced off the edge of the cliff!

SSSCCCRRREEE! The stall-warning horn screamed as the plane floundered in the air. "Put it down, put it down!" Jeff squalled. "We're gonna stall, put it down! The plane's not flying, we're fucked!" She could hear his gasping, and his thrashing became more frantic. He was as scared as she was.

The stall-warning horn continued to shriek, joined by Jeff's distraught caterwauling. The plane still wasn't flying!

Fifty-one knots . . . fifty-two knots . . .

Taylor shoved a handle down to retract partially the flaps as the Cessna continued to dive down the cliff's side. Out of the corner of her eye, she could see the downslope stones disappear behind the plane's wings, mere feet away.

Without conscious acknowledgement, she retracted the flaps further, and the airspeed increased as they tucked in. While the plane continued to rush down the side of the cliff, her heart pounded wildly.

The upper edge of a tree line loomed downslope. Spruce trees sprawled across the cliff like a chain-link fence, preventing any escape. The plane would have to pick itself up over them, and she wasn't sure that it could. The wail of the warning horn told her the plane still wasn't flying. "Come on, come on!" she screamed, her words muffled by its blare.

She had to do something. Terrified by her approach to the barricade, she shot a glance at the airspeed indicator, *willing* it to rise. Her hands gripped the control yoke like a vise—every muscle, every tendon in her body strained against it, urging the Cessna to fly.

The white needle quivered at the bottom of the dial's green arc: fifty-three knots . . . fifty-four knots. . . . It moved so slowly—she ached to nudge it ahead.

Then it hit fifty-five knots! She had flying speed—she had succeeded!

Suddenly energized, Taylor yanked back on the yoke and the Cessna shot away from the slope. The tops of the spruce trees tossed as the prop blast whipped the tender shoots.

VVWWOWWWwww! screamed the Cessna as it streaked past the treetops. The blades of the propeller bit into the air as the plane blasted off the cliff like a shuttle rocketing up from Cape Canaveral.

She nearly collapsed when she felt the plane respond to her grasp. The airspeed indicator continued to climb into the normal operating range, and she thought she had never seen such a welcome sight. Relieved beyond belief, she exhaled and executed a turn to the west, heading for Bethel.

TWENTY-NINE

Taylor reset the frequency dial on her VHF radio, positioned the boom mike over her mouth, and thumbed the push-to-talk switch. "Bethel tower, four-two-three-two-quebec is thirty east, inbound. Requesting an ambulance to meet me at the ramp with a trooper escort."

"Four-two-three-two-quebec, Bethel, state emer—"

The controller's reply was drowned out by Jeff's frantic cries of, "No, no! I'll make you a deal! Hear me out!"

Swiveling around in her seat, she blotted out the static-filled words from the tower and looked at him with puzzlement. "And what are *you* talking about?" she asked.

"Don't get the troopers involved, Taylor," he said in a wheedling voice. "Please. It's *me!* Don't do it."

An oily expression crossed his face. She'd never seen anything like that before, and it amazed her. He was a consummate actor, able to shift his expression from savage anger to pitiful supplication in seconds when it was needed.

"I can cut you into the deal, into the profit," he urged. "Both Shumock and Blaskovich are gone, I need another partner. You'd be perfect. Nobody'd suspect you, and you'll be back in Anchorage pretty quick. You can be my liaison in town, you can ship the stuff out to me, no problem.'' Insincere flattery dripped from his words. ''And you're a lot smarter than those other guys. You'd be a real asset. How about it?'' A rustling sounded when he moved to reposition himself. ''Just tell the tower you only need the ambulance, not the escort. Untie me, let the medics take me to the hospital. When I get there, I'll tell everyone you saved me and you'll be a hero. You'll look great, everyone would be talking about how good a pilot you are.'' He gave her one of his winning smiles. ''What'cha say, deal?''

She gaped at him, astonished. ''What? Do you think I'm enough of a slimeball to agree to that because there's money in it? Because it'd stoke my ego? Forget it, asshole! No dice!'' Shaking her head, she glared at him. ''An hour ago you were choking me to death, you think I forgot about that? A week ago you tried to kill me with my own airplane, a day ago you did the same thing to Blaskovich. I figured you'd try something like this, but I thought you were smart enough to know I wouldn't go for it.'' She turned around to the panel, and laughed. ''I hope you realize you just screwed yourself big time by saying anything about the booze-running. Thanks for giving me more stuff to pin on you, you're making the troopers' job a lot easier. . . .''

''Hey, it wasn't me that rigged your plane. . . .'' he pleaded.

''Yeah, right. You expect me to believe you? You're a fucking lia—''

Another call from the tower broke through her words. ''Three-two-quebec, three-two-quebec, did you copy? Please state emergency, I didn't read your reply.''

She glanced back at Jeff and smiled smugly. ''I've got an injured man on board,'' she transmitted. ''Wanted by the troopers. Contact Officer Pedersen at the Bethel headquarters to get the escort.''

''Bethel copies. I'll get the hospital and the troopers on the line.''

As she let go of the transmit switch, she moved her

hand to shield her eyes from the glare of gold and pink ahead. "Looks like a lovely day for an arrest, Jeff. Bet you thought I'd never figure it out, but you filled in all the blanks for me."

Guttural curses filled the cabin in answer to her remark. "Goddamn it," he barked. "I had you, you were so fucking stupid at the beginning. . . ." She ignored his snarls and gazed on the snow-covered tundra below.

After five minutes of intermittent outbreaks from Jeff, complete with disparaging comments on her skills as a pilot and her personal attributes, she started to pick up the low profile of Bethel. The sight comforted her. It meant an imminent end to her adventure—she'd had as much excitement as she could take that day.

"Bethel, three-two-quebec is now seven east for landing," she relayed to the control tower. Her steady voice displayed no evidence of her struggle in Merrill Pass, and she smiled at that. She liked to think of herself as unflappable, though the afternoon's images contradicted that.

Oh well, no one had seen that part.

"Three-two-quebec, Bethel," the tower replied. "You're cleared to land, runway three-six. Wind calm, altimeter thirty-oh-four. Traffic is a blue-and-white Twin Otter just clearing the runway, ambulance and escort standing by."

"Three-two-quebec copies, landing three-six."

She banked to the left and guided the Cessna through its turn into the landing pattern. The end to the day's events was approaching, and she was ready.

When she taxied onto the ramp by the terminal five minutes later, two paramedics raced to meet her, hoisting a stretcher. "Other side?" yelled one, pointing to the right cockpit door.

She jumped down from her seat and trotted around the nose of the Cessna 185, beckoning to the two men. Opening the door, she began unpinning it from its frame. "I gotta get this off before you can get him out," she told the nearest attendant, as she tugged on the fastening pins.

While pulling the door off the jamb, she noticed Officer

Pedersen approaching. The unfamiliar young trooper at his side matched his purposeful stride. Even from twenty feet, she could see the puzzled expression on the older man's face, and she wondered about it. Was he unhappy for some reason?

"What's all of this stuff wrapped around this guy?" a paramedic quizzed her as he leaned over Jeff. "He supposed to be tied up?"

Her gaze darted from the nearing troopers back to her former lover, now tightly bound. She grinned. He'd suggested tying each other up during past sexual escapades, but she doubted he had this in mind at the time. "Well, I guess it doesn't matter now that we're back in Bethel. You can remove the belts. You can see how torn up he is—I doubt he'll put up any fight with you guys. I just had to keep him away from me."

Both paramedics stared at her for a moment, then bent to their task. After entangling Jeff from his restraints, they gingerly extracted him from the plane, careful of his injuries. Startled looks continued to pass between the two men, and she shrugged happily in response.

By the time they had Jeff strapped down on the stretcher, Pedersen and the other trooper had reached the airplane. When the paramedics lifted the stretcher into the ambulance, the senior officer gestured at his partner to follow them. Once the back board and the trooper were stowed in the vehicle, it sped off toward the hospital.

"What's the deal here?" Pedersen asked, waving at the disappearing ambulance. "Who was that? What was he doing in your plane and how'd he get injured? When the call came in for an escort, I thought you had Shumock. I couldn't figure out how you got him, but . . ." He studied her face inquisitively. "Anyway, we were after *him*. ATC ID'd him as the pilot flying that 172. We came to get him, but the WAT dispatcher said he'd taken a Twin Otter into Anchorage." He frowned and gazed to the east. "Shit. He's probably long gone by now."

"No, he's not gone," she reassured the trooper. "He's lying dead in the middle of Merrill Pass. That's where the other guy came from, too. He's Jeff Davidson, another captain for WAT.'' Arching an eyebrow, she launched into a detailed explanation of the past two days.

As she expounded on her struggle with Jeff and the dangerous takeoff from the pass, Pedersen's gaze widened. "I can't say I would've risked that much,'' he acknowledged. "Especially for someone that tried to kill me. Not once, but twice.''

"Yeah, well, I didn't have much choice. Didn't want a murder rap.''

Pedersen squinted at her as he digested what she'd said. Then he nodded when it dawned on him. "He might've been involved in the Blaskovich crash, too. We checked into it and the plane had been tampered with. We went out to the wreck with a mechanic who found things wrong with the plane that couldn't have occurred in the crash. Whoever set that up was really lucky that the bad weather made the crash look like a real accident.''

Pedersen jangled his vehicle keys as he turned up his jacket collar. "I'll need to talk to you some more, Miss Morgan, probably tomorrow. I need to finalize everything, bring murder and attempted murder charges against Davidson.''

"That's fine, I'll be here. Call first so you can catch me between flights.''

"You're going to work tomorrow, after everything that's happened today?'' Pedersen peered down at her in bewilderment, then raised his eyebrows. "Well, you're pretty gutsy. Anyway, I do want to thank you for your help in this matter. At the beginning, I thought you'd just interfere in the investigation, but now I can see that there wouldn't have been an investigation at all without your input. Thank you again.'' He reached out to shake Taylor's hand, then turned toward his sedan.

She watched him drive off, then shoved her hands in her pockets and ambled across the apron.

When she pushed the terminal door open, she spotted Dan Mackenzie standing behind the TAC counter. He was leafing through a magazine absently. He glanced up from his reading material and set it aside. "Hi, there," he called. "I didn't hear you taxi in. You got the 185 out there?"

"Yup. That and more." Walking toward him, she exhaled deeply. It was a tremendous relief, just being back in the Bethel airport terminal. She never would have thought the tacky room could offer such comfort, at least not until she thought she might not see it ever again.

The sight of passengers restlessly waiting for departing flights pleased her; their poses were so nonchalant, so unhurried. They didn't look like anything had troubled them all day. The odors wafting downstairs from the café reminded her that she hadn't eaten since the morning, and the grumbling of her stomach felt good.

"What do you mean, and more?" Dan quizzed her. He glanced down at her hand, then looked up and caught a glimpse of her black-and-blue neck. He started. "What the hell happened to you?"

Shrugging, she smiled tentatively. "I had a little trouble in the pass on the way here." She sketched the details of the last two days for him, as he gaped. She ignored his expression and continued her story. "So, I guess I've found the people behind the smuggling. Davidson, Shumock, and Blaskovich. I always suspected Blaskovich, once I found out about his trip to Chevak, but Shumock was a complete surprise." Then she shuddered. "So was Davidson."

Dan nodded slowly, then reached out to pat her hand. "You must feel pretty good about yourself."

"Well, yeah. I kept my promise to Kittie Avakana, and the booze-running is done with. And that slimeball Davidson will do time. Shumock and Blaskovich have already paid for *their* involvement."

"Well, I'm proud of you. You got all the loose ends tied up." He winked at her.

She squinted at his uncharacteristic expression, then gestured at the phone next to him. "I got to make a call. Wanna hand that over?"

When he pushed it toward her, she grabbed the receiver

and dialed. After two rings, a familiar voice answered. "LifeLine Air Ambulance, this is Steve."

She started. "Steve? What are you doing answering the phone?"

"Oh hey, Taylor! You calling from Bethel? Made it okay?"

"Uh, yeah." She squirmed, hoping her voice wouldn't betray her. She wasn't about to tell Steve what happened over the phone—that called for a face-to-face. "Made it in just fine. Interesting trip. I'll have to tell you about it."

"Interesting trip? What do you mean?" She could hear the suspicion in his voice. Had she said too much, in only two words?

"Oh, you know," she hedged. "Merrill Pass and everything. I'll let you know when I get home."

"Oh, okay. Everything went alright then." His tone had brightened, and she stifled a sigh. "Well, don't forget to tell me about it when you get home," he added.

Her eyebrows rose. "I won't forget. Believe me, I won't forget."